Simpson's Homer

Simpson's Homer

JOHN MALCOLM

First published in Great Britain in 2001 by
Allison & Busby Limited
Suite 111, Bon Marche Centre
241-251 Ferndale Road
Brixton, London SW9 8BJ
http://www.allisonandbusby.ltd.uk

A catalogue record for this book is available from the British Library

ISBN 0 7490 0586 6

Printed and bound in Spain by
Liberdúplex, s. l. Barcelona

JOHN MALCOLM is the author of twelve previous Tim Simpson mysteries, as well as a number of books on art and antiques. A former Chairman of the British Crime Writers Association, John Malcolm lives in a Sussex village with his wife.

With grateful thanks to David Pearcy, of National Police Training, Bramshill, for the original spark, to my old friend Mick Rooney, RA, for Torre Pellice, and to my son Sam, for he knows what.

Chapter 1

It was a warm September morning, misty and ripe, when I was peremptorily summoned to be told, by his agitated nephew, that Sir Richard White had definitely gone off his rocker.

Outside, the mendacious bustle of the City of London was taking place in buildings starkly modern and fustily ancient. Rumbles of traffic, murmurs of people and the distant drone of an airliner vibrated beyond the windows. Inside, the feathered mahogany panelling of the traditional Bank director's office, waxed and gleaming, looked down upon a scene of agnate distress.

"Mad." Jeremy White snapped crisply, staring at a fax on the broad surface of the opulent desk in front of him. "Barking mad. Completely round the twist. I knew it would come, sooner or later." He gestured dramatically at the sheet of paper. "It's finally taken hold."

"It?"

"Senile dementia. No other explanation is possible. He has become a Harpic type. Clean round the bend."

I suppressed a cry of protest at this eruption of dated RAF slang. Jeremy White is a yachtsman, not an aviator. Charitably, I thought the deliberate colloquialism conveyed how upset he was, so refrained from comment. His condition suggested that discretion would be better than disapproval.

My tactful silence merely provoked him.

"Pretty suspect, I've always thought," he snarled.

"What?"

"That hobby of his - visiting the battlefields of the Hundred Years War. It may have seemed harmless at first, bit of an anorak sort of thing, kept the old boy off the streets, semi-retirement occupation, describe it how you will. A reasonable way of combining history with gastronomy but one never knew. There were always doubts about it. Other members of the Board often smile condescendingly about Richard's hobby, affecting an amused tolerance, but you can tell they aren't altogether impressed. All that preoccupation with France: grisly battles and fine cuisine. Once more into the breach. Two fingers up in a V-sign for archers." He shook his head irritably. "Shakespeare and Joan of Arc. *Moules* and *Montrachet*, followed by *Entrecôte Chasseur* with a modest bottle of *Chateau Rausan-Segla*. A smokescreen over an irreversible decline. Quite cleverly done, I suppose."

I sat down carefully on a buttoned leather armchair and refrained from making an instant response. The last time I had seen Sir Richard, his mind seemed sharp enough to me. I was indebted to him, as well as rather fond of him, in several ways, despite conflicts long ago. His so-called retirement to the Dordogne, at a time when the area was fashionable with prosperous English, had not removed him from executive activities. He maintained a small Paris flat in the *Seizième* and was frequently to be found there. It was Sir Richard who had been most involved with the Bank's French partners, Maucourt Frères. Several lucrative and prestigious projects had resulted from his peripatetic presence on the Continent. True, I had not seen him for a considerable period, having been dodging across the Atlantic on various other matters over the last year or so, but a year is not a very long time. Sir Richard's decline, if indeed it had occurred, would have had to be swift. His wife had died some years ago but he showed no sign of mental or emotional deterioration when he made the decision to indulge his hobby more fully.

It seemed to me that ingratitude was in the air. The Board had been happy, at the time, to have a senior volunteer cross the Channel to engage in an expansion long delayed by their own dilatory procedures. They had wished him well and gone back, with relief, to the safety of quotidian preoccupations.

His nephew, however, was glaring at me across his desk

with a rather mottled expression below his tousled blond locks.

"Well don't just sit there looking like a stuffed owl. Say something."

"I am distressed, Jeremy, to hear the news. And very surprised. What form, may I ask, has this onset of insanity taken? Seizure? Frenzy? Catatonia? Incontinence?"

He scowled at me momentarily out of loyalty to an important relative as much as at the flippancy of my response and made another gesture at the offending document in front of him.

"Italy" he growled. "My God, Italy now."

"Italy?"

"Not so much Italy, I suppose, as Savoy." He passed a hand over his brow as though to test for fever, causing a gold link to flash on the snowy white cuff projecting from his pinstriped worsted sleeve. His blond hair fell over his forehead and the cufflink flashed again as he pushed the offending locks back. "It appears that Richard has expanded his historical interests eastwards from the Dordogne into the Duchy of Savoy. A reversal of civilisation's usual trend. It seems it all started when he made a journey from a conference in Lyon over to Belley."

"Belley?"

"The home town of Brillat-Savarin, celebrated epicurean author of *La Physiologie du Goût*. A visit, in homage, as might befit anyone seriously interested in gastronomy as much as medieval history." An interrogative eye lit meaningfully upon me and his teeth flashed in a quick grin. "You're familiar with Brillat-Savarin's famous gastronomic work, of course?"

"No."

"Neither am I. After Belley it appears that, pursuing a somewhat dated Savoyard connection, Richard strayed from the Bugey over the Alps into Piedmonte in order to enjoy the mushroom season."

15

That got my approval. "How very civilised. No evidence of insanity there, Jeremy. The Italian treatment of the *boletus* mushroom - ceps, the penny bun - has much to commend it. *Risotto al funghi, or* even better *funghi fritti,* or alternatively *porcini al -* "

Jeremy made a tense gesture of interruption. "Stop that! For God's sake don't you start! Things are bad enough without you joining in this contagious madness! As Richard wishes you to do."

"Eh? Wishes me to do what?"

A savage look of satisfaction lit up my employer's face. "Ah! At last! You show interest when your own welfare suddenly becomes threatened, eh?"

"My welfare? Threatened?"

His mouth drew into a puckered downward bow. "Richard has become concerned, it would appear, with Waldensian Protestant history and England's involvement in it from Cromwell onwards." He clutched tightly at the offending fax as though to injure it. "Dear God, Cromwell. *Cromwell.* And Waldensians. Whatever next? If only he could have kept his idiosyncrasies to the Hundred Years War! But no, that's not enough! Now we have Savoy and the Waldensians to contend with!"

I have to admit that these references floored me. "Waldensians?" I enquired.

"A sect, Tim, of early Protestants living in an obscure Alpine valley long before Italy even existed. Persecuted by the Catholics until the mid-nineteenth century. Defended, apparently, in some way by Cromwell."

"Cromwell? Isn't he a bit modern for Sir Richard's taste?"

A flicker of a smile came at last to Jeremy's face. "Indeed, one might think so. Until recently, Mad Talbot and Castillon marked the limit of Richard's interests. Nothing after 1453 and the Field of the Cloth of Gold enthused him at all. Now, however, another craze has affected him." The smile vanished. "God knows what we shall end up with if his interests proceed in double-century jumps of this kind." He leant forward to glare at me. "Let me apprise you of the severity of the current imbroglio. Uncle Richard is most insistent that you be sent to investigate, with him, the possibility of the Bank's involvement in some aspect of local Alpine history. To wit, Waldensian evangelical activities and the promotion of related British and foreign tourism."

"What?" I almost shouted.

The glare was replaced by a look almost of pleasure. "I am glad that the full horror of the situation has finally struck home to you. At last I have your attention, have I? The Bank is hardly likely to benefit from what Richard says would be a prestigious international cultural PR exercise with - let me see - potential ramifications in several countries including those as far-flung as - wait for it - Switzerland, Uruguay and Argentina."

"Good God."

"You may well call upon the Deity. As the Waldensians apparently did when being butchered in the seventeenth century. As much good will it do you as it did them. They had to fight like tigers to survive. And enlist Cromwell."

"I can't possibly go to Italy. I'm due up in Newcastle the day after tomorrow."

Jeremy smiled cruelly. "As well I know. And wish you to be there."

"Well, then. Tell Richard I can't be spared."

He shook his head sadly. "If only it were as simple as that. If only this fax had not come through on an open machine in the main office yesterday, causing widespread speculation and insolent hilarity amongst our licencious staff. If only three other members of the Board - including the new demon, Shauna Spring - hadn't seen it."

He rolled another significant eye at me. Shauna Spring was a new Board member, adopted from the ranks of celebrated City females, females celebrated usually for their iron-hard and prominent performance over an inglorious organisation

17

of a semi-official nature staffed by grovelling unfortunates of both sexes. Her alarming presence on the secretive White board was apparently the result of concerted action by discontented minority shareholders. Due to my cross-Atlantic preoccupations and relatively low status I hadn't met her yet, but rumours of her acerbic character had reached me from various sources. I rolled a significant eye back at Jeremy in some sort of comradely male understanding.

He sighed deeply. "If only all three, separately and individually, hadn't buttonholed me and said that this is absurd and must stop. I mean, banks sponsor all sorts of amazingly esoteric cultural and artistic projects, like UBS Warburg and this Impressionism thing at the National" - it was a meaningful leer this time - "which one finds remote from the business of banking. PR people think up all sorts of hooleys to succour. But Waldensians? An obscure religious movement with a branch in Bahia Blanca? One must tread with extreme caution where politics and religion are concerned." A look of scandalous reminiscence spread over his face. "There was that group of breakaway Dutch Baptists, you may recall, whose finances we handled until those awful revelations of misappropriation and extraordinary misconduct by the founder and his principal deaconesses. The papers made hay of their altar-rail activities. Water on diaphanous vestments and appallingly uninhibited misbehaviour. Deeply embarrassing. We must at all costs avoid a repetition of that. The Board members are very alarmed. They insist that you comply with Sir Richard's request and get to him as quickly as possible. Not to carry out whatever his fax implies but to report back on both the proposed Bank involvement and on Richard himself."

"As the Board's spy, you mean?"

He bridled. "I wouldn't put it as crudely as that. No, indeed. As a trusted and valued employee with a remit to report objectively and professionally on Richard's - well, Richard's - "

"Condition? I'm not a medical man, you know."

"Of course you're not! But" - his tone became a little softer, almost wheedling, as he went into a recitation - "you have our trust in these matters. You have handled Richard excellently in the past. He clearly has the greatest confidence in you. Projects of his you have assessed before have received the most professional treatment."

"Thank you."

He waved the ironic interruption away.

"I, no damn it, we have every faith in your ability to act with tact and discretion should it be necessary."

"What about Newcastle? The timber business?"

"That will have to wait. You have no other involvement there, have you?"

"Um, no. No, I haven't."

He peered at me suspiciously. "You're hiding something from me. I can tell at once. Oh God, it's not an Art Fund matter is it?"

"No, no. Nothing like that, Jeremy."

He scowled. "I don't believe you. But I know you too well to press the matter at this point, when you're being sent safely off to Torre Pellice."

"Where?"

"Torre Pellice. Where Richard awaits at the local Albergo, doubtless sampling the *risotto al funghi*. "

"Torre Pellice? Where the hell is that?"

Jeremy smiled another vulpine smile. "It is a small place at the start of a remote Alpine valley near Pinerolo. Which in turn is not far from Turin. Your flight to Turin is being booked for you. You leave in the morning. Buy yourself a map at the airport. Or ask the car hire company how to get there; it's not very far."

"Turin? An odd coincidence. Isn't that where Geoffrey's arranging finance for a new electronics consortium?"

He gaped at me. "How did you know about that?"

"Geoffrey told me."

Geoffrey Price, our departmental accountant, had long been involved with Jeremy and me, particularly in the Art Investment Fund we had initiated long ago. He is a good friend, not at all a bad fellow considering he's an accountant, with a Rover car, several children and a keenness for cricket.

Jeremy frowned his most disapproving frown. "These potential and very confidential international projects are not for washroom gossip, you know. This is absolutely top secret. I'm surprised at Geoffrey."

I frowned back. "We never gossip in washrooms. Geoffrey and I meet at the Pig and Whistle from time to time so that we can keep up with relevant developments. Now that good City lunches are so few and far between, the old methods of informal communication have retreated before a wave of sandwiches, usually consumed in front of PC monitors. It is very distressing. Immobility is all the mode." I gave him a reproving look. "Geoffrey and I have had to make our own luncheon arrangements."

He waved aside my implied criticism of his lack of hospitality. "Life is altogether more serious these days, Tim. The survival of this Bank is remarkable in current circumstances but it rests on a knife edge. It is a case of all hands, et cetera, et cetera, as well you know. Lavish lunches are out. As for the Turin thing, it has come up via our local banking connections. But we are only part of a syndicate. It has nothing to do with Richard's extraordinary behaviour and you do not need to contact Giorgio Deserti or anyone from the Piedmonte branch. That is not your project." He leant forward to fix me with an offensive stare. "I repeat, it is highly confidential. We do not need you to complicate things."

I became indignant. "Me? Complicate things?"

He held up a cautionary hand, like a policeman restraining recalcitrant traffic. "You know very well what I mean. Your habit of interference is legendary."

"Oh, is it? Perhaps I'd better not go, then."

"For God's sake! This is a delicate but simple brief for

which the Board has chosen you! Uncle Richard is getting very old! We need to limit any potential damage! Will you please do as I ask?"

"Yes, Jeremy. Of course, Jeremy."

"Just get to Richard quickly and report back as soon as possible. We would not want Giorgio and his acolytes to find that an important member of our family, and a major current Board director, is suddenly becoming *non compos mentis* for God's sake. That would be very embarrassing at such a critical moment."

"Yes Jeremy. Very good, Jeremy. Everything shall be done as do the Italian Bersaglieri."

He scowled. "What?"

"At the double."

"Oh. Good." He managed to look mollified. "My apologies to Sue for taking you away at short notice but needs must when the devil drives."

"I suppose so."

I rose to leave, but he held up the same traffic-restraining hand.

"Your clandestine subterfuges for the Art Fund in Newcastle will have to wait." He brooded for a moment, thinking deeply. "Not that I can think of any artistic celebrity particularly connected with Newcastle on Tyne, of all places. Can you?"

"No Jeremy" I said.

But I was trying to.

Chapter 2

As it happened, just about that time, Henry Weaver had got in touch, phoning me at the Bank one afternoon when I really could have done without the interruption.

I hadn't heard from him for months. Hadn't particularly wanted to. He went back a long way but I didn't think of him as a very intimate friend. Everyone has someone like Henry in their lives, a leftover from past existences, dogging them with odd appearances at least-expected moments. Not always welcoming moments, because such contacts usually mean demands, sometimes for emotional sustenance, sometimes for money. But Henry wasn't a sponger in the financial sense; he just let you pay for the meal, or the drinks at the pub, on the occasions when he decided to regale you with his presence. For which, in some way, you were expected to be grateful. He never touched me for a loan; it was just time he wanted, and attention. That was it; he needed attention, like an old dog that greets you with ebullient, hairy affection for far too long.

As far as I knew, Henry was solitary. Had been for many years. He claimed to have been married once, but his wife had long gone. He rarely referred to her. "I have", he used to say, "retired hurt here to the seaside like Jack Knewstub, marooned with his kettle and birdsong. I am following the trail of many who, in countless biographies, one reads of as having failed in life and gone to live in Hastings."

I remember smiling at this glancing reference to the brother-in-law of Orpen and Rothenstein. Henry and I shared a penchant for esoteric art biography as well as another common interest in old films. Jack Knewstub wound up in Hastings after an art gallery venture in Chelsea which earned him the enmity of his hero, Augustus John. The New Chenil, which Knewstub had managed disastrously, was the epitome of the old joke about how to make a small fortune from an art gallery: start with a large one.

"Knewstub came down here to escape his creditors and live cheaply." Henry would say, then look wistfully at me.

There was not a lot I could do for him. He made a sort of living as a business consultant, working from home, which was a flat on the borders of Hastings and St.Leonards, without a sea view. Henry Weaver was one of hundreds of thousands of business's walking wounded, the early-redundant, industrially shell-shocked male scrap heap. His speciality was industrial market research, mainly statistical stuff, with some fieldwork, telephone mostly, but not much. When he could get it.

The bank had its own in-house researchers, all eager beavers. There was no way I could get him work for the Bank. From time to time I'd recommend him to someone looking for a freelancer, pass his name to a project manager, things like that. It did land him the odd contract here and there but he never seemed to get much by way of repeat business, a steady flow.

"How's the desk research going?" I used to ask him on our rare meetings. Then I'd watch his eyes slide sideways at the implication of hours spent in passive contemplation, of time ebbing in seedy libraries while he leafed through heavy Kompass reference books, catalogues, DTI statistics and trade magazines. Or plagiarised old Economist and other market research reports as he rubbed shoulders with muffled students making illegible notes for hopeless Business Studies or Trade and Tourism courses.

I knew bits of that life once, when I started.

"The *bibliographical* research" he would correct me mildly "is going well. I have a new commission to undertake."

Sometimes he'd tell me what it was: a report on imported hand-loom towels from Madurai, or the North American market for transformer laminations in neon lights, or changes in the Italian shoe industry. Sometimes he didn't bother. Sometimes my expression upset him. Henry was sensitive. I felt a pang of guilt, often, as I looked at old Henry.

Old Henry? Why did I call him old? I suppose because he was three years ahead of me at school, something which led to nastiness once. I told someone, in his hearing, that he went to the same boarding school in Buenos Aires as I attended for a couple of years, which set his teeth on edge because I didn't say we were 'at school together'.

"What Tim means" he'd said to the someone, with a contemptuous twist to his mouth "is that I was three years ahead of him. That's why he won't say we were at St.George's together, the supercilious bastard."

Then he scowled at me.

Well, I nearly answered, at school three years is three long years. Effectively like three bloody decades, quite apart from the fact that he was in a different house to mine. Different boarding houses were different worlds. At school, I didn't know him at all. It was long afterwards, when we met at a London film club, that he claimed old-boy status in my life. There was something a little too jovial, too eager, about him on that first reunion. The distant figure I remembered, slim and muscular on a games field where an older team was playing while we juniors watched, had changed. It pressed its burly, wool-waistcoated friendship on me as though we had been close pals. Henry was lonely. I was a rare sight: a figure from his imagined schoolday past that didn't know too much, hadn't followed his career very closely. He wanted me to be part of something I wasn't. He wanted people to believe that we were at school together in a way that, although technically correct, wasn't what the statement usually means. It gave him a sort of credibility, a more substantial existence, in a place where the past was so often to be avoided. In much of Hastings, the past is better not to have happened. My cool accuracy upset him. I didn't do it again. I indulged him, meeting him from time to time in different places, never having to talk much because Henry, like so many old and solitary people, needed someone to rant at.

Now he had surfaced again, like a shabby old whale blowing a snort above choppy water.

"Dear old Tim. *Que tal, pibe*?" His voice on the telephone sounded hoarser than before, his throat sandpapered perhaps by the passage of much cigarette smoke and even rougher sources of alcohol. "I've been thinking about you, dear boy."

"How kind. I am well, thank you."

"That art fund of yours at the Bank. Does it only buy British art?"

"Technically, yes. But we do buy works by foreign artists which have a British content of some sort. Monet in London, for example. Or Rodin's maquette of Gwen John."

"*Macanudo*. Bully for you, my boy." Henry coughed, painfully. "If that is the case, I think I may have something for you."

"Something? What sort of something?"

"My Geordie origins, always rumbling in the background, have returned to succour me in my time of dire need. A small but palpable inheritance."

"Geordie? I didn't know you were a Geordie. You've never mentioned it before."

"Not something one emphasised too much amongst those English snobs down in B.A. But my grandfather's family were a very decent bunch of Newcastle engineers originally. It's what got them down to Argentina, like yours."

"Ah. Something else we have in common, then. Not Newcastle, I mean. Engineer families in South America."

"Yes. All history, now."

"True. But what is this something you may have for me?"

"It's a watercolour. Before you reject it, I think we should view it together."

My heart sank. Watercolours, to Jeremy, are the artistic embodiment of feeble, British amateurism. He's wrong, of

25

course, but his opinion is entrenched. He would not take kindly to a watercolour.

"Where is it?" I asked, cautiously.

"Up in Newcastle, actually. I've been left a small terrace house by my dear aunt Myrtle and the watercolour is in it. Bit of luck, really. She's the last but one of my maiden aunts. Only old Enid left now, in Whitby."

"Oh, really. I see."

"You sound about as enthusiastic as a Muslim confronted by a pork chop. Newcastle's too far and too provincial for you London men, is it? Not like New York or Frankfurt?"

Not as far as it is for you, I remember thinking, immured in that shabby flat in St Leonard's.

"As a matter of fact, Henry, it isn't. I have business to transact in Newcastle at present. Not art. To do with timber."

It wasn't worth explaining once again that White's Bank originated with the importation of rosewood from Brazil by the original White sometime during the Regency, when rosewood became popular. The trading had given way to merchant banking in importance, but timber interests had always remained, with activities dotted about the country.

"How very appropriate. And timely. We could meet there and you could buy me a large dinner."

"Hang on, Henry, hang on. What is this watercolour? Who's it by?"

There was a brief, cagey silence. Then he spoke again, cautiously. "I think, dear boy, that's best left for the moment we meet. *Pas devant les domestiques*, and all that." There was another pause as he waited for my reaction. "*En boca cerrada no entran moscas, tu me sabes*?"

First time I'd heard a telephone line called a domestic servant. And Henry was mixing his French with old Spanish saws about keeping one's mouth shut.

"You're very cagey" I responded. "Watercolours are not exactly the stuff of international cloak and dagger, Henry."

"Oh no? You never can tell, dear boy. The walls have ears.

Think of Tom Keating and his Sexton Blakes. Apart from that, the north-east coast can be a very turbulent place."

"Oh God, Henry, this isn't about another daub of Dunstanburgh Head with a shipwreck under the castle? Or Flamborough with fishing smacks in a storm, is it? Not another? Every hack painter of the nineteenth century did one of those."

"No it certainly is not!" he snapped. "Flamborough's in bloody Yorkshire! I'm coming to you first for old acquaintance's sake but if you're going to act all toffee-nosed, I'll hoick it straight to Sotheby's."

"All right! All right! Keep your hair on! As I say, I'm going up to Newcastle anyway. I'll take a butcher's at your picture while I'm there."

"Good" he said, sounding appeased. "I'll meet you up there on your next visit. Be worth your time, Tim. I wouldn't waste it, you know that."

"You're not going to tell me more?"

"No, I'm not. You can spend a bit of your life on tenterhooks. Like I have to most of the time. I'm not giving you the chance to prepare beforehand. I want to see your face when you first set eyes on it."

"Very theatrical."

"In life, as in the theatre, timing is all."

What he meant was that he'd arrange to get a dinner or a lunch out of me before we could view this probably dismal coastal watercolour. We made arrangements to coincide with my next visit and he rang off.

Now, I'd have to cancel. I'd be in Turin.

I tried calling him but he was out. His ancient combined phone, fax and answering machine clicked uncertainly into a crackling tape message about talking after the bleep. He hadn't got round to email yet. How Henry ever convinced anyone of his statistical research efficiency was a mystery. I'd never have hired a researcher with such antediluvian office equipment.

A mental picture of Henry, in his habitual dark blue blazer, check shirt and club tie above traditional grey trousers, all far from fresh, came to me. Below rather tousled hair, tinged with prematurely speckled greyness, his crinkled blue eyes radiated what Jonathan Meades, in an historic programme on the bohemian aspects of Hastings, called the bruised amiability of the fallen. Yet Henry would not have liked the association with Bohemia, even though Hastings has an appropriate district of that name. He saw himself as a sort of academic, or an old-fashioned tutor, using the regurgitated knowledge gleaned from his shabby sources to engage the sympathies and respect of his listeners. He would smile like an apologetic tinker as he opened his old black leather briefcase and spread his second-hand statistics in front of them. And more often than not I think they would smile back. There was something undeniably engaging about him in a bookish way that called for reciprocal sympathy and interest even though, for many of his clients, cold intellect must have recognised little scholarship and much plagiarism.

I left an apologetic message saying I'd be in touch again soon and forgot about him until I went home.

Chapter 3

"Well really" Sue said, sitting down in the big armchair near the mantelpiece and picking up the thimbleful of Grand Marnier I had poured her, "I think that Jeremy's quite unreasonable."

· "Unfortunately he has the Board at his elbow."

"So the Board's unreasonable, too. You've been away a lot over the last year. If you're not careful, William will start to wonder who on earth you are."

The Simpson sprog, at that moment tucked safely away in his cot but capable of disruption at any time, was coming up to a year old. He had, so far, had little coherent to say but, whilst generally of a sunny disposition, was capable of expressing basic emotions with great force. Sue was doing very well in the role of mother and had come to a useful arrangement with the Byzantine organisation of the Tate Gallery at Millbank, which to me seemed more redolent of a civil service under the Ottoman Empire than anything else. Under it, she retained her job as a curator and specialist in Impressionism and, with the assistance of a part-time nanny, kept William in order too. There is something to be said for current legislation on maternal rights after all, even if it does rather strain the distaff side at times.

"I am only too conscious of my duties as a modern father. On the whole, up to now, they have been pretty secondary. Later on, they will undoubtedly develop. And to be realistic, I haven't been away for more than a week at a time."

"It still seems to have been a lot. And nursemaiding Sir Richard is hardly what you're supposed to be paid for."

"On the contrary, anyone who works for an organisation which is primarily a family concern almost always has to play nursemaid from time to time. Fortunately the pay does not reflect nursemaid rates. The bonus this year will be very luxurious."

"I thought you were having a tough time."

"We are. The fact that we haven't been swallowed by some enormous German, Swiss or Japanese monolith is remarkable. But what is called a tough time in the City is not what a stoker in a hot pie factory would call a tough time. Men who are used to being paid great fortunes even when their organisations are losing money have quite different concepts of tough times. Like the late Piers Hargreaves, for example, who absorbed large sums whilst destroying going concerns."

Sue shuddered. "I do not want to talk about the late Piers Hargreaves. It seems a long time ago, now, that his nihilist influence was invading our lives and he met a sticky end. There have been times when your acquisition of paintings for the Fund has been carried out at costs far greater than the actual sums paid over. Where is the Wyndham Lewis painting, *Kermesse*, now, by the way?"

"On loan to Toronto, fittingly enough. Although Wyndham Lewis had a fairly dismal time there."

She took a sip of her liqueur. "Things have been very quiet on the Art Fund front lately. I see the headlines and wonder, amongst all these record auction prices, how you will find good paintings to acquire at reasonable cost."

"I know. I have always been really keen to get a good Newlyn School painting, but Phillips sold that Stanhope Forbes one, *The Seine Boat*, this year for around one point two million pounds. To an American, of course."

"Of course" she said, dryly.

"Well the previous auction high for a Stanhope Forbes was ninety-six thousand. I always wanted to get one for the Fund, ever since I saw *The Health of the Bride* at the Royal Academy. Bit of a leap, to go over one million just like that."

"Perhaps you should think about Elizabeth." She gestured at the wall where an Elizabeth Stanhope Forbes painting of hers ranged next to an Alan Gwynne-Jones still life of mine. "She was very good, too."

"And was originally a Canadian, like Lewis."

"True. In that case, I'm not so sure. For security reasons."

It was consistent of Sue instinctively to recommend Forbes's wife, nee Elizabeth Armstrong. Our flat in Onslow Gardens reflected something of our divergent tastes. Sue has a Sylvia Gosse still life and paintings by Laura Knight - there was a Newlyn painter for you, for a while anyway - Ethel Walker and Dod Proctor plus a Stanley Spencer watercolour of a suburban angel with washing line. She hasn't managed to oust my big Clarkson Stanfield seascape of a vessel in full sail on the Medway from over the mantelpiece yet, nor to conceal my print of Dorelia by Augustus John and sketch of a soldier by Orpen. She has, however, managed to give more prominence to her Picasso print of a geometrically dismembered woman and her Hockney.

There was getting to be a bit of crowding for space, which the advent of our first child, young William, was emphasising as well. I was starting to think gloomily that we might have to move to something bigger, which economics would force to be further from our places of work, but kept putting the thought aside.

Sue has an uncanny knack of bringing up the subject of the Art Fund and its penchant for violence at moments when I would prefer her not to. The Bank's Art Investment Fund, which Jeremy and I started long ago, was designed to cater for clients who wished to invest in art without actually owning a Rembrandt themselves. Originally conceived for prosperous clients intent on capital gains rather than income, it has done rather well financially but has caused considerable mayhem at a personal level. There is something about art as a form of speculative currency which attracts not just the genial fraudster but also the predatory, the vengeful and the just plain lethal. We had had our dangerous moments. A period of quiet for over a year or so had been very welcome, especially when parental responsibilities had to be considered. Not that parenthood is any reason for retreating into a shell; indeed, it brings all the more necessity for activity. But unless it was just straightforward auction purchasing, my responsibilities for the Art Fund set alarm bells ringing in Sue's mind.

But no, I thought, a watercolour of the north-east coast is hardly likely to bring a combination of Bill Sykes and Hannibal Lecter out of the woodwork. I'm not particularly enthused by watercolours, even though I own one of Bosham harbour by Wilson Steer.

"You've gone quiet "Sue said." And you've got that broody look you get just before something lethal connected with the Art Fund crops up. What is it this time? A Sickert, perhaps? Or Bevan? Something that you can use to burrow in the seedy recesses of Camden and Kentish Towns?"

"Not again, Sue. I've done that."

"What then?"

"Oddly enough, it's a watercolour."

"A watercolour? Surely your Art Fund is far too grand for a watercolour? Only a Cotman, or an original Turner, would justify the purchase of something so English, so mild-mannered and subfusc, as a watercolour? The Art Fund isn't going into cottage garden painting by any chance, is it?

"I hear you, my dearest. And no, we are not. It is simply that Henry Weaver has asked me to look at a watercolour he has inherited, the next time I'm in Newcastle.

"Henry Weaver? Isn't he that shabby old chap who drives a dreadful brown car?"

This was all too accurate. Henry Weaver drove one of the most awful cars of my acquaintance: a brown Allegro estate of unlovely antiquity and little performance. It was a late seventies model, considered by many to be the least desirable in a long line of undesirable British motor cars. He was obstinate about it, refusing to scrap it against all advice, claiming that it would be prized as vintage one day whilst, contrarily, extolling its lack of attraction to thieves. You could leave it anywhere, he said, no one would touch it. He wouldn't listen to my remarks about it's effect on potential customers. You could hardly present it, I told him, as the vehicle of a successful, self-employed researcher and businessman.

"Unique" he would rasp back at me. "As a *cachila*, it is absolutely unique. They'll never replace this sort of engineering."

His treatment of the vehicle belied his enthusiasm for it. Henrys attention to its servicing gave credence to the old joke about the statement in car ads claiming a vehicle to be maintained regardless of expense. He never spent anything he could avoid spending upon it. A mechanic friend called Sammy Simes, out on the Icklesham road, despairingly tried to keep the car legal, using spares from breakers yards and charging only ten pounds an hour for his services, but it seemed like a losing battle.

"That's Henry "I said to Sue. "But he isn't so old, though he may seem it. He went to St.Georges at the same time as I did."

"Oh, yes." Her expression turned mischievous. "I remember him saying that you were at school together."

"Thank you, Sue. Your memory is, as ever, flawless."

"Well a watercolour from Henry Weaver up in Newcastle of all places isn't going to cause any earthquakes. I'm surprised that you're taking the trouble. Shouldn't you tell him to trot it along to a good auctioneer?"

"Most probably. But I will be going to Newcastle anyway, so it's no great sacrifice. And you know how it is with Henry. These old friendships have their obligations. The poor guy has had a very rough time."

"*Noblesse oblige*, eh Tim?"

I thought of throwing a cushion at her but she caught my expression immediately and smiled at me, melting my heart.

"It's very kind of you, sweetheart," she said, before I could respond. "I'm glad that my husband hasn't allowed merchant banking to destroy all feeling for unfortunate old acquaintances.

You've always been kind to Henry, even if some of those films he drags you off to are decidedly esoteric."

She paused and looked pensive. "And there can't be any harm in a watercolour of Newcastle, can there? No harm at all."

"No," I answered. "There can't."

Which made both of us dead wrong.

Chapter 4

The drive from Turin to Pinerolo was a doddle. To the south west of the city is a flat, mostly agricultural area, with things like maize and pollenta gradually giving way to kiwi fruit, apples and walnuts as you come off the level and start to climb. Much of it looked like the prosperous suburbs of a wealthy city rather than the approach to wild Alpine valleys. Pinerolo was once Pigneron, with proper Vauban fortresses, associations with Fouquet and much earlier Romish palaces, now all gone. I didn't have time for all that. I pressed on, past Bricherasio to Torre Pellice, to the start of where Italy winds up into France, long the cultural influence of this region. No wonder the Francophile Sir Richard had homed in here, following his Savoyard nose.

The weather was fine but mature, with a hint of misty autumn just starting to soften the light. Torre Pellice soon came into sight and I turned off the main road into the town, negotiating a narrow shopping street before finding my way. The Albergo Del Centro was placed in a side street but it was built round a courtyard, with a restaurant the principal feature of the ground floor and hotel rooms in the balconied wings above. At the entrance there was a huge wicker basket full of big beautiful mushrooms, boletus all of them, brown and rounded to justify their Italian sobriquet - *porcini* - little pigs - and, if you bent to them, giving off a wonderful musty aroma. Next to them was a small blackboard with the dish of the day chalked upon it: *Funghi Fritti*. My stomach juices perked up appreciatively.

Past the mushrooms, in the entrance lobby, stood Sir Richard White, cool, tall and spare, clad in a fine check sports jacket, light grey trousers and crisp cream shirt with silk tie. He glanced down at his gold wristwatch briefly before his thin, lined, beaky face looked fully at me.

"Excellent" he said. "Well done, Simpson. Your timing is, as ever, impeccable."

He held out a hand and I shook it formally, finding it as dry and sinewy as the man himself. At the same time, his words sent warning shockwaves through my brain.

Simpson?

The surname jarred; Sir Richard and I have long been on close enough terms for him to call me by my Christian name. After several hazardous experiences together I have earned the right to do the same with him. Normally, in private or at the Bank with family, we are familiar. I tend to keep respectfully to his title in front of strangers. Why this sudden, formal, slightly condescending use of my surname? Had our relationship suddenly become indefinably remote, distanced by a psychological change in the man? Was his fax to Jeremy evidence of mental aberration? Or was this a warning of some kind?

"Sir Richard" I responded courteously, letting the hand drop. "I hope you are well?"

He nodded shortly. "Thank you, Simpson. I am in excellent health. You, I have to say, look your normal robust self. I am glad to see that you keep fit. This is an interesting region but it can be a taxing one to explore on foot. We will not do that just now but, if you would care to check in to the hotel and put your case in your room, I will meet you outside at my car. I wish to drive up to Bobbio whilst explaining my ideas to you and describing the regional background. There is an opportunity for us here."

"Very good, Sir Richard."

No pause for coffee, no time to relax. Lunchtime might be only half an hour off but it seemed that the *funghi fritti* were not going to get near my stomach. I checked in with a pleasant hotel proprietor's wife, took my bag upstairs and put it in my sparse but clean single room. There I washed, dried my face, looked at my broken nose in the mirror and told it silently that there was both a rummy aroma and more to this than met the eye. The nose, detecting no aromas in particular apart from soap, looked flatly back without comment. I went back downstairs and out into the street, looking up over the rooftops to enjoy the steep hillsides rising to rocky edges on high above the buildings.

Sir Richard's Jaguar saloon was parked not far from my hire car. He gestured for me to get in without comment and, negotiating back to the centre of town, turned left past the Town Hall and proceeded out along a straight road - the Via Arnaud - past what looked like municipal buildings or perhaps a museum and library, on either side. Further on came a handsome terrace of nineteenth century houses set back behind a hedge, with front gardens in an almost English manner.

"Beckwith's houses for the Professors of the College," Sir Richard said, gesturing towards them.

"Oh really?"

"Beckwith himself is buried in the cemetery we shall pass to our left on our way out towards Bobbio."

"Indeed?"

A vision of Jeremy's face came to my mind after this exchange. Mad, it was mouthing, gone absolutely bonkers, told you so.

I managed to suppress it.

"I take it you are unfamiliar with Waldensian history?" Sir Richard kept the Jaguar, a continental version with left hand drive, running smoothly along the road towards the rising, rugged mountains in the distance.

"Not my forte, no, Sir Richard. Protestant martyrs of some sort, I understand."

He treated my comment as confirmatory evidence of ignorance. "The name Waldensian is said to come from Valdo, a merchant of Lyons who chose Christian poverty in the Middle Ages. It could however, come from the Valais, i.e. people from valleys. There is dissension on this. They are also known as the Vaudois. Be that as it may, Valdo and his followers, a religious community here, were excommunicated and became Calvinist. They abolished Catholic worship over a wide area in these mountains during one hundred and fifty years. To their credit in 1532 they produced the Olivetan Bible, the first translation of the whole Bible into French, even though it was not their language. They spoke a version of Provençal. It remained the standard French Bible for three hundred years."

"Good heavens." To humour rather than to scoff was clearly best policy. "So they made a considerable contribution to French religious life?"

He nodded approvingly at my attention. "But they disagreed with Catholic practices. They were typical Protestants to whom the written word was more important than graven imagery. Reading the Bible, and eschewing paintings as juvenile condescension, was all to them. In 1655, following examples set in 1386 and 1560 by the Duke of Savoy, the armies of France and Savoy invaded the valleys and massacred a large part of the population, here in what are known as the Cottian Alps."

"Cottian?"

"From Cottius, a pagan king of possibly the first century AD."

"I see." I didn't, but so what?

"Many of the people were inhumanly tortured. They had always defended themselves stoutly but numbers and treachery overcame them. Lurid depictions of their treatment were circulated. Other European Protestants were outraged. Particularly Cromwell, who was absolutely incensed. He refused to sign a Treaty with France, which had been about to be signed, berating the King and Cardinal with his fury. More importantly, he sent a livid message to the Duke of Savoy, saying that if he didn't stop this persecution forthwith, the English fleet would be sent to bombard Nice in retribution."

"Nice? Why Nice? Bit far away, isn't it?"

"Nice was part of the Duchy of Savoy."

"Oh. I see. An early example of gunboat diplomacy, then."

"Indeed. And it worked. The Waldensians, although much decimated, were granted a sort of peace. However, upon the Revocation of the Edict of Nantes in 1685 - which led to all those Huguenots coming to England - Louis the Fourteenth forced the Duke of Savoy to try extermination once again. Horrible measures ensued, in which Irish mercenaries were used. After more remonstrations by Protestant powers, a handful of survivors were sent into exile over the Alps into Switzerland."

"But that was not the end of the story?"

Jeremy would accuse me of humouring the old idiot too much. What had I to lose? Lunch looked like a goner anyway.

Sir Richard gave me a sharp glance, as though to check my attitude, then resumed. "Indeed it was not. A man called Arnaud led the Waldensians back in 1689. About 800 started out but they were down to 600 by the time they'd crossed the Alps in appalling circumstances. However, the survivors were ferocious and full of religious fervour. Large forces of French tried to stop them but were absolutely routed."

"A tough lot, these Waldensians, then."

"The feat is known as the Glorious Return. The Duke of Savoy gave up. He allowed them to settle back here but they were confined to their valleys like Jews in ghettos. Some moved to Germany. Ah, here we are, coming into Bobbio Pellice."

The road, moving ever upwards amongst rural valley landscapes with a river flowing to our left, had passed isolated Alpine farmhouses and walled fields through one small hamlet called Villar before approaching Bobbio. Ancient stone buildings mingled with later and modern edifices. There was a square and a church. Or two churches. We passed through, out past another sort of square until we reached an Esso filling station on the outskirts of town. Sir Richard pulled off the road and parked by a strong stone wall overlooking the valley, with its rushing stony river below. He got out so I followed.

He took off his jacket, folded it carefully and put it on his seat. Then he moved away from the car and stood in his shirt and tie without speaking by the stone wall, as though expecting something. It wasn't very warm and the procedure was the reverse of normal. Puzzled, I looked about me to see how, at an angle, the wall crossed the road, leaving a gap like a gateway, to go higher up past a renovated workshop building to what looked like a small sluice gate controlling a side stream. I turned back and sat on the top of the stone surface - it wasn't very high - to look at Sir Richard White with my most quizzical expression.

I was hoping to get some sense, rather than the exposition of historical trivia, out of all this.

"It is here" he announced, in response to my look "that Cromwell financed the dyke."

"The what?" Grief, I thought, this is hardly Holland. Did he really say a dyke? Why has he taken his jacket off? What in hell is he up to?

"Cromwell's Dyke. In winter the river often flooded the town, causing misery and hardship. Cromwell agreed to finance a dyke to help his fellow-Protestants. A flood barrier, in effect. It has been known, ever since, as Cromwell's Dyke. In gratitude for his having it built."

"So where is it?"

"You are sitting on it."

I grinned, looked at him, jumped down, and walked a pace or two away to look at the run of the wall more carefully. The air up here was keener and the feeling more mountainous, even though the real mountain peaks were away in the distance to the north of us. It was a mundane scene: the garage pumps, a few parked vans, a workshop, the road leading back into the village. Above us the sky was becoming cloudy. We might have been in North Yorkshire or Northumberland except for the Alps rising high beyond. I began to get a strong feeling of unreality. Had he actually gone doolally?

"He didn't build it really, though." Sir Richard was watching me intently.

"What?" I frowned at him.

"The dyke. Cromwell raised a National Fund for the Waldensians and sent them money but he died before any dyke could be built. Two elders went to England but by that time Charles II was on the throne and they got short shrift. He said he didn't consider himself bound by any engagement made by a usurper, a tyrant and a regicide, nor was he responsible for his debts."

"Bastard. He had Catholic sympathies anyway. I suppose he spent the money on Nell Gwyn?"

"This wasn't built until the early eighteenth century. But it has always been called Cromwell's Dyke in gratitude for his support."

He was still watching me intently but he looked keen and alert, not dispossessed of reason. I closed my eyes and then opened them again. I'd had enough. More than enough. I moved nearer to him.

"It's time to end this, Richard."

His eyebrows lifted. "End what? What do you mean?"

"A dyke that isn't a dyke called Cromwell's when it isn't Cromwell's in a place up a blind valley - the road doesn't go through to France, it's a dead end, however scenic - that has no relevance to anything the bank is doing. And remarks about some geezer called Beckwith who I've never heard of, nor his professorial houses." I looked back at the car and his jacket as comprehension dawned. "We are out in the open air where no one can hear us. Come on: what's all this about?"

Suddenly he smiled. It broke his austere face into a warm, even benign countenance.

"My dear boy. I knew I could rely on you" he said. "I expect they think I've flipped my lid back in London, do they?"

"Er, well, let us just say they are concerned, Richard."

"Very tactful. How about some lunch? You must be peckish. There's quite a good local restaurant and bar just down the road. We can savour the *funghi fritti* at the Albergo tonight."

"Lunch would be great. And tonight would be fine. But - "

He held up a hand. "Don't say anything confidential while we're in the car. Or while I've got my jacket on."

I gaped at him momentarily before I realised I had fully understood. Then I nodded.

And at that moment, my mobile phone rang.

Chapter 5

Sir Richard frowned. "I hate those things. I absolutely refuse to carry a mobile phone."

"Indispensable for we lesser mortals" I answered. "Mind if I answer it?"

He turned back to look over Cromwell's low stone dyke below, to the left, where a sports ground of some kind lay on flatter land near the rushing river. "Go ahead."

"Tim Simpson" I said, into the instrument.

"Tim?" The voice on the phone was hoarse, a bit like Henry Weaver's but not his. It had a stronger, more practical edge to it.

"Yes" I answered. "Who's that?"

"It's me. Sammy Simes. I had to twist your secretary's arm at your Bank to get this number."

"Hi, Sammy" I said, quickly recollecting Henry's long-suffering garage man. "How are you?"

What on earth could he want?

"I'm all right. This is not about me. It's about Henry Weaver."

"Henry?" I frowned. The name usually brought out a frown of some sort in me, even if humorous rather than exasperated. "What about him?"

"He's dead, mate. Bloody dead, he is."

"What?" My tone made Sir Richard turn slightly from his perusal of Bobbio's green sports field surfaces to look at me as I exclaimed. "Dead?"

"As a doornail." Concern for mortality, or maybe just tobacco, made the tones even hoarser. "Crashed, last night. On the A21. At Whatlington. You know, where they're always crashing. Coming back late from London, he was. Fell asleep at the wheel, they reckon. Where they all do. Smack into an oak tree. Copper pal, drops in to my local newsagents every morning for a packet of fags, told me when I went to get mine, just now. He knew the car, you see. Seen it here. Gave me quite a turn, I can tell you."

"Christ. Henry Weaver dead. This is a shock. A real shock."

"Right. He said the other day I was to tell you if anything happened to him. So I thought you'd want to know, soonest."

Temporarily, the implication of what he'd just said went past me.

"He - he was in the Allegro?"

" 'Course he was. Didn't drive anything else, did he? Didn't have a spare Rolls handy, nor a Jag in a lock-up, secret, did he? Not the car's fault. Not at all. Write-off, it is, though. Absolute write-off. Junked."

"Not surprising."

"Not half. It's not exactly robust, that car. They reckon Henry was a bit over the limit, too. Drink, that is. At least, that's what the copper hinted."

A thought occurred to me.

"Was there - I mean - was anyone else involved? Or hurt?"

"Nope. He was alone. Well he would be, wouldn't he? You ever know anyone want to go in that thing?"

"No. I suppose not."

There was a rasping half-chuckle from the other end. "You weren't thinking he had a bird with him, were you?"

"Not really, no."

"Never knew of one, did you?"

"Can't say that I did, Sammy."

I was answering on automatic. My mind had gone temporarily numb. The message I left on the answerphone, I thought: did he get it? Why an accident now? Why now, just when he'd come up with a painting for me to look at? Only a watercolour, but a painting none the less. Was this the Art Fund's evil genie at work again? What would Sue have to say?

"You all right?" Sammy Simes demanded, at the other end of the line.

44

"Yes thanks, Sammy. Bit of shock, that's all."

"Sure it is. You take it easy, now."

"One car less to mend, eh, Sammy?"

Sammy Simes's car repair shop, out on the Icklesham road, was housed in a sagging, corrugated-iron barn in a cluster of wet farm buildings down a rutted inland track. In winter, freezing wind blew through cracks in the boarding. Frost nipped the air when rain wasn't driving in through a big doorway left open for the light. Sammy was kind; he kept old Henry's Allegro going for many years after it should have dropped to bits. He had sources of used spares at low prices and never charged Henry more than ten quid an hour for his time.

"Thank God for that" he responded. "That car was a real dog. I hated it. The engine wouldn't knock the skin off a rice pudding. But I'll miss old Henry. Pedantic bastard. There was a lot more to him than he let on, I reckon. We'll never know. I mean, he managed to stoke the Allegro up fast enough to kill himself, which is an achievement. Take care, Tim. I've told you as I promised. See you at the funeral."

"You too, Sammy." I nearly turned the phone off before a thought struck me. "Sammy?"

"Yes, Tim?"

"Did you say the crash was at Whatlington?"

"Yeah, that's it. Somewhere beyond the Royal Oak pub. A bend on the road."

"The Royal Oak." My Waldensian surroundings faded around me. A vision of Henry's face came to my mind, Henry and I discussing biography and Hesketh Pearson on one of several sessions at Porter's Wine Bar in Hastings Old Town then later, much later, over a steak at the Royal Oak.

"Anything wrong, Tim?"

"I don't think so, Sammy. But I'd be grateful if you could do something for me."

"Sure. What?"

I braced myself carefully. "Could you look at the car? You

knew it better than anyone. Maybe your copper pal could let you. Tell him you just want to satisfy yourself it wasn't the car 's fault."

There was a brief, tense silence. Then the voice came back, still strong, if anything stronger. "He fell asleep, Tim. *Asleep.* At the wheel. That's what they said. There was nothing to do with the car."

"I heard you. I'm sure there's no responsibility of yours, Sammy. All the same, will you do it? Please? I'll pay for it. An examination, I mean."

Another pregnant silence. Then, rather resentfully: "Why? What for? What's up?"

I shook my head for my own benefit. "Nothing. Just me getting the willies, Sammy. The heebie-jeebies. Just for reassurance, will you do it? Please?"

The voice on the other end went into a sort of reflective mode, as though assessing what I'd asked for carefully. "He was a bit funny when he brought it in the day before yesterday. Said if anything happened, I was to tell you."

"Anything happened? What sort of anything?"

"Didn't say. I thought he was a bit odd. But now something has happened, hasn't it? He had a meeting, he said. Was in a hurry. To tell you, though, if anything happened. Gave me your number at the Bank. I thought he was strange. Maybe he'd had a drop."

"What did he bring the car in for?"

"Indicator switch gone. I fixed it. Only a fuse."

"Did he say where his meeting was?'

"He said Croydon this time, I think. Otherwise he'd have gone by train. He'd been going up to London quite a bit, by train, recently."

"Look Sammy, I'll come and see you when I get back. I promise. But have a quick look at that car. All right?"

"Well maybe, Tim."

"You know it better than anyone. Just the obvious. Please?"

"Don't fancy it, Tim. Bit grisly, really."

"Please."

"Well, for you I'll try. The police have got it, I think. Then it'll go to a wrecker's. It'll have to be soon."

"Please."

"OK. 'Bye, Tim."

"'Bye Sammy."

Sir Richard White was watching me carefully, holding his car door open. "Bad news?" he enquired.

I looked round at the high lush fields and woods of Alpine Italy, the Esso filling station, the rough stone wall attributed to Cromwell, the looming mountains shutting out France. Nothing like the road past the Royal Oak at Whatlington, nothing at all. Why there, though, Henry? Why there?

"A friend." I answered Sir Richard. "Killed in a car crash."

"I'm sorry. Was he close?"

"Not that close but" - I never thought to hear myself say it - "we were at school together."

Chapter 6

"You took the hint well," Sir Richard said. "You are always commendably formal in front of strangers. I wanted to let you know that strangers might be present. Not in substance, but in effect, maybe."

"Since when?"

"Since I saw something alarming, something I wasn't supposed to see, in Belley."

We were sitting in a homely café-bar cum restaurant near the bus terminal in Bobbio. At a long table across from us a group of old men were playing dominoes, croaking in local dialect between the clack of counters and sips of strange dark drinks in small glasses. Above them, on the wall, hung a big faded photograph of a reunion of wartime prisoners from a Piedmontese Alpine regiment, showing men ranged in ranks like a school photograph with names carefully printed under. There were a lot of them, in blazers and suits, and they looked serious, like schoolboys are meant to do on those annual portrait occasions, except that there's always some joker who grins. I had eaten roast veal and was feeling better. A jug of light red wine had helped, too. Trying to decipher the faces, I wondered how many of the old men with their dominoes had been in the photograph when it was taken sometime in the fifties.

The fifties: I wasn't born then, nor was Henry Weaver. He was gone, now. The sense of emptiness, pushed back by the meal, began to return.

Sir Richard had another jacket on, one he'd taken from the boot of the Jaguar. It was a light wool check too, browner than the first one. He looked cool and collected but alert, like a stringy, elderly thinker dealing with an interesting problem, a chess move or a crossword clue or a brain teaser requiring the identification of a key word, concept or connection.

"I found one small device on the back of my jacket lapel" he said. "And I'm sure another is somewhere in the car."

"Bugs?"

"Listening devices of some sort. The one on my jacket I found quite by accident. I've left it there to allay fears. It would be logical to assume that there is one on or in my car somewhere. It is the most accessible place."

"Logical, yes. But they would have to have a remarkable range. And how did all this come about?"

He paused, thought for a moment, and sat more comfortably in his chair. "Have you ever come across Brillat-Savarin?" he asked.

"No."

"Interesting chap. Lawyer. Cousin of Récamier, whose wife Juliette, in a painting, made the couch famous. A survivor, like Talleyrand, of all that revolutionary turmoil. Went to New York to avoid the guillotine, taught French and played first fiddle at the John Street Theater. Came back, became quite an important judge, survived political upheavals and wars, wrote a bit of stylish pornography then, in the last three months of his life, produced *La Physiologie du Goût*, which is not a cookery book but a discussion of eating in its widest sense. Almost as soon as he was famous he dropped dead."

He turned and waved at the only waitress to order coffee. I sat without speaking. Sir Richard, I began to think, has been on his own for too long. All this history. How old must he be, now? Late seventies, certainly; he was in SOE during the war, when he met Charles Maucourt, Eugène's elder brother, now gone. That gave us our relationship with Maucourt's. He could be knocking on eighty, Christ, he must be knocking on eighty. He's remarkable for his age, well come to think of it, so many of them are, these days.

Henry Weaver never would be, though, not now.

Not that I ever thought of Henry as being a candidate for a ripe old age. Why not?

"Brillat-Savarin was a provincial from Belley" he went on. "Ever been there?"

"Never."

"Nor had I. There was a meeting in Lyon I had to attend concerning various bits of industrial financing. It finished on a Friday lunchtime. I re-read the book not long ago and decided, out of sheer curiosity and having the weekend free, to drive on the motorway to Chambéry after the meeting and turn off via St.Genix to go to Belley. It's not far; about fifty miles as the crow flies. If there were no suitable hotel I could always pop over to Aix-les-Bains and stay on the Grand Avenue de Lord Revelstoke."

"Very grand" I murmured. "Revelstoke was, of course, the banker, Baring, of Barings, now no longer with us due to the attentions of a currency dealer."

"Correct. And tragic. There are very few of us left, Tim. White's is a survival, some might say an anachronism."

"Let 'em." So was Henry, I thought, an anachronism well before his time, poor bastard. Maybe he's better off. No: that's the sort of smug thought people use to brush a death out of their thinking. Have you asked Henry whether he's better off? What would he reply?

"Quite so. But it shows how one mere slip can demolish the work of generations. A fact which will bear thinking when my narrative is complete." He paused, thought again, then went on. "Belley was charming. An old cathedral city fallen into quietude by being passed over in favour of Bourg-en-Bresse. Belley was once the capital of the province of Bugey, itself part of the Italian Duchy of Savoy. The region was annexed by France after the Treaty of Lyon in 1601. It had already fallen under the sway of the Burgundians of François I. Then Henri IV converted to Catholicism in order to end French religious wars and defeated the Dukes of Savoy. Bugey became permanently French. Centralisation ensued, eroding local laws and customs. Paris created a new *département*, called Ain, of which Bourg-en-Bresse was made the capital rather than anywhere further south. The Bugey was summarily abolished. Conqueror's rights, I suppose, but the effects of regional downgrading were predictable."

"End of local autonomy?"

He nodded. "Belley became a backwater. The people, who felt closer to Savoy than to Paris, resented this but had to accept the destruction of many of their traditions from distant, centralised controls."

"Even more lessons for modern times."

"Quite so. Belley is hardly a city, now. A small town above the Rhône, would be a more accurate description, in a remote, picturesque, rugged area but with little pretensions for visitors. There is an Episcopal palace and the Grand'Rue, a main street of rather flat historic façades to town houses which conceal fine Renaissance courtyards. Brillat-Savarin was born at number sixty-two. His father was a prosperous lawyer, part of the local elite. It was said that due to the boredom of life in such provinces, cooking and food were a major preoccupation, one from which Brillat-Savarin later drew his inspiration."

Coffee arrived and he paused as it was served. The old men suddenly all laughed together at some clever move of the dominoes, a cackling mixture of triumph and despair. One of them stood up, looked across curiously, more at the elderly Sir Richard than at me, then moved away towards the bar, empty glass in hand. I put a lump of sugar in my *espresso*. The elderly interested in the elderly; did Sir Richard play mental dominoes, fitting matching numbers to matching patterns in that active, experienced brain of his? Did Henry Weaver when he carried out his desk research?

"I parked near the Cathedral," he continued, stirring his own *cappuccino*, "and went for a stroll round, including the Cathedral itself, which I entered. My car has French registration but I suppose a Jaguar is a little unusual and may attract attention. I was about to leave the Cathedral, perhaps half an hour later, when I saw three people looking at it. Their backs were to me but there was a familiarity about them, something that made me move back behind a convenient newspaper and postcard holder right in the entrance. They didn't see me, I'm sure of that. When they turned, I got a shock. One of them was Shauna Spring; I recognised her immediately. Do you know her?"

"No."

"Then you must accept my assurance of her easy recognition. Another was Jacques Charville."

I must have gaped. "Jacques Charville? The squeaker at Maucourt's?"

He pulled his mouth down at the corners in a humorous reaction to my description. "I had forgotten that you have not been over to Paris for quite a while. Charville, as a researcher, may have been the - the squeaker, as you put it - at the time of your involvement in the carpet industry affair three or more years ago, but he is no longer a mere squeaker. He is Head of Research at Maucourt's."

"What? Good Grief! Little Jacques Charville?"

"Indeed. Times move on, Tim, and people move with them or perish. Eugène Maucourt professes himself very impressed with Charville, in that rather disdainful way Eugène has with those who supply him with essential information. He was responsible for the promotion and the enlargement of Maucourt's research facilities."

"Heavens. Jacques may be a good little beaver, but I don't see him masterminding a dam."

"You have a way of putting things which cuts to the bone. I agree with you and of the younger generation so does Eugène's great-nephew Christian, who you know well. But I am in a delicate position vis-à-vis Maucourt's despite being a board member. It is not for me to comment on internal appointments. Eugène regards Charville as a technician, the mechanic to his vehicle, as it were, and steers in his own grand way confident in the knowledge that the facts fed to him for his decisions are reliable. It is this aspect which disturbs me."

"You mean what the blazes was Jacques doing in Belley, of all places, with Shauna Spring and - who was the third person?"

Sir Richard's face set. "An Italian entrepreneur from Turin called Bertrasconi. I recognised him, too. Head of Officine Bertrasconi, a maker of electronic instruments on a grand scale. A man who has absolutely disdained the consortium which we, and Maucourt Frères, are involved in setting up as part of a syndicate."

"Oh dear. The thick plottens."

"Charville must have recognised my car. He knows it from its parking place when I occasionally brave the Faubourg St.Honoré."

Maucourt Frères premises are behind the Elysée Palace, in a street which actually crosses the Faubourg St.Honoré. They have a fine, late eighteenth-century building with imposing double-arched doors which lead to a courtyard once for carriages, overlooked by long Directoire-style windows in three stories whose floors creak the creaks of old, fine, seasoned timber. Other parts of Paris might sport technological skyscrapers and monolithic blocks of modernist architectural merit but Maucourt Frères preserve the seemly façades of yesteryear.

"What on earth was Jacques doing? What kind of research gets him together with Shauna Spring and this Bertrasconi at the same time as we and Maucourt are involved in a highly confidential project in which there is, clearly, a conflict of interest?"

"Precisely my thoughts."

"That must have given 'em a turn. Seeing your car there in Belley, right out of the blue."

"I imagine it did. Although they couldn't know whether it was just pure chance or whether I was stalking them."

"You'd be a poor stalker to be so obvious."

"True. I thought that, too."

"Why Belley? I assume that you were the only fan of

Brillat-Savarin's there, that day, unless the other three have taken to gastronomic history, too."

He smiled in agreement. "One from England, one from Paris, one from Turin. The one from England was - I checked discreetly back in London - actually attending an international financial conference in Geneva organised by some quango or another. She goes to such things regularly, due to her past involvement. Charville had attended the same meetings as I had in Lyon, but for only part of the time. He left before me, giving the impression that he was going straight back to Paris. So you have Turin, Lyon and Geneva as your starting points. All three cities are a bit public, a bit risky, in which to meet. Somewhere central to them, like Chambéry, might be more discreet, or even Aix-les-Bains, but they too have many visitors."

I nodded. "Always be good when you travel. You never know who you'll bump into."

"A wise precaution at all times, Tim. If, however, you were driving from Turin to, say, Paris, taking the Fréjus tunnel rather than Mont-Blanc, heading north to the A42 autoroute to Bourg-en-Bresse, then the A6 past Chalon-sur-Saone, Belley would be smack in line. Who ever goes to a backwater like Belley? But it is a convenient place, and a discreet one, for the key protagonist - Bertrasconi - to stop in and meet the others while on one of the many pan-European journeys he makes in his Ferrari to various factories. Shauna Spring could nip down from Geneva in less than an hour. Charville's journey would, like mine, also take no more than an hour."

"That means prior collusion."

"Indeed. Many questions raised themselves in my head as I cowered behind the postcards. I was fortunate; I had caught them at what must have been a very brief moment, for they walked briskly away from my car and were quickly out of my sight."

"They obviously didn't want you to see them together."

"Evidently. But how could they know whether I'd seen

them or not? Bertrasconi's Ferrari is distinctive but there are many Ferraris about these days. Who would associate him necessarily with that one? Charville drives an unremarkable Renault Laguna and Shauna Spring, presumably, had a hire car. They must have been agitated by Charville's confirmation that the Jaguar was mine, but they would look foolish if they moved precipitately on the assumption that I'd seen them. I was nowhere in view. Whatever meeting place they used, presumably a restaurant or café, or even just one of the cars, had not yielded a sight of me. Yet my car was not clandestinely parked, quite the opposite. They must have assumed that I was in the Cathedral, acting touristically."

"But that was still worrying."

"Exactly. Hence the bug or bugs."

"How on earth did one get on to your jacket?"

"I'm coming to that. Once I thought they'd left and the coast was clear, I came out from behind my postcard rack. My first instinct was to get in the car and drive away with all despatch, but then I reasoned with myself. If I left precipitately, it would confirm that I'd seen something disturbing and was away in all turmoil. By taking my time, making sure they were gone, it might convince whoever they might leave to watch me that I was, in fact, taking a leisurely look at a quaint place without any external motive. So this I did. I went to a café, ordered a cold beer, and sat watching the world like any idle tourist."

"You didn't see any more of them?"

"Not at all. Wherever they'd gone, they'd disappeared completely. I think they probably made off in different directions - at least, Bertrasconi and Spring did, but I think they left Charville behind to follow me."

"Ever elected the squeaker, our Jacques. His bad luck that the other two are so highfalutin; they'd never do a tailing job."

"However it was decided, I was followed once I drove off, I'm sure of it, now."

"By a Renault Laguna?"

"Probably. I'm afraid I'm not very good at driving with one eye in the rear mirror these days and one Renault Laguna looks much like another to me. At the time, I was uncertain. But now I'm convinced that I was followed to Aix."

"You stayed in Aix-les-Bains for the night?"

"On the Grand Avenue de Lord Revelstoke. A small, private, exclusive hotel - the *Vieux Bedeau* - I have used before."

How very appropriate, I thought, for Sir Richard to stay at an hotel called the Old Beadle. Precisely the sort of function he is so talented at performing.

"My clothes were hung up for me by the room valet who carried my case in from the car. It's that sort of place. After making a few calls - one to check where Shauna Spring was supposed to be - I eventually went out to dinner. My mind was highly preoccupied."

"I can imagine."

"I did not feel in any way endangered. After all, the three might have a perfectly good explanation for their meeting. They might not think I had seen them, so might take no action. I decided to wait and see if Charville came up with an account of his meeting the following week, when I would be in contact with Paris. Shauna Spring might produce some account before or at the next syndicate meeting; after all, Bertrasconi might be making secret overtures, overtures that would upset things in many directions and need great care. There might be legitimate reasons for discretion. I am, as you know, inclined to give people the benefit of the doubt."

"You are indeed."

"The following morning - Saturday - I went out to get a paper while the room valet packed my things. It had got warmer and, on my return, I decided to change my jacket, which had been hanging with two others in the wardrobe overnight. I asked the valet to put the new one on the bed for me while I used the bathroom, and to pack the one I'd taken off. When I came out, everything was packed and the valet

56

stood holding the jacket for me to slip into. Which I did. I drove off wearing it. I discovered the device, just like a small calculator battery, behind the lapel by pure accident, when I stopped and turned, twisted in my seat, to get a better look at my road map. The lapel folded over and the cold metal touched my neck."

"Must have been a shock."

His face suddenly looked old. "It chilled me to the marrow. I felt violated. I could also assume that my car had been similarly dealt with. I was being permanently scrutinised. It meant that the meeting I had seen was clandestine for illegitimate, possibly criminally fraudulent reasons. No one innocent plants bugs. I had definitely been followed and someone had, very quickly, arranged to tag me so as to find out what I knew. Presumably the valet was bribed."

"They must have moved very quickly. That would be arranged by Bertrasconi, almost certainly."

"My assumption as well. His organisation probably produces such things. My focus shifted to Turin. I suddenly needed a reason to be in the area of Turin so that I, and maybe eventually you, could start to find out what on earth was going on. Make discreet enquiries. It is, in fact, the mushroom season around Belley and I thought that to go to the Turin area on the pretext of mushrooms only would seem false. It was then that I remembered Captain Stephens's book."

"Who?"

"Captain R.M.Stephens. A retired naval man who lived in Cooden, the golfing area of Bexhill-on-Sea. He wrote a slim volume entitled *The Burning Bush* all about the Waldensians in the Cottian Alps. I picked it up some time ago on the Left Bank in Paris. A paperback curiosity. I will arrange for my copy to be sent to you. It is an account of the Waldensian history, which I have summarised for you, as well as a sort of tourist guide. The English connections with these valleys might be developed in some way, for tourism. The English like to ramble and there is excellent mountain rambling here on footpaths designated by the Italian authorities. It is much cheaper than Britain to stay here and the food, if I may say so, is better by far in value as well as execution."

"You don't need to convince me. Eating in England is currently either exorbitantly expensive or not much cop."

"We have financed tourist projects in the past. I concocted a fax which made no reference to what I'd seen in Belley, proposing an examination of a possible tourist project, of which the current Waldensian Church might approve, with suitable religious study groups thrown in. Ecumenical, emphasising the international connections, historical, a sort of healthy foreign version of walking in Yorkshire or Scotland. People do it in France and Spain, walking to Compostela and so on; why not here? *Mens sana in corpore sanum* but with better food and drink and some spirituality thrown in." He grinned. "I styled the fax on the lines of a senior, rather detached board member's suggestion, rather like a Bishop addressing the House of Lords."

"You overdid that part."

The grin broadened. "I sent it deliberately to the open office fax, not Jeremy or anyone else's private one. That way I'd be sure of the news spreading."

"You were right. Shauna Spring saw it. Her concern, along with other board members, was expressed in terms of mental condition. I doubt if she's still worrying about your presence in Belley or the possibility that you know she was there."

"About which she has told no one." His face went serious. "This could be very important. We only have to get entangled in one major industrial financing disaster to be weakened severely. Which would mean at best a take-over and at worst disappearance."

"Surely this syndicate doesn't commit us to that extent?"

"It easily could. When you speak of major restructuring in Europe, speak in billions."

"What do you want me to do? Jeremy was most emphatic that I should steer clear of Turin."

"So I assumed, too. It will be an advantage for you, initially. Turin will be for me to cover, as will Paris, also initially. I want you to go back and cover London. You may raise your eyebrows at being hauled all this way simply to be sent back, but this tourist concept, if it is to remain a suitable red herring, needs a little London spadework. I have arranged a meeting with a suitable contact for myself, Emilio Bonnetti, at the Egyptian Museum tomorrow after you go back. I have used his services before. I shall also visit the Waldensian Church in Turin. You need to be at the Bank in order to get fully familiar with the electronics syndicate and to check on Shauna Spring. Then we shall team up again. I'll call you on that awful mobile thing or at your home if necessary, for security."

"Jeremy won't like my poking my nose in. Unless I am to enlighten him on the real reason for my interest?"

He gave me a shrewd look. "I think that the importance of this matter is such that Jeremy would be unwise to exclude you. However, I leave you to deal with Jeremy as you think fit. You have worked with him for years and are of a much nearer generation. Proceed as your experience dictates."

My experience: a shiver went down my back as a brief mental vision of Henry Weaver's academically-inclined face flitted past me. Fortunately, Jeremy knew nothing about Henry. It seemed that there would be little reason to explain the Newcastle connection to him, now. That space was empty. The thought made me feel cold. Losses of that kind bring John Donne to mind. In front of me, Sir Richard White's lined, angular face waited expectantly, his expression slightly softening as his eyes searched my face for enlightenment on my thought processes.

"Richard" I finally said, feeling the cold feeling creep over everything "I don't think you should do this."

"Why not?"

"If there is a criminal fraud in the offing, and it seems that there is, with all due respect it is not the sort of thing for you to be stalking. People engaged in major frauds can turn very dangerous."

He smiled. "I'm touched by your solicitude, Tim. But I do not think the little - squeaker - Jacques can be dangerous. Nor, despite her abrasive reputation, is Shauna Spring likely to embrace violence as a normal procedure."

"Which leaves Bertrasconi. From what you say, a man of considerable resource and territorial ambition. All the more reason for not going to Turin. Leave him and his devices to me."

He shook his head. "Which leaves Bertrasconi, as you say. If you go to Turin, suspicions might be aroused much more than if I, an old buffer, go there to pursue my strange but just credible project. I shall be very circumspect. And, if it sets your mind at rest, in Turin I shall ask Emilio Bonnetti to make any practical enquiries, or moves, that might alert Bertrasconi to my presence and interest in him. Although if we are careful, such an alert will not arise."

"Who is Bonnetti?"

Sir Richard smiled. "A businessman. A consultant. A market researcher. One man in his time plays many parts."

"I've never heard of him."

"Oh no. He is very low profile." He fished inside his jacket and got out his wallet. "Here is his card. It tells you nothing apart from a telephone number and a correspondence address. Maucourt's have used him many times for their Italian information. In Italy, you need an Italian."

I looked at the card, took out a pen, and made a note of its bland details. "All the same, Richard, I'm not happy about you going off on your own."

His face clouded slightly. "I'm not completely senile yet, Tim, even if no longer able to deal physically with sabotage. And once you have done the London part, I will have you back with me, won't I? That's why I sent for your reassuring and protective presence."

"OK. If that's what you want."

"I do."

I knew there was no likelihood of changing his mind. Further suggestion that he was past it would irritate him. I decided I'd better proceed with what he asked. I nodded in acceptance and said: "This London spadework for the tourism project. Is it simply a general survey?"

"Ah. I was coming to that. There is the Beckwith aspect to deal with."

"Beckwith? Of the professorial houses? Who's he?"

He smiled. "If you have finished your lunch, I will pay for it and, while we drive back to the Waldesian Cultural Centre and Museum, tell you all about him." He stood up and gestured for the bill. "Beckwith's story will educate and enlighten our listeners, whoever they are. It is at once remarkable and tragic."

Chapter 7

The Waldensian Cultural Centre was interesting, if you're interested in Waldensian culture. Beckwith's story was more gripping, if you're English. The *funghi fritti* were brilliant, if you like mushrooms. Sir Richard was in good form all through dinner and ordered the very best wine. His eyes were bright with anticipation. It occurred to me that he'd become very bored with the life of a solitary, elderly Continental banker, semi-retired and mostly on liaison work, respected for his experience but regarded as a museum piece by people who do not expect a milestone to march along the road. He was excited, anticipatory. I warned him, as tactfully as I could, to go carefully and promised to keep in close touch. He didn't really listen to my cautions.

The next morning I said farewell, got in my car and drove back to Turin. My flight was delayed and I didn't get into Heathrow until mid-afternoon. I went home, to the pleasure of Sue - the nanny was on a day off - and did the fatherly thing with young William, who was pleased to be with me, or at least gave that impression. While playing with him I gave Sue a version of the events in Belley which had got Sir Richard on the hop. She expressed suitable concern, although industrial espionage of a financial nature doesn't get her particularly agitated. Business matters are business matters to Sue: dull, in other words, and probably always unethical anyway.

About the news of Henry Weaver, things were different.

"Oh God! He hardly had time to phone you before he was a goner!"

"An accident, Sue. A car accident. On the A21 at Whatlington, where other accidents have occurred."

"And a painting in the offing for the Fund! It runs to pattern!"

"A watercolour. Just a watercolour. You said yourself the Fund hardly bends to watercolours. It's probably a wash by someone like George Stanfield Walters, when out on a tour of the north east. Fishing smacks and chaps with lobster pots. There's no chance we'd buy something like that. I was just humouring old Henry, that's all. I was pleased that he'd had a little inheritance. A watercolour is hardly the basis for some dreadful demon to get loose."

"Dear God. You don't hear from him for ages - "

" - months, you mean - "

" - then he comes up with a painting for the Fund. Within a day he's snuffed out like an old brown candle."

"Coincidence. Could have happened any time. Henry and I have known each other for years."

She shook her head in frustration. "I never could understand what it was you had in common to talk about. You said yourself that he wasn't known to you at school, at least hardly at all."

"Films and biography. It was very much firmed up after our involvement with Moreton Frewen, remember? It got him very interested. He always hoped I'd come up with another contact like that, something maybe to do with East Sussex again. That he could explore from St.Leonards. Henry was a great cowboy film fan. He reckoned that despite what all the critics say, *Stagecoach* was the greatest Western ever."

"What's that got to do with Moreton Frewen?"

"In the short story on which the film is based - by Ernest Haycox - there is a gaunt bony Englishman with a huge hunting rifle on the stage. He uses it to good effect when the Indians attack. When Frewen went out to Wyoming in the '70s he carried a huge four-barrelled elephant gun with him. And he took his bride to Wyoming on the Deadwood Stage. Henry reckoned he was the model for Haycox's Englishman. Who doesn't appear in the film. Ford dropped him."

"Was Henry an expert in Trivial Pursuit?"

I chuckled. "You might say that. Anyone who spends too much time on research in libraries, or makes biography a hobby, becomes an expert in Trivial Pursuit."

As I spoke, I thought of the Royal Oak at Whatlington, but decided not to go into all that. Sue wouldn't like any further associations to complicate her view of Henry's death. We went back to dandling young William between us, getting him to gurgle happily.

Altogether it was the sort of day you look back on and say was a blank work-wise, but a restorative from the family point of view. A pleasurable blank to some extent, but a blank nevertheless.

I needed it.

Next morning, as soon as I'd got installed in my office at the Bank, the phone rang.

"Mr. Simpson?"

The tone was educated, professional, cautious, not quite hushed but lowered, like someone probing for an unknown, perhaps even hostile, response.

"Yes?"

"I am speaking to Mr. Tim Simpson, am I?"

"You are. In person. Can I help?"

"My name is Harding, Mr.Simpson. Brian Harding. I am with Franklin, Jones and Harding, solicitors. In the London Road, St.Leonards."

"Oh yes?" The name sounded vaguely familiar, but I couldn't place where I'd heard it.

"We act on behalf of Mr. Henry Weaver. The late Mr. Henry Weaver, I should say. You have heard the news?"

"Yes I have."

"A tragic matter, Mr. Simpson. Very sad. Absolutely unexpected and shocking."

"Indeed."

Christ, I thought, this is quick. Poor old Henry only snuffed it a couple of days ago. The lawyers are circling like - no, I'd better not think like that. It's their job, after all. But there are usually all sorts of formalities after a crash like Henry's. That take time. Aren't there?

Why was this lawyer contacting me?

"I am contacting you because we hold his will in our safe, Mr. Simpson. I would just like you to know that we can make it available as soon as you wish."

"I'm sorry?"

"Mr. Weaver left it with us for safe keeping, you understand. It is here. You may collect it whenever you wish."

"I see. No, I don't. Why would I want to collect it?"

The tone became frosty, reproachful, almost critical. "Because, Mr. Simpson, as sole executor, I assume you will wish to see the correct procedures observed and the terms of the original will properly fulfilled."

"Eh? Sole executor?"

"Good heavens, Mr.Simpson, do not tell me that you are not aware that you are Mr Henry Weaver's sole executor?"

"*What*?" I almost shouted. "Me?"

"Yes indeed. The will is quite specific. Mr Weaver had us draw it up a year or so ago. Let me see; yes, about eighteen months ago. Surely he can not have failed to ask you, and to advise you? Let you have a copy or a draft? He felt most strongly that you, as a responsible person as well as a friend, would be entirely suitable."

"Good God. Did he?"

Memory flooded back. An evening at a London film club meeting, when we'd watched an obscure *film noir* about sinister crooks and their doxies in Valence, of all places. Henry was adept at French regional accents, using those nasal tones that go with *Les filles de Valence, les plus belles de la France* and so on. After the film he insisted we went to a Soho wine bar, to practice while our ears were still full of *bavardage*. He drank a lot and got maudlin. He said he was staying up in London with a friend who was working late, so was glad I could keep him company for a while. I wondered, at the time, if it was a woman he was staying with, but didn't ask; I never enquired too much into Henry's private affairs for fear of receiving another depressing dissertation on the lines of Jack Knewstub.

"If" I remembered, now, he'd asked, rather late in the proceedings, his appealing, crinkled expression taking on a wistful sort of look "*if* I asked you to be my executor, would you agree to do it, Tim?"

"Executor?"

"Of my will." He lowered his head and spoke in hushed tones, as though a massive inheritance were involved. His tie had gone skew and the blue eyes were getting slightly bloodshot.

"Will? Good God, Henry, we're not that old yet, are we?"

He tapped the side of his nose. "You never know, old boy. You never know. Can't be too careful. Dying intestate's a bad business. All sorts of buggers try to horn in on your leavings. Especially the tax man. And lawyers. Not to mention spurious cousins from Australia. Australia is full of spurious cousins and similar con men. Argentina has none, of course."

"Important, are they? Your leavings, I mean?"

He raised himself up a little in hurt dignity and gave me a reproachful look. "Mine will not be a fine mansion, nor a noble carriage to convey. But it would be reassuring to know that one's modest appurtenances, one's sentimental residue, would be handled with proper concern, in the way one would wish. Not just given the old heave-ho into the Filsham rubbish tip by some house clearance villain."

I repented of my initial reaction. "Sorry, Henry. Put that way, of course I would. But let me know when you decide to do it, so I know what I'm in for. I've never been an executor. Besides, I may predecease you."

"That's very unlikely, given your robust constitution. Try not to sound too enthusiastic though, will you, dear boy? Or flattered, of course. As a banker, I thought you might bring some *gravitas*, a sort of official endorsement and substance, to the settlement of my humble, but to me affecting, affairs." He drained the last of his glass of red wine. "I shall bear your kind if hesitant acquiescence in mind. Now, how about another entirely appropriate bottle of that flavourful Côtes du Rhone? In view of our association with Valence this merry evening?"

So he must have done it. Put me down as his executor, I mean. Perhaps, in the amnesia of the morning after - he drank much more than I did that night, even though I had to foot the bill as usual - he convinced himself of my agreement. He must have told this disapproving Harding that I was fully *au fait* with my responsibilities, whatever they were. Until now, I had put the matter entirely out of my mind.

I felt more than just a pang of conscience. Henry obviously attached importance to what must be his pathetic possessions at the time and wanted someone he could trust to dispose of them as he wanted. Not taking the prospect of his death seriously, I had responded inadequately, unfeelingly, even with mockery. On the whole I had learnt to be tender in dealing with Henry but there were times, times I now recalled and regretted, when I was probably less than considerate.

And now, his possessions were not quite so pathetic as they were.

A mental image of the will containing instructions perhaps to scatter his ashes onto the heaving surface of the Channel, or even into the bins of some market research library, or in a dubious Soho film cellar, flashed half-humorously, half-worriedly into my mind. What would be the personal effects of a year or more ago that were so important to Henry? I would be responsible for his funeral expenses. I would have to deal with the watercolour, now, whether I liked it or not. And the terrace house his aunt had left him in Newcastle; who was to benefit from that?

"Mr. Simpson?" Harding's voice cut in on my thoughts.

"Yes. I'm still here. I hadn't realised he was serious when he asked me. To be his executor, I mean. He raised the matter, but didn't confirm it to me."

"Oh dear. The will is quite specific."

"It's no problem, Mr. Harding. Or shouldn't be. I have little experience, but doubtless I'll find out. It's the least I can do for Henry."

"That's very kind." He sounded relieved. "I think you'll find the official booklets most helpful. Most helpful. The Registrar's office people are enormously useful. You'll need the doctor's details and so on to get a death certificate from the Registrar but it's all very straightforward, once they've satisfied themselves about the cause of death, and that is already a formality."

"I see." I began to feel gloomy. "I'll have to get probate and go through all that malarkey, I suppose."

"The probate office in Brighton is most helpful. I don't think you'll find it much trouble, Mr. Simpson. Or that the estate will incur tax liabilities, since they commence only above two hundred and thirty thousand pounds."

What did a funeral cost? At least a grand, I reckoned. That Côtes du Rhone might turn out to be even more expensive that I'd thought at the time. No, surely not; there was a small house and a watercolour as collateral, now.

"I see. Well OK, I'd better come in person and pick up the will, then."

"Excellent. We are open normal office hours. We'll get you to sign for it, of course. I will arrange for the authorities to pass over the possessions he had with him, including his house keys."

"Oh. Thank you."

"There will be a fee outstanding to us but we'll send that to you later, of course."

"Of course." I tried not to sound too dry.

"Thank you, Mr. Simpson."

"Thank you, Mr. Harding."

I put the phone down. It promptly rang again.

"Tim?" The tones were rich and fruity. "Jeremy."

"Good morning, Jeremy."

"You're hardly gone than you're back. Great heavens, was it so simple?"

"Well - I suppose - "

He brooked no hesitation on my part. Jeremy was either all fire and dash or deep reflection. In the main, his instincts were to fire from the hip as soon as quarry came into view

"I'm waiting! All agog! Get in here at once and enlighten me! Before I have to report to the Board!"

"Very good, Jeremy. I'm on my way, Jeremy."

So it was that, heavy of heart, and appointed executor for the first time in my life, I went to spin a tale to my employer.

Chapter 8

He sat with his mouth slightly open, as though the information was too breathtakingly preposterous to allow his jaw to close.

"You are," he interrupted at one point, "suggesting that a Protestant emphasis in relation to Catholic persecution, one whose history apparently makes events in Northern Ireland take on the all the tempo of a vicarage tea party, is the basis for attracting British tourists? To this remarkable enclave in the same country as that in which the Pope resides?"

"I do not think that the religious aspect should be too pre-eminent, Jeremy, although it is integral with the character of the area. It forms part of a background tapestry, so to speak, as might say Huguenot history in parts of France or, indeed, events in the Spanish Netherlands when one visits the Low Countries. In this case there is an international Methodist penumbra. The persecuted Waldensians established communities in Switzerland, Uruguay and Argentina apart from links elsewhere. One travels in these places for more modern reasons, evidently, but so much is known of the more well-travelled areas that these, how shall I put it, not undeveloped but lesser-known regions might have a novelty, a freshness lacking in the well-worn paths of Tuscany and canals of Venice, perhaps."

"Freshness and the canals of Venice could provide a resounding oxymoron. The place stinks."

"Quite so, Jeremy. It is a different sort of tourism that one invites."

"Ha! What sort?"

"Walkers, hikers, those interested in nature and history. The mountains are very fine. A sort of grander Cumbria or Wales, with perhaps a spiritual approach."

"Oh God! The thonged sandal and rucksack brigade! Fat lot we'd get out of them!"

"There are gastronomic aspects, especially in the mushroom season."

"September or October? When all their kids are stuck in school?"

"There is a large market segment of active, retired people to whom such excursions would appeal."

"Buy shares in Saga Holidays, should we?"

"There is a strong English interest which might exert an influence. Not just Cromwell. There's Beckwith."

"Who the blazes is Beckwith?"

"General Beckwith lost his leg in the last throes of the battle of Waterloo, whilst still a Colonel. He was on Picton's staff. The loss of the leg meant that he was put on the retired list after months of agony. It was the end of a career for a man whose whole family were military. Not only were they all generals but one of them founded the 95th - the Rifle Regiment to which he belonged. He had gone through most of the Peninsular War and had almost survived Waterloo unscathed even though Picton was killed early on. It must have been bitter. By chance Beckwith, waiting to see Wellington at Apsley House much later, picked up a book by a cleric called Canon Gilly, who had interested himself in the Waldensians. In the nineteenth century they had fallen into a parlous state in their valley ghettos. Gilly's book persuaded Beckwith to make the Waldensians his cause. Which he did, stumping on a wooden leg up those fearsome mountains to found schools and build chapels, some of them at his own expense. He lived in Torre Pellice. He arranged the building of a College and fine houses for professors. In 1848 the Protestants were at last emancipated and he arranged to build a church in Turin. He's something of a local hero. He loved children. Late in life he married a local girl and after a spell in Genoa he died in Torre Pellice. Six months later his wife bore him a daughter. It's a poignant and elevating story."

'Any art about those parts? Galleries?"

"Er, no."

"Medieval palaces?"

"No."

"Sculpture?"

"None."

"Crafts?"

"Not really. The museum has examples of local, agricultural implements and - "

"Fine buildings?"

"Only the Waldensian - "

"Swimming? Fishing? Discotheques? Beaches? Fun fairs?"

"You're being bloody negative, d'you know that? Bloody negative! The area is not developed! It is beautiful and productive and mountainous. That's the whole point!"

"And you're lying about something!" He held up a hand as my mouth opened. "No! Sorry! I take that back. You are being economical with the truth. You are dissimulating. Come to the point: is Uncle Richard dotty or isn't he?"

"He's not. In no way. Far from it."

At this there was a silence. Jeremy stared at me, long and thoughtfully. After a while he spoke, softly. "Have a coffee, Tim?"

"Thank you, Jeremy."

He made the necessary telegraphic signals and his secretary, Claire, brought coffee, muttering to him that there was not much time before the Board meeting. Then she left us. We sat holding coffees, looking at each other. His gaze was absolutely steady. After a while he said:

"How long have we known each other?"

I put my coffee down on the corner of his handsome mahogany partners' desk with a deep sigh. "All right, Jeremy. I surrender."

He banged his cup back into its saucer with a crack that nearly broke it. "Why is it that Uncle Richard always does this to you? Why?"

"Does what to me?"

"Sets you off in a counter direction to mine? Subverts you? Sends you underground? Makes you downright shifty?"

"That's not true. He always acts in the Bank's best interests. And I am, as you know, your obedient servant."

"Rubbish! Balderdash! If you were that, we'd have been finished long ago. I can't stand sycophants, never could."

"I know. And I'm sorry to have seemed to try to hoodwink you. Not that it was deliberate or clearly planned. I just wasn't prepared. It's a complex story and I wasn't sure how to handle it. Now I'll tell you the truth."

And I did.

All of it.

At the end, he sat back and whistled softly.

"Wow."

"So you see, Richard had to find a way to alert us, to get me out there, whilst at the same time giving the impression to these conspirators that he's a harmless old fogey. I thought you'd react badly to my - complicating things- as you put it."

"He did the old fogey part all right. All too convincingly. I wonder if they still think he's harmless. If there is harm to be done."

"That's what we don't know. That's why I didn't want to react too quickly. Even the bugs might just be a harmless precaution."

He pulled his mouth down at the corners, in the same sort of family grimace that Sir Richard did.

"Hmph" he said.

"If there is harm in the offing, the proposed Waldensian project might be just too absurd to wash, do you think?"

"It might be." He stood up, looking at his watch. "The crunch comes in a few minutes, when I report to the Board. I can flannel them with some sort of guff about Richard perhaps overestimating the lure of these Methodist valleys but that there may be some possibility which you, with reservations, can take a quick, cheap look at. Discuss with suitable tourist contacts et cetera, et cetera. No risk of our being

73

embarrassed by Richard while you do it. And no decisions are required today."

"They'll like that."

His mouth turned down again, grimly humorous this time. "You are an irreverent bastard, Tim."

I stood up as well, to grin at him. "One of the principal Anglo-Saxon characteristics, as exemplified by Hesketh Pearson's description of W.S.Gilbert: truculent, humorous, pugnacious, irreverent."

"He got you both to a tee. I must go. The key will come during our revision of projects. I shall listen to Shauna Spring with great attention. The utmost attention, in fact."

He shot his cuffs, giving another gleam of gold linkage, and smoothed his long blond hair back from his forehead. As Claire came in unannounced, bearing a folder of papers for his meeting, he brushed an imaginary crumb off the sleeve of his faultless pinstriped jacket. Then he let his similar trousers fall into sharply-creased, narrowing curves, like a cavalryman's, to break over the instep of his polished black leather shoes. He took the folder with a gracious bow and murmured his thanks. Claire stood to one side and winked at me. At the door, he turned back to look at me with one piercing stare.

"The very utmost attention" he said.

Then he was gone.

Chapter 9

I went back to my office, tried to get on with some work, stared out of the window a lot, muttered to myself even more about things like Hesketh Pearson's adjectives for Anglo-Saxons and filled in over half an hour of suspenseful time before the phone rang.

"Tim? Tim Simpson?"

"Hullo?"

"Is that you, Tim?" The voice was hoarse, strong, demanding of confirmation.

"Yes it is. Who's that?"

"It's me, Sammy. Sammy Simes."

"Oh, right. What news, Sammy?"

"I've got to see you, Tim. Soon. Urgent."

A cold tinge crawled down my back. "See me? Why? What news?"

"I got to the Allegro. My copper mate fixed it for me. Just to set my mind at rest, he said. He thought, that is."

"And?"

"It's with a pile of other junked cars. People don't half go off the road round here. Anyway, I had a go all over it."

"And?"

"I - I don't know what to tell you. I knew that car backwards. Someone tampered with it."

The cold tinge turned my spine to ice. "Tampered with what?"

"Brakes. Hydraulics. And the steering: the linkage had been got at. Very subtle. Not to mention the seat belt fixing. Very cleverly unshipped. Anything he hit, the seat belt fixing'd come clean out. Shear off. Which it did. So Henry went straight into the wheel, then the screen, smashing both. Quite apart from the car rolling over and breaking his neck. After it hit the tree it rolled off the road. Severe cranial damage is given as the cause of death. No witnesses, no one on the road at all."

"Not outside the Royal Oak?"

"The smash wasn't at the Royal Oak, Tim. It was nearly a mile down the road. Still Whatlington, but getting towards the Sedlescombe straight, where everyone opens up and they have those nasty smashes at Stream Lane."

"Why did I think it was at the Royal Oak?"

"The first reports are always a bit off the mark. It was very late. After closing time. No one about, according to my copper pal. Henry was coming back from Croydon, remember?"

"So the car was tampered with up there?"

"Jesus, Tim, how should I know?"

"Sorry, Sammy."

"Why did you ask me to check the car? Why? What do you know?"

"Nothing, Sammy, I swear. Absolutely nothing. It was just a premonition. A ghost whispering in my ear."

"I'm all a-shiver now. It would have been better to have let sleeping dogs lie, Tim. It won't bring Henry back, this, will it?"

"No, it won't. But we may find out why it happened."

"The police aren't treating it as suspicious. He was a bit over the limit according to them. The car wasn't found until the next day. It'd rolled off the road into a bit of thicket. No one would report Henry missing, would they?"

"No, I don't know of anyone. Have you told anyone about this? About your look at the car, I mean?"

"Christ, no."

"Not even your copper pal?"

"He wasn't there when I did the survey. Just told the yard man it'd be OK, then shoved off to a burglary in Silverhill."

"So you've told no one but me?"

"No, of course not. I'm freaked. I don't know what to do."

"Keep calm, Sammy. Keep calm. Tell you what: write it down. Just jottings if you like. A brief report."

"What for?"

"To clear your mind. I find it helps a lot to see what you're thinking or calculating down on paper. It clarifies things. Sketches, diagrams, anything. Don't go back to the car, though, not yet."

"You don't need to tell me. I'm dead twitchy, Tim. Who'd want to do that to Henry? Whoever it was knew what they were doing. You'd have to know the car well, and have suspicions, to look for evidence of the tampering."

"Write it down. Now. I'm coming down to Hastings tomorrow to collect stuff from the lawyers and look in Henry's flat."

"You are?"

"Yes. I've just heard that I'm Henry's executor. So I have to do all the necessary."

"You're his executor? You? No wonder he said to contact you if anything happened."

"Why on earth did he do that, Sammy?"

"Search me. He was going up to London quite often but by train. Then he comes in with the switch gone duff and, while we're chatting, comes out with your name. I couldn't really understand what he meant. I certainly didn't know you were his executor."

"It was news to me, too, I can tell you, Sammy. As soon as I've finished in St.Leonards though, I'll come over and see you. I promise. We'll go through what you've found out. Then we'll decide what to do. All right?"

"All right, Tim." He sounded relieved. "Thanks, mate. I'm glad you're on the job. I'll be here all day. Look forward to seeing you."

"Don't forget: write it down."

"Gotcha."

He rang off.

I leapt up in more of a jump than anything else and went to the window to stare out at nearby buildings and walls. It was starting to rain and spots spattered the window, obscuring the view. It didn't help. Nothing was going to help. Henry was dead and, if Sammy Simes was right, someone had deliberately killed him. Murdered him. Arranged his death or severe injury. Put it how you like.

Why? Why?

Why kill harmless Henry Weaver? Just beyond the Royal Oak? Could Sammy be mistaken? No; Sammy was efficient, and there was more than one point at which he'd found evidence of tampering. He couldn't make so many mistakes.

But for a watercolour? Just a watercolour? Surely not, yet the timing shrieked that this was no coincidence. Someone murdered Henry within a couple of days of his calling me about a watercolur for the Art Fund. That thought could not be stuffed away in a conveniently amnesiac pigeonhole and forgotten.

My office door swung open and Jeremy strode in like a blond Goth on the rampage. He was breathing heavily. His mouth was set in a line.

I gaped at him in surprise as I tried to conceal my mental turmoil over Henry with a bland expression. "Board meeting over already? That was quick."

He shook his head. His eyes had a deep-set stare that showed emotional strain. "Suspended. Not over. Suspended, in view of the news."

"News? What news?"

"Uncle Richard was found dead in his car late last night. In Turin. Near the Egyptian Museum."

Chapter 10

"How old was he?" Sue asked, as we came off the dual carriageway and plunged into the hedged, winding narrows which lead down to the valley village of Lamberhurst.

"Seventy-seven," I replied. "He was twenty, apparently, when he was parachuted into the Doubs by SOE, who in 1943 thought his French good enough to pass for, at worst, an Alsatian."

"I don't suppose you ever see life in quite the same way again, once you've done something like that."

"I don't suppose you do. Which may explain why, at the age of seventy-seven, you still think yourself capable of going off on a cloak and dagger operation in Turin, involving a meeting with some shady character at the Egyptian Museum. Although it may well be that, having passed the middle of your life in perfectly respectable investment banking operations, you revert to a youthfully rash pattern of behaviour when senility approaches."

"I thought you said that his mind was still as sharp as ever."

"It was." I frowned as we slowed through the quaint high street and surged back up the hill the other end. The A21 beyond Pembury is a tedious road, even if charmingly rural in places, and I was anxious to get on.

"And he does just seem to have had a heart attack."

"That is according to first reports. But the Italian authorities are as scrupulous as ours when it comes to irregular deaths in unattended motor cars. There is to be a port mortem. The Bank's representatives are in full attention but the law has to take its course. No different from this country. It is surprising how state services which in life leave much to be desired, in death work with extreme efficiency."

She was silent as we sped on towards Flimwell, with its

traffic lights. She had insisted on coming with me, and I was glad of it. William was well looked after by the daily nanny. I was in a turbulent mental state. Without being told about Sammy Simes's findings, Sue was already gearing herself up for trouble. I might have tried to put her off, but Sir Richard's death had left me feeling isolated, exposed with my secret knowledge of events in Belley, now shared with Jeremy and Sue. The sense of loss was acute, much worse than the death of Henry Weaver had brought on. It would be an exaggeration to describe Sir Richard White as some sort of father figure, a replacement for the early loss of my own parent in distant Callao; we were not as close as that. But he had often provided me with a senior element, an experienced judge of life in a sort of long-stop position, one whose help I had invoked on occasions when events at the Bank had moved against me. On other occasions I had not needed to invoke him. He had moved in splendid anticipation to assist me, providing mentorship and support at a level necessary to pull the hounds of ambitious, predatory executives off my trail and to ensure that what we both wanted came to pass.

More than that, though, we had been friends. Despite the difference in ages, there had been that rapport which comes with some indefinable empathy, unexplained, not clarified or embarrassingly expressed, which two Englishmen find themselves enjoying after only very few meetings. Of course there had been tacit respect on either side, invisible boundaries and frontiers carefully retained and untested. He was of the loftiest echelons of the Bank. Jeremy and I had unseated him, years ago, but he had come back via his French citadels and re-established himself once again as a power at the top. He had decided to use my talents for his own ends on one memorable project, which led to his disarming offer of friendship, without any rancour for the past. I accepted gladly, for he was a man of great talent as well as charm. It was flattering to be gathered into his circle of intimates or, at least, to one as intimate as he allowed. His war experience and natural reserve kept him always behind a certain emotional barrier but, with me at any rate, the underlying warmth was clearly expressed.

Jeremy still had his reservations. The family bond, strong but abrasive, placed him in an entirely different position to mine. No man can serve two masters, sure, and Jeremy was always my first master, which well he knew, but sometimes Richard had run him close. I guessed Jeremy was having mixed feelings about the loss of his uncle.

After the immediate shock of the news, we'd agreed to discuss the next steps once we learnt more about the way he died. We looked askance at each other as we agreed this, each knowing what the other was reluctant to say: it might just be a heart attack, it might, but why now, and there? What sense of timing did Fate have, if there was natural explanation?

Sue had moved instinctively to my side. Her fears for the strange effects the Art Fund had produced before, and now the Turin episode, which under normal circumstances would have pushed her into a long-established, almost schoolmistressy attitude to my activities, were today suppressed by her love and sympathy. At the same time, she was as curious as I was over the question of the watercolour. Such mysteries, deep down, always thrilled her. Her artistic expertise, far deeper than mine, would be invaluable and I was relieved to have her with me. There was also the benefit of her presence during the rather morbid business of attending to Henry's affairs.

"It is" she now said, "just a little too coincidental, Tim, that he should die at this precise moment, isn't it?"

My mind had strayed for a moment to Henry Weaver and I had to jerk it back to Sir Richard White.

"Too convenient by half."

"And if there is something horribly sinister about it, where does that leave you?"

"Eh?"

"They, if there are a they, must know that you were the last person to see him. Even if it was ostensibly to discuss this spurious Waldensian tourist project, they must wonder what else you talked about. If Sir Richard had only gone to Turin to visit the Waldensian Church, things might have been reassuring, but by meeting this Bonnetti man, he might have aroused suspicions."

"If someone knew he was meeting Bonnetti. I think he'd have arranged that where he couldn't be overheard."

"So where does that leave you?"

"It depends what I do. What course of action I take."

"They may not wait. If we hear that his death was suspicious, we'll know that they must have rumbled his little subterfuge. They'll be watching you like hawks."

"I agree, but only if we assume that there is something dodgy about his death."

"Tim, they must know he'd seen them. They must. Why would Sir Richard meet this Bonnetti man otherwise?"

"If he did meet Bonnetti. If they know he met Bonnetti, or intended to. He might just have died, Sue, beforehand. Although his presence near the Egyptian Museum argues otherwise. There are imponderables to clarify yet. If one can clarify an imponderable."

"I should assume the worst if I were you. The worst. Be very careful, Tim".

"Let's wait for the news from Turin. We've got enough to deal with over Henry Weaver for the moment."

We had passed through Hurst Green and signs for Robertsbridge, now bypassed over to our right, came up. They reminded me of Henry Weaver once again, joking about the journalist and broadcaster, Malcolm Muggeridge. A newspaper interviewer had described Muggeridge, who lived nearby, as having a 'strange liking for the Hastings hinterland'.

"We are" Henry chuckled as we quaffed a pint at the Royal Oak "in the Hastings hinterland, Tim. Unexplored territory to those London folk. Unbelievable that we're only fifty-odd miles from the capital, yet a hinterland apparently exists. Like darkest Africa. To journalists, anyway."

I laughed at the time. Now memories of the Royal Oak had a quite different significance. One that was taxing my mind.

"Whatlington." Sue interrupted my thoughts. "This is where it happened, Tim."

"Not just yet. We have to pass the Royal Oak first."

We came round a curve beyond a chapel converted to a fireplace centre and a garage. There, in front of us, at an angle to the road, was the Royal Oak Inn, an old, weatherboarded posting house of great antiquity. I slowed, pulled off the road, and parked in front of it. At that time of the morning it was closed. But the memories flooded back.

"Henry was a great fan of Hesketh Pearson's, you know," I said to Sue, after a moment's silence.

"So are you."

"Yes. I am. He wrote biographies that are stylish, with a true understanding of the theatre because he'd trod the boards himself in his youth. His *Gilbert and Sullivan* is first class. Not a modern type of biography but first class. There was a hell of a lot more as well as theatrical stuff. Whistler, Shaw, Wilde, Dickens, Conan Doyle, Shakespeare, Tom Paine, dozens of 'em. The Lives of the Wits. Henry Weaver had read 'em all. Pearson was a friend of Malcolm Muggeridge and Hugh Kingsmill, actually co-authored books with them. Muggeridge wrote some of his best stuff in tandem with Pearson, even though he might not have liked to admit it. *About Kingsmill*, it was called. Henry got it - Kingsmill and his brother Brian, both Lunns of the travel agency, were another pair of Hastings crocks, living round Ore somewhere - but he wasn't really interested in Muggeridge's bit. He went for anything by, and about, Hesketh Pearson."

When I stopped Sue looked at me, looked at the façade of the pub, and raised an eyebrow in query.

I closed my eyes for a moment, then opened them to stare through the windscreen at the white-weatherboarded façade. "One evening Henry made me bring him out here. He said the Cronins, the couple who ran the pub, did first class steaks. Which was true. I can see Henry sitting at a table inside there, eating a 12-ounce ribeye, as though it were yesterday. Tim, he said, I'll tell you something about this inn that you don't know. During the war, the Muggeridges lived down that side road, which leads to Battle. Mill House, quite big place. There's a vineyard down there now. They moved to Battle and Robertsbridge later. Opposite Mill House is a bumpy track that goes into the countryside, crossing the main London railway line. About half a mile or more along it, is an old red brick farmhouse called Wood Place. Hesketh Pearson and his first wife Gladys moved there to be out of the blitz. Muggeridge went off to Washington in '41, leaving his wife Kitty alone with four children for the umpteenth time. Pearson used to call at Mill House to collect his post every morning because the postman wouldn't trudge all the way up the muddy lane from the main road. Pearson was estranged from his wife, Gladys; their son was killed in the Spanish Civil War. He would be in his late fifties then; handsome, educated, witty, splendid company."

"Oh, Tim, I can guess what comes next."

"I'm sure you can. One thing inevitably led to another. Every Tuesday night, Kitty and Hesketh Pearson used to walk up the lane to this pub. Muggeridge was upset when he found out about the affair, but he was hardly in a position to complain, not with his own record of dalliances in Russia and India, let alone with neighbours and wives of various sorts round here. He even started one on the train up to London on his way to meet another mistress. Later on there was that spectacular affair with Lady Pamela Berry. Anyway, he and Pearson remained friends."

"Very civilised, Tim."

"Perhaps. I remember Henry looked round at this point in the story, as though seeking to see Kitty and Pearson's ghosts. I said that the place must have been very different then; pokier and darker, with Saloon and Public Bars separate. They've opened up all the stud walls now and put in a new bar counter. Pubs have become more respectable. That didn't faze Henry. There was a historical magic to the place for him. Pearson had been here, to this pub in front of us, every Tuesday, in love with Kitty Muggeridge, sixty-odd years ago."

"How did he know all this?"

"From Richard Ingram's book on Muggeridge. Bought for fifty pee, paperback, at the Book Jungle in St.Leonard's. You asked if Henry played Trivial Pursuit. For modern biography, he'd have been an expert. He even quoted Michael Holroyd's autobiography, *Basil Street Blues*. Hesketh Pearson helped Holroyd with his first book, on Hugh Kingsmill. Henry had all Hesketh Pearson's books, even a potboiler or two. Picked up for pence in Hastings and St.Leonards second-hand shops, of course."

"Of course."

"Which is why it's so ironic that he should be killed here, or near here. Why here? Why not somewhere else?"

"Like Sir Richard at the Egyptian Museum, you mean?"

"Yes."

Why, I thought, should the car's tamperings affect it just beyond here? Why here? This pub had significance for Henry and I don't believe in coincidences of that sort.

Sue shook her head. "Tim, this is getting quite a way from Croydon. It's just coincidental that he should be tired, fall asleep at the wheel around here. He'd have been driving for more than an hour or so, at the end of a long day. And if he'd had a drink or two up in town, all the more reason."

"Except that he didn't fall asleep at the wheel. The wheel was put to sleep on him."

"What? Tim, what are you saying?"

I started my car engine. "I'm afraid I've got bad news, Sue. Something I've been concealing from you. Let me confess while we get down to Hastings and St.Leonards as quickly as possible."

Chapter 11

I said that it's surprising how, though you may find them dilatory and frustrating in life, state services work well in death. This turned out to be true. Doctor's, Coroner's and death certificates, of which you need to get more than one original from the Registrar so that you can send them off to all sorts of organisations like insurance companies who insist on an original, not a photocopy, can all be obtained from sympathetic, brisk and competent people. They carry out their functions smoothly. The State may deny you a proper pension or health attention when you're alive, but an oiled machine clicks into place once you're gone. Despite the proffered sympathies, the kindly help, there is almost an air of relief, of having got another one away. It is as though they set up the social and medical services to speed the parting guest.

I found most of this out later, once I started to function as Henry's executor. I called first at the rather drab office of Mr Brian Harding, of Franklin, Jones and Harding, solicitors, in the London Road, St.Leonards. I have never been sure where Hastings and St.Leonards overlap but this was central to the latter. At the end of the long, sloping street, flanked by shops and a great stone churches, the brown waters of the English Channel danced in breezy, chopped rhythms under a distant flat horizon. Bracing was the word that came to mind. Shops that dealt in second-hand clothes and the uneconomic emptyings of innumerable attics were prominent. There were betting shops and prominent National Lottery sales outlets. Like Jack Knewstub, we had arrived at the end of a line.

Mr Brian Harding was grey suited, grey haired, sympathetically deferential, perhaps relieved that there was someone to hand things over to, someone to pay a bill. He murmured condolences. I had to sit down in his office, having left Sue in the car outside, to explain how long I'd known Henry and smile bashfully over my unexpected executorship. He passed over keys, documents, a will in one of those special, long envelopes that wills come in, not a Post Office job with the standardised, inscribed words in Gothic - Last Will and Testament - on it but a sober lawyer's envelope suitable for foolscap. It had Franklin, Jones and Harding's name and address printed on the outside. I put it together with the other things and he got me to sign for them after scrupulously checking my identity from the passport I had the foresight to carry with me. I thanked him, and left.

Then we went round to Henry's.

I'd been there once, long ago. Henry usually preferred to meet me elsewhere, looking for cheer and change. He bought the upper storey flat in Kenilworth Road, he told me, for seventeen thousand pounds because, as a three-bedroom flat, it was cheap even when he bought it. He didn't need three bedrooms, of course, but he had impedimenta, mainly book impedimenta, to accommodate. Kenilworth Road, a long cliff of seaside houses going up the hill and fronting onto the back of what's left of Burton's Regency development, saw no seas and was not expensive. In a way, it was typical that Henry should choose to live there, using the imagined past, as so many people do, to blot out the present. There were times when, voice dropping to a hush, he wittered on about James Burton as though referring to a genius rather than a speculative builder-contractor who put up one of his period's equivalents of the Costa del Sol. It is not as though the original architectural panorama remains; over the years its brave corpus has been invaded, penetrated, scarred, despoiled, mugged, surgically dissected. Blocks of flats and suburban houses sporting garages with tin doors have been inserted into the wooded bluffs. Even the archery ground's handsome crescent now faces not an open sward for bowmen and women but a glass and concrete technical college, like a Regency buck confronted by a mammoth skinhead.

And yet, and yet; there are still some grand houses round

about, I once had to admit to Henry over wine in the Hastings Old Town. Even one by Norman Shaw, one of my favourites, plonked down into the Regency with late Victorian, sham-Tudor bravado before turning, inevitably, into a nursing home.

We pulled up outside the divided house. Together Sue and I strode up the stone steps to the front door set in the bayed terrace to enter the hallway. A wide staircase confronted us. It was typical that there was no security, just cracked encaustic tiles and emptiness, the smell of stale ash and cabbage. Stained walls and partitions told of division into lesser purposes. A metal, multiple post box with each flat's number, each segment lockable, hung on the wall. I opened Henry's with one of my keys and found nothing but an electricity bill. We went upstairs, avoiding touching the banister rail or the walls. There was no one about. No one. How the denizens of this building occupied their time was something we didn't want to know. I didn't think they were at work. A damp smell hung in the air.

I got out the key and we opened the door to the top flat. An entrance corridor with doors going off it confronted us and we turned, almost automatically, into the front room overlooking the street.

The room was surprisingly airy. There was a good fireplace with a gas fire in it, a red three-piece suite in quite smart condition, a table with two upright chairs, a hi-fi, television and video machine, small bookcases, a standard lamp, a mirror over the mantel. It was conventional, quite clean, almost suburban. There was a big print of Whitby harbour on one wall. A faint smell of cologne, or perhaps aftershave, hung in the air. Outside, through the bay's sash windows, I could see that the sun had fallen on dark trees and stone triangular pediments of the later Burton's large houses across the road, giving them a radiance like hope. Beyond them the gardens and the sub-classical architecture amongst which Henry had liked to feel he lived, as though its mere presence lent style to his life, were warming as the strong rays intensified. But Henry would be cold, alone in a box in a mortuary.

The house was oddly silent.

My eye strayed to the crooked bookshelves on the inner wall where some of Henry's treasured volumes were carefully arranged in lost ranks. Then I looked at the table, where papers covered in notes and books were surprisingly littered; usually, Henry was neat and meticulous, avoiding the chaos that usage lends to such references. Perhaps death had interrupted his normal procedures. Against the table leg leant, sagging in empty expectation, a portfolio for larger sheets. Henry was gone. His research, his reading and endless biographical absorption were all over. His breath was a ware that had not kept. The lonely man had no successors and many of his books would be binned along with him, not perhaps reduced to ashes somewhere and scattered, but pulped for cardboard and newsprint.

"This is dismal" Sue said. "Let's look at the rest of the place."

There was a kitchen, which was quite respectable for a bachelor, a bathroom ditto, then the main bedroom. A double bed was neatly made, looking unused. On the floor beside the gas fire was a white bone china cup and beside it a very small cafetière with black coffee grounds in it. On the mantelpiece stood an inevitable clock, still ticking, a china dog, a box of matches and two Goss candlesticks. An easy chair, a big dark oak wardrobe and a dressing table with the same faint smell of cologne completed the furniture. On the walls were a big mirror and a small oil painting of chrysanthemums in an octagonal Mason's Ironstone jug, by a '30s painter called Florence Engelbach, a lady who Henry tipped to be highly collectable, like Allegro cars. Opposite was a print of Stephenson's Rocket. Geordies, I thought, and railway engineers; to Buenos Aires to run trains. Otherwise, I wouldn't have known Henry.

A single room had a single bed in a corner, a bentwood chair and an ironing board open in the middle of the floor.

Clothes were scattered on the bed. This, evidently, was Henry's laundry store. We moved on to the last room in the place.

It was arranged as a study. A commercial oak pedestal desk, with an office armchair, occupied the space under a window which looked over the garden and congested backs of houses in Carisbrooke Road. The walls were lined with books, ceiling to floor. There was a large table with two old leather-covered chairs drawn up to it. The table and the desk tops were covered in papers and files in rather untidy heaps. I sighed loudly.

"This needs a lot of time to sort out. This is not just a day-excursion job, Sue."

"It certainly isn't." She was looking about her curiously. "He really was a bookworm, wasn't he?"

"Not just a bookworm. He was supposed to be a market researcher. A statistical man. With a biographical hobby." I shook my head sadly at the papers. "After a day spent digging up figures, he spent evenings digging up lives. Not just evenings, I imagine, when he was short of work. Days, too. Long, long days."

I walked over to what looked like a book-built wall and ran a finger along the battered spines until I came to a row of Hesketh Pearson's works. Five pence was what Henry liked to pay for old books, at boot fairs and village jumble sales. For Pearson, though, he was prepared to pay a bit more. What was it he'd said about him? It must have been recent, because I remembered him quoting Michael Holroyd, from whose *Augustus John* he'd got the Jack Knewstub reference. Henry had picked up a review copy of *Basil Street Blues*. A year or so ago, perhaps. Now it came back:

"Pearson brought his characters into the present, Tim. Holroyd, to whom he was something of a mentor, says that he didn't bother with all that dreary documentation that modern scholars use to justify their existence. He relied on good anecdotes, quotations, primary colours and solid structure. He was fascinated by human nature and wrote for love. Bit of an amateur that way, I suppose. Full of gusto. Something of a ladies' man. Great, active fellow."

A wistful look came over Henry's animated face as he said this, as though he wished he could have put his biographical enthusiasm into practice, like Pearson, taking Muggeridge's wife briskly up the road to the Royal Oak rather than allowing his bibliographical compilations somehow to sap his energies.

Sue's voice broke into my thoughts, as though reading them. "It seems to have been a very unhealthy life. Did he ever get any exercise?"

I turned away from the books. "He went out to film clubs. He liked gangsters and Westerns, mostly. That was all that *Stagecoach* stuff. He claimed that *Stagecoach* saved the Western from extinction in 1939, when the genre had run out of ideas. He's got books on John Ford somewhere in all this lot. And Moreton Frewen, with all the Churchillian and Jerome and even Sullivan connections, let alone Wyoming, Buffalo Bill and the Deadwood Stage."

"What an odd life" she said, softly. "What was it for?"

"Hmph. I'm not qualified to answer that." I moved to the desk and started to leaf through the disorganised papers, frowning to myself. "I don't even know if he got my message."

I pressed the relevant key on Henry's dusty telephone message recording machine and got a hissing, crackling tape with odd bleeps on it. It was not even one of the more modern units that has a bright woman's voice saying "you have no messages". After a certain brief spell of crackling silence, it clicked itself off, with a wink of light from red to green.

"He must have got the message, then. It's been erased."

I went on with my search. Under a circular from a credit card company - credit? Henry? - and an offer of free double glazing, was a solicitor's letter with a Tynemouth address. There was a heading "In re the will of the Miss Myrtle Weaver, deceased, of 11, Gordon Terrace, Cullercoats."

"Oh look, Sue, here's the start of the whole thing. That must be the maiden aunt and the house she left him. The watercolour's up there, according to Henry. Bloody miles away. In a place called Cullercoats."

"What?"

Something about Sue's voice and its sudden, sharp note, made me look up.

"What what?"

"Where? Where did you say the aunt's house was?"

She stepped across and held the letter, so that our two hands were grasping it together. I gestured at the text.

"Cullercoats, Sue. Never heard of it. That's what it says: 11, Gordon Road, Cullercoats."

"My God!" her eyes were suddenly shining. A pink tinge infused her cheeks but the rest of her face had gone white. "Cullercoats! It could be Homer!"

"The ancient Greek?"

"No, no, no, Tim! Homer! Winslow Homer! The American! The watercolour could be by Winslow Homer!"

"Why?"

"Winslow Homer painted in Cullercoats! In 1881 and '82! In watercolour! At the turning point of his career! Fishermen and elemental, sculptural women!" Her hand came off the letter and gripped my arm, nails digging in. "If it's one of his big ones, it's worth an absolute fortune!"

Chapter 12

"A fortune? A fortune? I thought that Art with a capital A was the important thing, Sue, not filthy lucre. At least, that's what you've always said to me."

She made a *moue* at this reference to her long-expressed, outward disapproval of the Art Fund's mercenary purposes. She was still glowing; the Cullercoats connection had got her really excited. When it comes to the crunch, Sue is just as keen a bloodhound as I am.

"What you don't know" she said, nodding at the solicitor's letter *in re* Myrtle Weaver, deceased, of Gordon Terrace, "because you're so locked into British art, and British art biography, is that Winslow Homer is big-time in America. Really big-time."

"Of course I know of Winslow Homer. They pay fortunes for him. He was a miserable old coot. Did elemental seaside scenes and lived on his own at Cape Cod, or somewhere equally bleak."

" Prout's Neck. Maine, not Cape Cod."

"Just as bleak. Bleaker, even."

"He wintered in Florida."

"Oh. Well anyway, he was one of those solitary artists. Rugged figures in roaring storms. And canoes, on empty lakes."

"Not all the time." She looked round the study. "He was probably no more solitary than Henry Weaver. He even painted stagecoaches."

"What?"

"Well, a stagecoach, anyway. Around his Civil War period, I think."

"Henry would have liked that. Cullercoats Geordies and *Stagecoach*. Quite the right artist for Henry. If the painting is by Homer, that is, not some dark, dank coastal daub by one

93

amateur or another. Although I doubt if Henry would have phoned me for that; he did have an eye of some sort."

Thoughtfully, excitement subsiding a little, Sue asked: "Who else would know?"

"About what? Oh, about the Cullercoats inheritance. I don't know."

She gestured at the envelope containing the will, which I was still carrying along with the keys. "Why don't you read it? It might provide some answers."

There's no gainsaying logic like that, even though I had instinctively delayed looking at the will out of some sort of natural reticence. I looked guardedly at the long envelope. It seemed like opening a box akin to Pandora's.

Henry's will: what winds would it unleash?

"Well go on, Tim!"

Carefully, I eased the envelope flap aside. A long folded document, typed 'Will of Henry C. Weaver, Esq.' slid out into my hand. I opened the stiff paper and started to read the narrowly-typed text, just a few words per line, with Sue peering impatiently alongside me.

This is the Last Will and Testament of me, HENRY CHARLES WEAVER, of Kenilworth Road, St.Leonards on Sea, East Sussex.

1. I hereby revoke all former Wills and testamentary dispositions.

2. I appoint TIMOTHY SIMPSON of Onslow Gardens, London, whose office is at White's Bank, Gracechurch Street, London, to be the Executor of this will.

3. I give to my Executor all my books, reference works and other literary documents for his own absolute use and benefit and declare that all administration expenses other than those arising out of a special Grant of Probate and the payment of duties necessary to secure such Grant shall be borne by my general estate in exoneration of the gift hereby made.

"Generous of him" I murmured, glancing at the serried shelves of battered volumes around me "but I'd be surprised if he expected there to be much by way of estate at the time he made this will. Grant of Probate indeed; where did he expect over two hundred thousand to come from?"

"It's just legalese standard phrasing, for Heaven's sake. They always use it to justify their fees. Turn over, Tim!"

I turned, obediently.

4. I give to my aunt, MYRTLE WEAVER, of 11, Gordon Road, Cullercoats, Tynemouth, my car, television set and all such electrical domestic appliances except kitchen appliances as may be in my possession at the time of my death for her own absolute use and benefit .

"The TV looks OK, but she'd have been a goner if she'd tried to drive that Allegro at her age. Lucky for her she snuffed it before it got up to her. What's left of it."

"Tim! Really!"

5. I give to my aunt ENID MAY WEAVER of 29, Smith Crescent, Whitby, Yorkshire, my steel engraving of Whitby, flower painting by Florence Engelbach and all such furniture, ornaments, cutlery, kitchen appliances and crockery as remain in my possession for her own absolute use and benefit.

6. Subject to the payment thereout of my debts and my funeral and testamentary expenses I GIVE all the remainder of my property and assets of every kind and wherever situated to my Executor TIMOTHY SIMPSON absolutely.

7. Should the beneficiaries named in Clauses 4 and 5 above predecease me I give all my property and assets of any kind and wherever situated to my executor TIMOTHY SIMPSON absolutely.

"Good God, Tim! He left it all to you!"

The will was signed, dated, witnessed by Harding and one of his clerks and stamped with the office stamp: Franklin, Jones and Harding, solicitors. I stood holding it, staring at the text in disbelief. Then I re-read it, twice. While I did so, Sue sat down on one of the two old leather-covered chairs. I put the will down, eventually, and sat on the other one. We stared at each other dumbly for a while. Then I rallied myself.

"There are a couple of questions here, Sue."

"A couple? Only a couple?"

"If he didn't expect to inherit the house at Cullercoats, then this was a will with his tongue in his cheek. What was left after all the possessions here had been passed to his aunts - just the books he left me - would be pushed to cover even a minimum funeral and any outstanding bills. Oh no, wait a minute; he owned this flat, unless I find that he'd mortgaged it."

I went over to the desk and rummaged amongst the papers, coming up with a bank statement for the previous month. There was a standing order paid to a building society listed amongst the outgoings. The remaining balance shown was overdrawn.

Sue was looking at me, expectantly, still looking a bit stunned.

"He must have got very short of money. He had a mortgage" I muttered. "Quite a substantial one, by the payment. What's left after that's paid off, when this flat's sold, together with the books, would have been all there was to meet funeral expenses and outstanding bills."

She looked at the shelves of books. "You don't know, Tim. There might be some valuable books there."

"Not in this tribute to Trivial Pursuit, there aren't, except by accident."

"You'll have to go through them to be sure of that."

"I will. All in good time." I was starting to feel real depression coming over me. "I bet there's negative equity on the flat." I looked at the will again, carefully. "He made no stipulations about cremation or where his ashes were to be scattered. Nothing about what kind of funeral. He's overdrawn by several thousand." I was beginning to feel bad. Dealing with a deceased, for me, brings on a sort of accidie. "If he didn't know about the aunt's house and watercolour coming to him, this may have been his last joke on me. Leaving me to carry the can, or rather cans, probably."

"And if he did? Know about his inheritance?"

"That wasn't for me, was it? He didn't expect to die young, did he? He probably thought he'd spend it well before this will would be invoked. Pay off his mortgage with it. If it can be paid off. Anyway, it's academic; he'd change the will if his aunts were dead."

"You don't know that. You were kind to him. Listened to him. I think you underestimate his gratitude."

"I don't know, now. I'm confused. He was glad of my company, as he was glad of anyone's who'd listen, but he called me a supercilious bastard, and he meant it. About being at school together, I mean. It was as though I'd denied him, distanced myself from him."

"That was a long time ago. You more than made that up to him."

"He was the kind of bloke to let it rankle. When you're that solitary, reluctance in acceptance assumes a great importance." I sighed, gloomily. "I've always had a guilty feeling about him. Maybe he did remember our conversation in the wine bar and my rather grudging reaction. Maybe this was his comeback."

"Oh, *Tim*." She got up and put her arms round me, her face close to mine. "Come on. I'm sure it's not like that. Don't look so depressed. You're letting this place get you down. He made you his executor. That's a compliment in anyone's language. He trusted you to carry out his provisions, to make sure his old aunts got his treasured bits and pieces if he died. He left you his books. His prized books. They were everything to him, weren't they? It didn't matter whether they were worth anything monetarily. Old books may just be old books, but they contained all of life's meaning to Henry. Everything that kept him going. He must have thought you were well-to-do compared with him. It may have been wishful thinking to believe you'd agreed to act as his executor, but there wasn't anyone closer he could ask to carry out his will, otherwise he'd have asked them. And I'm sure there'll be a positive balance on the flat. Sure of it. Come on, Tim; cheer up. Take it the right way, not in doubt and ill-feeling. It's not like you. Be positive. Think; you may even own a Winslow Homer!"

That made me grin. I gave her a squeeze back. "You're right, Sue. *De mortuis nil nisi bonum*, and all that. I had an affection for Henry. The thought that he might have made me executor in resentment gives me a horrible feeling. Even if the will, ironically, before he had time to change it, passes an unforeseen inheritance to me. Whatever the inheritance turns out to be. Come on, let's go and see Sammy Simes. Leave all this for later. A bit of fresh air will blow the spiders away. We need to know what really happened to that car."

"Good. That's better. Much more like you. Let's go."

I went round the flat to make sure that everything that should be turned off at its root was turned off. Another electricity bill wasn't going to boost my morale any further, that was for sure. I locked up carefully and we got in the car, negotiating our way out along the seaside promenade and up towards the Old Town and Ore, following the Rye road.

"Isn't this rather a long way for a car to go for repairs?" Sue asked, as we ascended the long hill and passed through the rather congested streets of Ore before emerging into the open, out past school and apartment blocks. "All the way out towards this Icklesham?"

I grinned. "Sammy was in Ore originally. Quite nearby, then. It's where he lives, but he needed a cheaper and bigger place, so he moved to this decrepit but big farm workshop. Henry had a thing about keeping one craftsman to look after his vehicle, and they could meet in the Old Town quite easily. In reality, it was to do with money. No one else would maintain his vehicle for the price, or bother with it, the way Sammy did. There was a friend of Henry's who was the same about an old Citroen *Deux Chevaux*; used to take it out to Brede for servicing because there are two lads there who really know those cars. Henry had a similar, slightly snobbish attitude. Sort of 'my man Sammy' sort of thing. Don't think Sammy appreciated that very much but he's been good to Henry. It's not exactly as though becoming an Allegro specialist has a long and prosperous future to it."

"I don't suppose it has. Tell me; why was everyone so kind? What was it about Henry?"

"I think" I replied grimly, "that it was a case of 'there but for the Grace of God go I' or something like it. And he had character. There was nothing suburban or Sunday supplement about Henry."

Signs were coming up: Fairlight and Pett to the right, Guestling to the left. Memories of taking Henry out to pick up his car gave me the correct place to turn off the main road onto an inland track between thick hedges towards farm buildings. Mud splashed under my wheels. The track went past a sagging gate, between two low brick buildings and into a bumpy yard.

A policeman suddenly stepped out in front of the car, hand raised.

I stopped sharp as Sue drew her breath. In front of us were a police vehicle and a paramedic ambulance, their garish white and red stripes glaring livid against the dull farm buildings. Over by the wide-open doors of Sammy's big corrugated-iron shed two ambulance men stood still, looking into the workshop. Their attitude chilled me to the marrow. Body language says everything. There was no urgency about these emergency men; just the still, chill look of immobility. They weren't doing anything at all.

The policeman was coming round to my window but I was out of the car before he got there.

He held up a hand.

"Sorry, sir. Can't allow you any further."

"What's happened?"

"Accident."

"Is it - is it - serious?"

The policeman's face was reddish, worn, experienced. He hesitated for a moment, clearly not sure what to say. I hurried to establish some sort of credentials.

"I know Sammy Simes quite well. He's expecting me."

"Then I'm very sorry, sir. I'm afraid it's fatal."

"What?"

"Yes, sir."

"But how?"

"It seems that a jack slipped while he was under a heavy vehicle. A farm labourer found him. We're waiting for a crane to come and give a lift so we can extricate the - the deceased. I'll have to ask you to move your car out of the way. Then I'll take your details, if I may, for the record."

Inside the car, Sue stared out, dumbly, white-faced. I moved slowly back from the policeman and got back into the driving seat.

Her eyes burned into me. "Don't tell me: he's dead?"

I nodded, silently.

"How?"

"An accident. A jack slipped. The vehicle he was under crushed him."

"How does a jack slip?"

"If someone wants it to, it can slip quite easily."

I started the engine, feeling numb. Three deaths, all connected with cars.

I hate coincidences.

Chapter 13

"Let me see" said Nobby Roberts, scraping the last scoop of fried egg yolk onto a scrap of bacon and spearing both onto a bit of fried bread "if I have got this right. May I summarise?"

"Fire away, Nobby."

"You say" he mumbled slightly, due to a full mouth "that this Henry Weaver died in a car crash the local police are treating as an accident but you suspect that his car had been got at?"

"Yes Nobby."

"You say this" he lifted a cup of coffee up to swill down the residue, found it empty, and signalled at a waitress "on the basis of a verbal report from a seedy garage mechanic called Simes." He smiled sunnily as the waitress promptly brought us both fresh coffee. "A mechanic so competent and successful that, working in a decayed corrugated-iron shed of minimal weather protection, he managed to kill himself by failing to secure a heavy lifting jack, one to which proper safety standards have to apply, so that a pickup truck fell on him."

"Now look, Nobby - "

"Hang on! Hang on! I am going through a sequence here. As a policeman, you understand."

"I understand. The wheels turn slowly, but turn they must."

"Quite so. Slowly maybe, but thoroughly, I hope. You have, as it happens, no motivation for either death, should suspicious circumstances be adduced to them, except for" - here he raised his now-empty fork in a gesture of caution - "a possible inheritance, probably of a modest character, in Tynemouth or thereabouts, some suburb, satellite, of Newcastle upon Tyne?"

"Cullercoats, actually."

He waved a dismissive hand. "Wherever. The key point" -

now the fork came round to point itself at a spot somewhere in the middle of my chest - "is who, one must ask, would benefit from such a death, or deaths, were such a death, or deaths, to have occurred as a result of criminal activity? Who is the one to get the filthy lucre, if filthy lucre there be? And the answer - admitted, I agree, perfectly frankly, openly and without reservation by yourself - is yourself."

"Ah. Well. I'm not quite sure whether there's much filthy lucre to be had or not. But you do see, don't you Nobby, that I didn't have any idea - "

"Which puts you" he interrupted, ignoring my response totally " to use popular police jargon, as seen on TV, *in the frame.*"

"God, how I hate those TV police serials. Do London coppers really talk like that? Still call their bosses 'Guv'?"

"They do, Tim. They still do."

"Appalling. You mean you are often referred to as 'Guv' by your underlings?"

"I am."

"Disgraceful. I would have thought that a Detective Chief Inspector, a Scotland Yard man no less, might command a better form of respect and title."

"Such as?"

"A minimum of Sir, at least. Or Your Honour, maybe. What about, as per the legal profession you admire so much, m'Lud, perhaps?"

"Now you are resorting to hyperbole. And becoming your normal irreverent self. The fact that you are paying for this breakfast does not entitle you to punt gratuitous insults at me."

We were sitting in a small Italian café on Victoria Street, not far from where Nobby would soon have to go to work. I have known him since we were at college together and we played rugger on the same side. Whereas in those days I was a stolid front row man, the ginger-haired Nobby swooped around on the wing. He joined the police after graduating and has risen remarkably, motivated by strong moral feeling and sharp percipience. For a time he was on the Art Fraud Squad, so we were involved in various escapades, to his distaste. Nobby views me with the deep reserve of a true friend of youth but his wife Gillian and I are close, in the most decorous sense of the word, and he has a high regard for Sue, so there is a deal of family mingling outside professional events.

"I would not dream of insulting you" -

"Ha!"

"-as well you know. It is just that before anyone starts to put me *in the frame*, as you so colloquially call it, I seek to make clear that I had no knowledge that I might be a beneficiary. Indeed, I was not even aware that I was to be the sole executor until Harding phoned me."

"That is what you say. What you claim. As might anyone culpable but determined to avoid justice. However" - he held up a hand to check my protest - "are we not jumping the gun a little here? Is your usual suspicious, adventure-seeking mind not working a little too luridly?"

"I don't think so."

He sighed. "No one has attacked you yet, by any chance, have they?"

"No. Not yet."

"How unusual. Normally, you have severely injured at least one assailant by now."

"Nobby -"

"Keep calm. If there had been an attempt of some sort, I would express less reservation. In these affairs, it is normal for you to attract murderous footpads like flies. On this occasion, nothing has happened."

"That's disgraceful. Do I have to get battered to death before you will arouse yourself from this torpor?"

"What do you suppose is the value of this Cullercoats inheritance? This treasure which you believe has stimulated such fatal pursuits? Of an unsuccessful, impecunious bibliographical researcher and a bottom-level garage mechanic neither of whom was renowned for their assets?"

"You can be a cruel bastard sometimes, Nobby."

"Realistic, you mean. How much?"

"I don't know. Sue and I are driving up to Newcastle this weekend to look. I've arranged to get the keys to Gordon Road."

He frowned. "You're involving Sue?"

"Try stopping her."

"Hmph. Not advisable, knowing your back history. However, it is not for me to interfere."

"You mean you're not going to do anything?"

"I meant in family affairs. I will do something, since you have asked, about events on the A21 and at this farmyard garage. You remember Inspector Foster of the Hastings CID?"

"Only too vividly."

"He is still in place. I shall ask him to make discreet enquiries. The Allegro should not have been scrapped yet."

"Bloody certain it shouldn't. I'm the executor. They have to ask me, don't they?"

He smiled crookedly. "You'll learn, Tim. You'll learn. Compared with an insurance assessor, you are peripheral."

"I'm obliged to you, Nobby. Deeply obliged. This will set my mind at rest."

"The least one can do. Since we were at college together."

I grinned at him. He looked the same as ever to me: wiry, ginger, quite fit considering he walks with a slight limp these days, keen-eyed, alert. College men see themselves the same as ever, year after year, until they drop, I believe, but there was little perceptible deterioration about him.

"How's trade, Nobby?"

"Brisk."

"Still after the big time gangsters? No shortage, I suppose?"

"None whatsoever. The sums get bigger, the networks more diverse." He looked at his watch. "I have to go." He stood up and began to tidy himself, picking up a newspaper. "I have to appear before a committee to testify on a complicated financial case. I do detest these quangos and committees of enquiry. All verbiage and no vigour. By the time their report comes out, the world has forgotten the case or the political lecturer has moved on to the next slide."

"Quangos? Not one of the redoubtable Shauna Springs's quangos, is it?"

He paused, frowning. "Why do you ask?"

I hesitated. "Nothing."

"Tim!"

"You know Sir Richard White was found dead in his Jaguar in Turin a day or two back?"

"I did hear, yes. What's that got to do with Shauna Springs's quangos?"

"I, er, um, nothing. Well, it's a long story. I wasn't going to bother you with it, since it's really an Italian affair."

"Italian?"

"Chap called Bertrasconi seems to be involved."

He sat down again, slowly.

"You are a focus for trouble, aren't you? Really a focus for trouble." He signalled to the waitress for another coffee. "Come on, tell your old friend Nobby all about it. You've got just four minutes."

"I thought you were busy."

"I am."

"Well, you realise it's all rather confidential. Confidential to the Bank and its affairs, I mean. I'm not sure whether" -

"Tim!"

"Yes, Nobby?"

"It is a serious offence," his teeth bared as he repeated what was, clearly, a formula he used only too often professionally, "to withhold information from a police officer during the course of an enquiry."

That set me back. I must have done a double-take at him. "An enquiry? What enquiry?"

He smiled at the waitress once again as she put another cappuccino down in front of him and added it to my bill. His ginger complexion lightened into a sunny radiance for a moment, then he turned back to me.

The smile disappeared. Concentration reddened his returning ginger look. He held up an admonitory finger. "You just cough it all up, Timmy. All of it; none of your usual omissions, selections, evasions or tampered evidence of any sort. I'll decide, subsequently, what you need to know about my enquiry."

Chapter 14

Once again, outside the windows, the bustle of the City of London brought murmurs of traffic, movements of people and the distant drone of an airliner to the ear. Inside, the feathered mahogany panelling looked down upon yet another distressed, congested countenance.

"My dear Tim! What the blazes have you gone running off to Nobby Roberts for? What on earth could he have to do with this matter? What possessed you? I am amazed that you should act, in an international affair which is highly confidential, poised on a knife edge, absolutely top secret, with such blatant disregard for the Bank's internal security!"

In another leather-buttoned armchair facing me, Geoffrey Price sat quite still, his face immobile in a way that, as a result of training, or perhaps simple acquisition by experience, accountants are able to keep their graven faces straight behind their thick spectacles. Perhaps I saw just a flicker, a mere shadow of humour glide across it but if so, it lasted only a fleeting second.

"Nobby is very discreet, Jeremy."

"Discreet? He's a policeman! A rozzer! Great clodhopping boots will be stamping over the whole area within minutes! Apart from persecuting hardworking motorists going about their legitimate businesses, these days they have nothing better to do than poke their noses into people's private affairs!"

Jeremy had recently picked up a speeding fine via a police camera and his language, on receiving the official summons advising him of the amount and the points docked on his licence, had been unprintable.

"Look, it came out quite by accident. I was talking to him over breakfast about quite a different matter, and - "

"A different matter? What different matter?"

"Oh nothing. Nothing, really. A private thing. Quite irrelevant, Jeremy."

A finger stabbed at me across the leather top of his immaculate partners' desk. "Stop! Stop right there! I can tell by your face! There's been some deadly event connected with the Art Fund, hasn't there? That would certainly induce a breakfast with a Robert. What are you concealing? Geoffrey and I are both executives of the Fund, remember, and are entitled to know. You're up to something, aren't you?"

"Not really. Well, sort of. A minor matter which has engaged my attention, you might say."

"A minor matter." It was almost a whisper. "A minor matter. I could see this coming last time we met. So you haven't mentioned it to us." He braced himself dramatically as though ready to receive a blow. "How many people are dead?"

"Er, well, that's rather an unfair question, Jeremy."

"How many?" he shouted, causing Geoffrey's dark eyebrows to twitch, just the once, over his horn-rims.

"Two. But - "

"Two! Dear God!" The cufflink flash was repeated as his hand struck his brow. "Two people are dead already! But! But! But me no buts! Cough it up! The whole story! All of it! Now!"

So I did. Well, an edited version of it, you might say, emphasising the possible lack of criminal background, the probability of pure coincidence, and so on. As emollient a version as possible.

It got him clean out of his chair. He did one of his two-steps up and down the office while Geoffrey and I watched in rapt fascination. For relatively early in the morning he moved quickly but, with a face that congested and a body that tense, rapid movement in a half-strut constituted the best form of relief.

"This is dire! Dire! You've done it again!"

"Jeremy, I have done nothing. Other people may have - "

"Don't deny it! Once the first death occurred, you set events in motion which led to the second!"

"That's unfair. Don't think I haven't thought long and through the night about Sammy's death being laid at my door. I have. But we don't know, yet, whether my suspicions were justified or not."

"They will be. Oh yes, they will be. It is written. It is written." He raised a stabbing finger and pointed it at his panelled wall as though, as in a play by Lord Dunsany, a disembodied hand was already scrawling prophetic messages about purple birds of doom across the polished surface. "It is written. Anything of this kind in which you have a hand will lead to a dreadful, a ghastly outcome. The indisputable fact is that your methods and contacts, if they can be called that, have once again led you into the criminal world. Here we are, a perfectly respectable merchant bank, of long standing and impeccable reputation - "

"Dealing in the world of insider trading, insurance swindles, currency gambles, takeover scams, third-party commissions, arms dealers, commodity manipulation, property hypes - "

"Stop that! Stop that at once! You wretch!"

"Jeremy, you are over-reacting. As I have explained to you, I have placed the matter in the hands of the police. As befits an honest citizen making a full and frank deposition. My fears may be groundless. The police have all the facts at their disposal. If Sammy Simes had time to write down any relevant points they will find his report, or notes, or whatever they are." I shrugged, and shook my head dismissively. "If they say there is no cause for alarm or suspicion, I will accept their verdict."

He paused in mid-hop, halfway across the carpet, and peered at me.

"You will?"

"Absolutely."

"You mean that? If the police tell you that the road accident was just an accident and that Simes's jack also slipped accidentally, and that in their highly professional view no further steps need be taken, you'll accept it?"

"Suddenly you view the police as highly professional, do you?"

He ignored my sarcasm. "You promise? Here and now, in front of me, with Geoffrey as witness, you promise? On your word of honour?"

"I promise. I shall accept the police's verdict. I shall do no more than carry out the melancholy requirements incumbent upon me as Henry Weaver's sole executor. Absolutely."

"And if they find grounds for suspicion?"

"Then the matter will be in their capable, highly professional hands, won't it? There is no room for amateurs in modern detection."

He stopped pacing. "I suppose" he said, gloomily, "that's about as good a promise as we can get out of you, under the circumstances."

"Yes, Jeremy."

"We'd better have some coffee."

"Good idea, Jeremy."

It was his form of peace offering. He summoned Claire and she dispensed coffee. We sat back for a moment as he reinstalled himself behind his desk.

"To business" he said, after taking a deep draught of a blend of Brazilian for strength and Colombian for aroma.

"Where were we?"

"You were about to advise us of some enquiry which Detective Chief Inspector Roberts is conducting into the affairs of this, this Bertrasconi's bank, the, the - "

"Baddy risk" said Geoffrey, speaking for the first time. At least, that was what it sounded like.

"Eh?" Jeremy glared at him, uncomprehending.

Geoffrey cleared his throat. "A little City joke, Jeremy."

"Why am I not laughing?"

"Let me explain. It has to do with abbreviations. In Italy, for instance, the highly respectable and successful bank, the Banco Di Risparmio Della Provincia Lombardia - the

Lombardian Provincial Savings Bank, to translate - is known, for short, as the Ba100riplo."

"So?"

"Bertrasconi is the prime mover in a bank called the Banco Di Risparmio Cottiano - the Cottian Savings Bank."

"Cottian?"

"From the Cottian Alps, Jeremy" I interjected. "Named after a pagan king, Cottius, of the first century AD, I believe."

"For God's sake, Tim! This is no time to be facetious."

"It's true, Jeremy. Richard told me. And it's interesting. The Cottian Alps, according to Captain Stephens of Cooden Drive, are where the Waldensians apparently- "

"Shut up! Just shut up!"

"Sorry, Jeremy."

"If I may resume." Geoffrey was unperturbed. "As soon as the jokers in the City heard that Bertrasconi had taken a major interest in the Banco Di Risparmio Cottiano, they immediately labelled it the Badirisc, for short." He paused to let it sink in. "Badirisc? Bad risk?"

"Dear God."

"Whereas in fact it uses the abbreviation Baricot on its correspondence and logos et cetera." Geoffrey smiled blandly. "It is only we in the City who still, surreptitiously of course, refer to it by its humorous epithet."

"You're just a bundle of laughs, you lot, aren't you?"

"It is this bank which would have been involved in the electronic consortium finance we are very carefully discussing, had its prime mover been interested in the consortium."

"Tim? Have you anything to say at this point? Useful, I mean, not some garbled idiocy about Cottians and Waldensians?"

"According to Nobby, there is some sort of enquiry going on into the affairs of Bertrasconi, especially this Baricot bank. He wouldn't say what it was, but it involves international police cooperation. There is a project of some sort in which

Baricot got involved, where money laundering is said to have taken place. He wouldn't tell me any more."

"Well, that's pretty useless. I mean, it's virtually par for the course in Italy. Money laundering, I mean. Hardly an honest lira in sight."

"Jeremy" Geoffrey's tone was gently reproving. "I think you should know that the Italian Government, and their police, have taken very severe measures against money laundering in recent years. They are very sensitive about the subject. The Northern Italian economy is a powerhouse far more effective industrially than ours and they wish to protect it from-"

"That's a laugh! The Italians have plundered the European Community of funds in every kind of investment scam possible for years. From olive trees that don't exist to vast construction projects that fall down, they're the masters of EC fraud. Look at the Banco Ambrosiano affair. Merely the tip of an iceberg."

"Be that as it may, their industrial expertise cannot be gainsaid. And they do still make things, which is more than can be said for us."

Jeremy bridled. "I'm surprised at you, Geoffrey. These negative views of our economy do no one any good."

"Facts are facts."

"Cutting back to the chase" I decided to interrupt, "we have a situation in which it appears that the consortium to be formed, and financed by syndicate in which we are to participate strongly, may be prejudiced by leaks from within our ranks. There is also the possibility that Bertrasconi, drawing upon the dubious funds available to him in bulk from the Baricot, or Badirisc, or whatever you want to call it, could act destructively in some way yet to be established, using insider knowledge. Or am I being too alarmist?"

There was a silence. They looked at me, uneasily.

"I realise" I continued "that this is a matter in which I am not supposed to be involved. Since, however, Richard involved me willy-nilly in what he had seen and feared, my involvement is already established. Even if it is, as yet, merely a peripheral involvement. Which reminds me, by the way: aren't we supposed to have heard from Turin as to the cause of death by now?"

"We have." Jeremy looked at a sheet on the surface in front of him. "Heart failure."

"Heart failure?"

"Good heavens, do I have to repeat everything twice in this place? Heart failure. That's what is the official cause of death."

"Just like that? No explanatory circumstances?"

"He was seventy-seven, Tim."

"All the same."

"What do you mean, all the same? Gadding about like an amateur sleuth at his age was not exactly the best thing to do, was it?"

"I did advise him against it."

"So you say."

"Heart attacks may be induced by a variety of means."

"The Italian authorities have carried out a thorough post mortem. They say they are satisfied although -"

"Although what?"

"There were, apparently, small light bruises on his wrists which are not entirely explained. Richard took some sort of medication for blood pressure and this could have caused such marks to arise."

"Any bugs - electronic listening bugs found about his person or the car?"

"No."

"So they must have been removed."

"If they were there."

"If they were there? What do you mean?"

"Did you see them?"

"No. I didn't. He didn't actually show them to me."

"Exactly. And now we have no confirmation that he saw

those three people in Belley except what you say Richard said he saw."

A red mist began to move across my eyes. Suddenly I began to feel isolated and exposed.

"Oh well, I suppose that means the whole thing is an invention, is it? Pure fabrication. Either Richard's eyesight was defective or he was ga-ga or I went out to Torre Pellice, ate hallucinatory mushrooms, came back and invented a whole farrago of absolute bloody nonsense, did I?"

"There's no need to shout! You really must watch your blood pressure, you know, Tim. Your face is quite *mottled*. I wonder sometimes whether this coffee isn't too strong for you."

I gaped at him, speechless, for a moment. Then I got up, went across to the tray Claire had left and filled another cup.

"If it's any consolation to you" he murmured across to the back I had presented to him "Freddy is not satisfied, either."

I turned to face him. "Freddy isn't?"

Frederick, Lord Harbledown, Jeremy's cousin, better known to his friends as Freddy Harbledown, is the senior member, socially anyway, of the White family. He combines a touching preoccupation with the breeding of thoroughbred Old English Sheepdogs with membership of the main Board of the Bank.

"Freddy has pronounced that it isn't good enough."

"What isn't?"

"This report. I won't dwell on what Freddy actually said because it might distress Geoffrey here, in view of his remarks about the Italian economic and professional miracle, but Freddy has ordered that another examination should take place when the body is returned to this country. Which it shortly will be, following our representatives' intervention in Turin."

"Good old Freddy. But why?"

"He says that one of his champion dogs died of distemper or something at a Milan show once and he's never trusted

Northern Italian medical skills since. Says they're absolutely clueless."

"Distemper, eh? A champion dog, what? These things mark a man, Jeremy."

He pursed his lips but kept calm. "They do. So we will obtain a second opinion. Whether we like it or not."

"Right. Good. I am glad to find that hereditary qualities, including the traditional suspicion of foreigners, still persist in the peerage. Thank you for letting me know, Jeremy."

He opened his mouth and might have blurted out a suitable retort had not Geoffrey Price coughed mildly, cleared his throat and spoke straight to him. "May we return to the central issue? Since I do have to carry forward the financial examination of this very taxing electronics project on which much of our future depends?"

"Of course, Geoffrey my dear fellow, of course. Please excuse these churlish diversions of Tim's."

Geoffrey's eyebrows flickered once again, giving me the faintest wink. Despite his thickly-rimmed spectacles, Geoffrey is known, in cricketing circles, as a deceptive, stonewalling batsman with an excellent late cut to the off. "There is no doubt in my mind that, following Sir Richard's sad demise, Tim should act as project co-ordinator for the London end of things."

"*What?*"

"He has filled that role many times before. Indeed, you may recall that actually it was his official position following the end of the Bellevie cosmetics affair. It is only recently - last year, in fact - that he has been diverted to the American business. I think he should step into Sir Richard's shoes in this project forthwith. He knows the Maucourts well, has worked with Jacques Charville and can, I am sure, work alongside Giorgio Deserti without problem."

"That is if he doesn't induce another whole round of fatalities amongst all those with whom he comes into contact, you mean? I can't think what you're about, Geoffrey. If what

Richard said is true, Tim would be the most unsuitable candidate. Give rise to instant suspicion."

"He would also" Geoffrey imperturbably ignored Jeremy's unnecessary remarks "be able to observe the Deva at close hand."

This foxed me. "The Deva?"

Geoffrey smiled gently. "Before joining us, Shauna Spring was Director of an organisation called Intradeva - the Internet Trade Development Agency. A quasi-governmental venture to encourage - some might say interfere in - the growth of Internet business. It ended in recriminations due to its involvement in some Internet launches of stock which bombed. While it lasted, she was known by her staff and some outsiders as the Deva. I need not explain why it is humorously pronounced with the long e."

"Indeed you need not." Jeremy was still acerbic. "Just a mass of wags, you finance wizards."

"She might view my appointment with suspicion and hostility" I said.

"I agree" Jeremy fluted. "Anyway, I wish Tim to be kept well away from the electronics project. Certainly until this dreadful Henry Weaver affair is resolved. I really think that all this Baricot-Badirisc comedy must be kept away from him. It's quite a separate issue."

"Jeremy." Geoffrey's voice had suddenly gone calm, much calmer than his normal, controlled delivery. I recognised it at once. It's a very bad sign. I am extremely fond of Geoffrey, who has been with the Art Fund since its inception, and have much to be grateful to him for, but fondness has to be tempered with the danger signs when he puts them out. Geoffrey is no fool. When he goes into his over-calm mode, it is as well to listen.

Jeremy caught but little of the tone. "What?" he demanded.

Geoffrey stayed calm, much too calm. He was going into one of his Real Accountant, Senior-Auditor styles of address, like a college tutor delivering a polite but formal indication to one of his charges that if he doesn't buck up his ideas and listen, The Grand Order of The Boot will be applied any time now.

"My humorous reference was perhaps ill-advised. It may have diverted you from reality. The involvement of the Baricot Bank is not something to wave to one side with a gay gesture. It has become a very large bank indeed. Very large. The Americans, the Swiss and the Germans may have made all the headlines here in London, but the Northern Italian powerhouse is not to be ignored. Baricot are setting about securing a major presence in London and Frankfurt. For obvious reasons. They are, rumour has it, looking to put a very large foot into the industrial and commercial investment banking field. They are intent on becoming a major European player. To secure their position in Italy they swallowed up a number of smaller investment entities, including banks like ours. Their methods were without scruple. Technically just about legal, but without scruple. Other aspects of their operations have been remarkable for a very rapid rate of expansion, one which has started to give rise to comment. I am not surprised that Nobby Roberts has filtered a gentle warning of his enquiries to us. There is no scope for sentiment in business. They want a bigger share of the London cake. If Baricot could swallow up this Bank of ours easily and cheaply, we'd be down their gullets tomorrow. We need to move quickly and decisively to clarify this very disturbing report of Sir Richard's."

Jeremy blinked. He has the sense to listen to Geoffrey and admires him, otherwise Geoffrey wouldn't still be with us, but Jeremy's instinct is always to avoid putting the brakes on.

"Of course, Geoffrey, of course. I hear everything you say. Very sage, as ever. But Tim's involvement, if seen to be imposed by us, must lead to suspicions. Especially after the ludicrous Waldensian affair. His reputation as a ferret - if you'll pardon the expression - is too vivid in the eyes of some of the Board. I can not see how one can just gaily, in an offhand manner, say oh, by the way, I've put our resident bull terrier into the electronics chicken coop. It just won't wash."

And as he said it, as though up on Olympus the Gods smiled to themselves, or like Fate quietly slipping the lead into the boxing glove, Claire came diffidently slipping through the door to face Jeremy's frowning countenance at her interruption.

She managed to ignore his disapproval.

"Jeremy, I am sorry to interrupt but Shauna Spring is here in my office. She apologises for the interruption but is most anxious to see you while all three of you are together."

Jeremy tried not to look startled, but he was. "Shauna Spring? To see all three of us?"

"Yes. She's very specific. Says she has to leave for another meeting soon and this is the only time she's got. Knowing that the three of you are together, she's very adamant she wants to see you. I said I'd do my best; she says it won't take more than a minute or two. There won't be another opportunity for a while."

Although disconcerted, Jeremy rose gallantly to the occasion, coming out from behind his desk in a swift recovery whilst shooting me a glance that spoke volumes about the need for discretion.

"By all means" he boomed, getting to his best mid-carpet reception point as quickly as possible. "By all means show her in."

Geoffrey raised a confidential eyebrow at me from behind his protective tortoiseshell screen.

"The most effective form of defence is attack. Prepare to receive spin bowling" he murmured. "Not to mention the odd googly. Better pad up thickly, Tim. See to the protective equipment. Down where things can hurt most."

Chapter 15

It is difficult, when you're expecting the onset of a dragon, to adjust quickly to the entrance of a lamb. Fortunately, Jeremy was busy greeting the modest arrival ushered in by Claire with due gallantry: making a leg, taking a hand, beaming broadly, raking a fall of blond hair out of his eyes and generally cavorting. So I had time, whilst Geoffrey and I stood up, to observe Shauna Spring at close hand before it was my turn to be presented.

I had expected something blunt, perhaps even with a straight fringe or square jaw, bulky or burly in form and scrubbed in appearance, to manifest itself. This, Sue would say, would be due to a typical, inbuilt male chauvinism about women successful in business, but in mitigation I must plead that her reputation, especially her reported performance in many meetings, was one which indicated a head-on, in-your-face aggression coupled with a viper's tongue. It took a substantial realignment of impression to adjust to this medium height, attractive woman with light brown hair, blue eyes and smooth complexion who cooed apologies at Jeremy and turned, all enthusiasm and smiles, to greet me.

Knowing that Sue would want a full sartorial report, I took in her grey suit, of slightly crumpled material, and instantly knew that, despite its modest, almost dowdy impression, it was an extremely expensive piece of tailoring. The length of skirt was not provocative, nor too long; the fit to the figure was not too loose nor too revealing, but snug enough for the observer to realise that the figure was good. The legs were shapely, cased in mid-brown stockings leading to dark shoes with heels that were not too high, nor too low, the toes not too pointed nor too blunt. The blouse under the jacket was silk but not too silky; its collar was open but not too wide; the necklace beneath it was not too thick a strand nor too thin, studded with gold, but not bright gold. Her eyes were set wide apart, her chin pointed but firm, her lips, lightly made up, quite full. Her cheekbones were not too high but well shaped, her forehead broad but framed by the light brown hair which someone had arranged very carefully.

She was an attractive woman. One certain men would prize for being so unostentatiously but appealingly turned out. One who women would admire for combining skill in business with a flair for this very cultivated, low key but carefully-perfected sort of appearance.

She was smiling at me as Jeremy stumbled out self-conscious introductions, showing even white teeth, not too small, not too big, not too white.

"This is a great pleasure!" Her voice was low, warm, full of humour. "I've been waiting to meet you ever since I joined the Bank. But you keep flying off to America. I'm beginning to think you're avoiding me."

"Really?"

"Of course! Tim Simpson of Art Fund fame. The one who gets the Bank so much good PR. I know people in the Arts Council who'll be green with envy when I tell them I've met you."

"Envy? I think they'll evince other emotions. I'm not altogether popular with some of them. Due to some of the things the Fund collected ahead of their pet galleries, I mean."

"Jealousy."

I smiled. "I'm not sure about that. But I too, am honoured. Your fame goes ahead of you. This is a real pleasure."

"Thank you, kind sir. Flattery from famous rugby players will get everywhere with me." The smile widened, then the eyes went past me. "Hello, Geoffrey; how are you?"

"Hello, Shauna. I am well, thank you."

She turned to Jeremy. The smile vanished and an expression of determination replaced it. "Forgive me for interrupting what is, I am sure, a grave conclave of the Art Fund and other erudite matters."

"Oh no, really -"

"But I wanted to catch you together before I have to go. It being Friday, I shan't be back until Monday afternoon or Tuesday morning. It's important that the electronics project doesn't lose impetus. Now that poor Richard is no longer with us, I mean."

"Um, yes, of course, of course."

"So I had the thought - I hope I'm not treading on any toes - that provided he's not deeply committed elsewhere, the ideal thing for all of us would be that Tim should take over Richard's co-ordination role right away."

Jeremy managed not to gape at her but his expression was a picture. "You think so?"

"Absolutely. You and Geoffrey are already involved at this end. Tim has worked with you for ages. He knows Maucourt's very well and I'm sure Giorgio Deserti will welcome him as a - no disrespect to the deceased, but - younger and more vigorous addition to the team. It makes sense. Entirely logical, I think. Especially in view of Tim's previous successes."

She gave me a quick, comradely grin, to which I bowed slightly.

Jeremy did a rapid recovery job on himself. "What an excellent idea, Shauna. I thoroughly agree. Tim and I will have to go through his current workload and revise some priorities but I'm sure we can arrange that."

"Good." She turned back to me and smiled again, warmly. "I shall look forward to working with you, Tim. I'm sure Geoffrey will brief you thoroughly as soon as possible. Then you'll need to go to Turin. Before the next round of negotiations, I mean."

My goodness, I thought privately, you can't wait, can you? Out loud, I said I would be delighted.

"Marvellous. Please forgive me, once again, but the opportunity couldn't be missed. The time was propritious."

She gave us a another quick, mischievous glance, like a

teacher who has caught three boys smoking behind the bicycle sheds but, on a boys-will-be-boys basis, isn't going to report them, and moved to the door slowly enough for Jeremy to leap ahead and open it for her. Evidently business equality didn't forbid such gallantry as sexist, or maybe she was just used to minions opening doors for her. She moved smartly through and was gone.

Jeremy closed the door in wonderment and turned back to stare at me in some discomfiture. "What the blazes was all that in aid of?" he demanded. "I don't understand it at all."

"It's a pre-emptive strike" I replied.

"What?"

I was going to quote Lyndon Baines Johnson; something about better to have me on the inside pissing out than on the outside pissing in, but Geoffrey beat me to it both in timing and decorum. He's good on nursery rhymes, is Geoffrey; he gave one straight to Jeremy.

"Will you walk into my parlour," he said.

"Eh?"

"Will you walk into my parlour, said a spider to a fly. 'Tis the prettiest little parlour that ever you did spy. And Tim is a spy." He took off his horn rims and began to clean them with a snow-white handkerchief, as though they had steamed up. "My goodness, she's showing enormous keenness on you, too, Tim. The signs were unmistakable. Do remember what happens to male spiders afterwards though, won't you?"

I grinned. "Only if, having delivered the coup de grâce, they don't withdraw fast enough, Geoffrey."

"How very coarse!" Despite his discomfiture, Jeremy's tone was reproving. "These rugby club analogies have no place in a respectable office."

"I sit corrected, Jeremy." I smiled at him sunnily. "And impressed by the speed with which, under feminine influence, you can change your mind. Geoffrey and I will now withdraw - sedately - and plan my trip to Turin."

He scowled. "You know damn well I had little choice. The

whole situation fills me with foreboding. But at least this will divert you from any possibility of breaking your word, your solemn word, over this damned watercolour."

"Absolutely, Jeremy." I nodded emphatically and stood up. Geoffrey followed suit and we shuffled out of the office, leaving him still scowling behind his big, mahogany, partners' desk.

It didn't seem the right moment to mention, yet again, my melancholy duties as an executor.

Chapter 16

Tynemouth, which has a rather elegant air after you have traversed the square miles of housing estates surrounding Newcastle, is across and down river from the famous coal city. With its ruined castle and abbey, it sits on the north bank of the Tyne at its corner with the open sea. Cullercoats is just beyond Tynemouth, round the corner of the river mouth if you head north towards Whitley Bay, up the blistering coast to pass yet further housing estates before you reach it. There are lumpy sandstone cliffs round a small bay protected by curving breakwaters with the usual entrance gap for harbour mouth. It was once an export site for coal and salt then, when that ran out, a fishing harbour for the small, flat-bottomed boats called cobles which abounded along the north-east coast. At a later time, it was a popular summer bathing resort for workers from Newcastle out on day trips. A hardy lot, not expecting the warm, soft-water luxuries of the modern package holiday.

I wouldn't bathe there.

I'm not sure what Cullercoats is, now. A big, redbrick marine research building, architecturally stark, and a similarly uncompromising redbrick lifeboat station were plonked on the sands a hundred years ago. These two buildings, with concrete railed steps in cascading slopes, fill the space close to the cliffs. The small bay is grey and the atmosphere enclosed. To the present-day, art-history conscious visitor, perhaps expecting the plein-air, broad expanses suggested by the canvases of a hundred years ago and more, it is as disappointing as Newlyn is to those whose impressions are formed by Stanhope Forbes and his followers. The beach looks small, disused, inactive, grubby and cluttered.

Newcastle being a long stretch from London, we had driven up in an easy stage or two, stopping at a reasonable motel on the way. William was safely in the hands of the nanny, who was pleased to have the flat in Onslow Gardens to herself for a Friday night. We were somewhat excited, hopped up, our blood buzzing with the prospect of discovery or of chance's wheel dropping the right coloured ball into our compartment, like a Lottery ticket holder in anticipation, on the edge of a Saturday night seat.

We swept along the bare front at Sue's request because she was visually agitated, searching with probing stares to find the exact location of Winslow Homer's most celebrated works. At first, seeing the stone facades of late Victorian boarding houses ranked along the wide clifftop highway, she made exclamations of disappointment. Then, seeing the sturdy pile of the Bay Hotel, she let out a cry of pleasure and called on me to stop.

"That's it!" she exclaimed. "There it is!"

Opposite the hotel, just across the road and set slightly below it, was a strange, brow-roofed building in the Arts and Crafts style, with a pointed clock tower and a spindle-balustered balcony glowering out to sea. It looked like something from Bedford Park or the studied, arty, village hall of some high-minded community set on Improvement with a capital I.

"The Watch House of the Volunteer Life Brigade," she crowed. "It's still here."

I peered at the long expanse of tiled roof, so redolent of the followers of Norman Shaw, the low windows under, and turned to look at her in query.

"Winslow Homer painted the local fisherwomen right here. Standing in gales looking out to sea for the returning boats, tense and anxious, or statuesque and brave. The Life Brigade House is in lots of his work, usually just a corner with that balcony and the turned, spindled uprights. It was their lookout in bad weather, built just two years before he got here. He must have stood at this very spot to do his paintings and sketches. Isn't that wonderful?"

I stared beyond the building out to what was, that day, a fairly calm North Sea. A ferry from Scandinavia was ploughing in towards Tynemouth. Otherwise the horizon was empty. The scene was mundane, casual, void of drama. Behind us, beyond the hotel, modern housing estates had supplanted old fishing cottages. Traffic drove past, close to the Watch House, along the front, on its way somewhere else. There were no pedestrians. It was hard to imagine any bustling, red-sailed, fishy activity here.

"Wouldn't it be great" she went on, impervious to this day and age, "if the painting was one of those he did here, with the Life Brigade House in it?"

"Why don't we go and see? Then we can come back here and compare views?"

"Oh yes! Come on, Tim. Let's go!"

I found out from a passer-by that Gordon Terrace was near the station, a row of older houses well back from the front. After a little searching, I parked the car at the end of the street and we walked along the terrace of stone and brick houses, each with a door opening on to the pavement and a front window at street level. Above were two upstairs windows, symmetrically placed over door and lower window, so that the ranks marched uniformly together to the blank end. Number eleven was half way along, unremarkable, unchanged, it seemed, from the time when it was built except for a coat of blue paint to the front door, perhaps renewed some ten years ago.

I opened up and we walked straight into a room about twelve feet square but with a staircase going up in line with the front door. A small fireplace, with a single bar electric fire in it, had a thin mantel over it and mirror above. A clock on the mantel, rather like Henry's in St.Leonards, had stopped ticking. Two armchairs and a tiny settee, covered in faded chintz, almost filled the room. There was a small TV set, a side table with knitting on a shelf under, and a magazine holder that could scarcely be called a Canterbury stuffed with old women's journals. A print of Queen Elizabeth the Queen Mother, teeth parted in an eternal smile, waving from the balcony at Buckingham Palace, adorned one wall. A net curtain and two heavier curtains screened the sash window. A patterned carpet covered the floor. There was a soft, sausage-like draught excluder for the front door. It was all very neat, clean, spinsterly.

There was not a watercolour in sight.

I went through to a back room, followed by Sue. This had an oak extendable dining table of 'thirties manufacture on bulbous false-Jacobethan legs, with four small chairs. On the table was a sewing machine. Another mirror on the wall, over another small, empty fireplace with a metal scuttle next to it. This was coal country, once.

Through the next door, further back, was a kitchen-scullery with a gas cooker and an old sink with a wooden draining board of the type they now sell as antique. A small table and dresser-cupboard stood next to a low refrigerator. There was a faint smell of pine disinfectant and fried fish.

Outside was a very small yard, surrounded by brick walls, with an outhouse, which must, once, have contained a privy and a coal store.

"Upstairs" I said to Sue.

The front bedroom was equally neat, with a single bed with an oak headboard, again of thirties style. There was a patterned eiderdown over the sheets and blankets. No duvets here. A bedside table with a lamp -

I heard Sue draw in her breath and turned quickly to look at the wall facing the bed. There was a painting hanging on it, in a place where the occupant of the bed could see it clearly, at night when retiring and in the morning as soon as she woke up.

It was a watercolour all right, framed and glassed, about two feet wide by eighteen inches high. It showed a cottage interior, with a table at a window, light filtering through, like Bramley's *A Hopeless Dawn*, but without any view through the small panes. A woman sat at the table doing something in her aproned lap, peeling potatoes perhaps, or carrying out another vegetable, household chore. Her head was bent in concentration and her loose clothes, brown and long, bagged around an ample figure of middle age. On a chair the other side of the table, a child, female, sat watching her across the clothed surface, on which a brief still life, of which a teapot, a cup and a seated cat were the first things to hit the eye. The child, now I looked closer, was wearing a creamy-coloured smock over a brown robe-like dress of some sort, and held a book in her hand. The tones were subdued, tawny, almost subfusc, and the effect was impressionistic rather than clear-cut.

It was an interior observation, domestic, feminine, rapt, conveying the feeling of life passing in these calm but tedious circumstances, from which women can draw joy in the company of a responsive child. This, I thought, is no elemental, masculine view of anything.

The scrawled signature discernible in the bottom left hand corner of the painting confirmed my feelings.

Laura Knight.

"Staithes" Sue said, out loud. "Laura Knight's Staithes period. It's typical of what she did then. Before she and Harold went down to Newlyn. It's not all that far off, I suppose. Down the coast towards Whitby."

"Another elemental, miserable fishing village. I've been there. Life perched on the edge, under the claustrophobic cliffs instead of on top of them, like here."

Her voice concealed her disappointment bravely. "Don't be so cynical. It's my fault. I shouldn't have raised your hopes so high. I know it's not a Winslow Homer but you did say you were looking at the Newlyn School. And it's worth a lot more than any daub of Dunstanburgh of the sort you feared."

"You've already got a Laura Knight, Sue," I answered glumly. "I don't want another."

"That biased against women's paintings, are we?"

"This sort, yes. If it had been a beach scene, or gypsies maybe, or one of her theatre jobs, or a young woman on a bed, I might be more enthusiastic, although she turned out an enormous amount. But not this brown study. Not my cup of tea at all."

"Talk about looking a gift horse in the mouth! A Laura Knight! Of the Staithes period! Early work! There are people who'd give eye teeth for this! It must be worth ten or even up to twenty thousand, Tim. Really! You're very difficult sometimes, you know."

"Sorry, but I'm not inspired. And I think ten thousand is nearer than twenty, going by her recent prices." I sighed. "Poor old Henry, though. This would have been a real boon to him. Sorted out some of his immediate financial problems, without doubt."

"Well it'll sort out yours. About funeral expenses and everything."

"Yes."

Anti-climax was seeping into my every pore. Jeremy would dismiss a watercolour like this in his most peremptory fashion. I left Sue studying the picture and went into the other, spare bedroom, where perhaps Henry must have spent the odd night on visits. There was nothing remarkable about it, nor the tiny, old-fashioned bathroom leading off the small landing.

That was it. I guessed the house to be around forty or fifty thousand pounds' worth. Say forty, for safety. With the Laura Knight, Henry might count on fifty thousand clear. Not bad for Henry. Worth a long drive for me and Sue, I supposed. But not what we'd hoped for.

"Come on, Sue. Let's put the watercolour in the car for safe keeping and I'll look up one or two local estate agents."

"All right. But I like it. I think it's a very good Laura Knight."

"It's OK, I suppose."

She gave me an appealing look. "Can we go back to the seafront? I want to view once again."

"Of course."

I carried the painting carefully back to the car and stowed it carefully in the boot. Then we drove back to our vantage point by the Bay Hotel and got out to stand by the railings at the Watch House, where Homer had done so much work. In front of us, the sea moved restlessly but not with the venom of his scenes. The atmosphere was quiet, retired. The only thing that came to my mind were lines from Albert and The Lion, concerning Blackpool: *No wrecks nor nobody drowned. Fact, nothing to laugh at, at all.*

"Tell me" I said to my beloved and art expert, after a length of silence, "what on earth brought a first-rate American painter like Winslow Homer to this dump, anyway?"

She smiled ruefully. "It's said he was thwarted in love sometime in the late 1870s. Before that, he was quite the New York clubman, a social animal. But he also took umbrage at repeated criticisms of his work. Or it may be that he'd reached the end of a certain phase in his painting and his inspiration. He told someone that there was too much similarity in the people and towns of America. If that was so, it seems to me that he could have gone West for variety. Anyway, he certainly changed. Something broke him. He became irritable, irascible, rude and definitely unsociable. He got away from America to England and, on the voyage over, someone recommended Cullercoats, rather than Newlyn, or Staithes, or any other fishing village, to him. So he came here and took a cottage with a high wall round it and only one entrance plus a studio at 12, Bank Top, with a view of the sea. It seems he really was looking for the sort of elemental women that fishwives represented."

"My God, he must have been upset to run away to this. A change from sophisticated American girls? In 1881?"

"Almost certainly. It seems odd, because he'd already painted at dangerous fishing places in America. Gloucester, Massachusetts, was one place, where they lost over a hundred men in one storm. So why come here to do the same?"

"Because of the women?"

She shook her head, thinking. "He did paint fishermen, too, you know. In fact there's a division evident in his work, which is said to have been deeply influenced by his stay here. Fishermen at sea, or beside it. Women and wives on land, in heroic stances. All working. It was nearly a 'never the twain shall meet' attitude between male and female. He did go down the coast as far as Flamborough, but where else is unknown, apart from his first arrivals in Liverpool and London, where he painted a sort of Whisterlian or Monet view of Westminster. Twenty months later he went back to America, where his family bought almost all of the land at Prout's Neck, near Portland, Maine. A rather exposed, elemental place, emptier than this."

"He really did get the hump, didn't he? Did he ever recover?"

"Not really. That was it. He travelled a lot subsequently, all over, but the family community at Prout's Neck was enough for him. He never married."

"Sounds like a great life."

"If Henry Weaver had been a painter, or writer, say even a biographer, his life might have been similar. At least there'd have been something to show for it, rather than a heap of books and some forgotten market research."

"Not in St.Leonards. A flat in St Leonards is no Prout's Neck. Hastings and St.Leonards are packed with Henrys. There was no family community for him, either. Even though Henry was married, once."

"Who to?"

I stopped to stare out at the scoured North Sea, emptied now, of its ferry. Something was bothering me about 11, Gordon Terrace, and it wasn't the lack of a Winslow Homer or the presence of a Laura Knight. "Actually, I don't know. He said he was divorced."

"Where? Where was he married, and where was he divorced?"

"I've no idea."

"Odd, isn't it, never to talk about it? Never to mention her by name or characteristics? To have no record of any kind?"

"No record?"

"Well I realise that you haven't had time to go through his papers properly yet, but even divorced people tend to have bits and pieces left over. Perhaps you'll find something in that desk of his." She shivered slightly. "I'd rather not go through it with you. That sort of thing depresses me terribly."

"It doesn't do me any favours either - that's it! I've got it!"

"Got what?"

"Sue, his aunt's house. The place is as neat as a new pin."

"So?"

"The Weavers were all neat people, I bet. Henry was very neat. I remember him as pedantic in many ways. A bit of an old maid himself. A neat sort of person, even if fallen from grace. Donnish, perhaps, would be a better description. A would-be academic."

"What does - you mean, his flat?"

"Yes! His flat! The papers were all disordered. Henry hated disorder of that sort." I bit my lip in agitation. "Sue, I believe someone went through that flat before we did."

"There was no sign of any entry."

"So they had a key. Someone who knew Henry well enough to have a key - or a lock expert - went in there, looking for something."

"Tim, as I remember it, the lock wasn't very sophisticated."

"The Yale wasn't. But there was a five-lever deadlock as well. You can't live in St.Leonards and leave your front door to a simple Yale. A standard yobbo breaker-in would have taken the telly, the hi-fi, any of that sort of kit. But they weren't disturbed. Just the papers."

"Why? What do you think they were looking for?"

I waved vaguely towards the car, where the Laura Knight reclined on the back seat. "They couldn't steal the house. So the painting is the only thing of value Henry had. Maybe they were looking for it."

"It's pretty terrible if they killed him just to get hold of that. Although ten to twenty thousand pounds is a lot to many people."

"To some people a few thousand pounds is a bloody fortune. Murder has been committed for a lot less. They could have been searching for this address."

She frowned. "Then I'm surprised they didn't find it. If they had, the door at 11, Gordon Terrace is no deterrent, is it? Yet the painting was undisturbed."

"No. It seems a hell of a lot of trouble to go to, killing Henry by an elaborate car method, breaking into his place to search his papers, disposing of poor Sammy Simes to hide the deed, being ready to come all the way here just to get hold of a Laura Knight, but not doing it."

"Unless" she said "there's something about this Laura Knight we don't know about. Its ownership, perhaps? Or the girl and woman in it? Or something else, Tim?"

"I don't know." Memory was flooding back. "It's odd because, when Henry phoned me, he specifically asked whether the Fund only bought British art. And I said that normally we do, yes, but we do buy works by foreign artists which have a British content. Like Monet in London or the Rodin of Gwen John."

"A Cullercoats Winslow Homer would fall into that category."

"Right. And Henry said *macanudo*, bully for you my boy, as though something like that was what he'd got. Well, a Laura Knight is as British as roast beef, or fish and chips. She came from Nottingham and painted all over England. Why would he ask that question if what he had was a Laura Knight?"

Sue smiled. "You mean someone took the foreign-artist painting that was in the bedroom away and substituted a Laura Knight? As a consolation prize?"

"Of course not. It's inconceivable. I just don't get it. Sammy Simes said he reckoned there was more to Henry than met the eye. Well it gets to be more every day."

Sue sighed. "You're right. I wonder if the old principle of *cherchez la femme* shouldn't be applied?'

"Oh? How?"

"Well, his wife, for a start. Or his ex, to be more accurate. I really would like to know something more about her."

"You sense the presence of a woman's hand in all this, do you?"

"There's no need to be sarcastic, Tim. A an ex-wife might feel she was entitled, emotionally if not legally, to some of his residue. The early years of struggle to be paid back, so to speak."

"So she nipped in, took a Winslow Homer, and put back a dull old Laura Knight she'd been fobbed off with, years ago, in its place?"

"Of course that seems far-fetched. She'd keep the Laura Knight as well if she knew about it. But Henry wasn't homosexual, was he? What ended the marriage? And did he have any girl friends?"

"None that would have needed money to take out."

"Then maybe the boot was on the other foot. They had money."

"Henry? Attract rich girl friends? With his brown Allegro estate and roomful of old books? Come on, Sue."

"I must admit it does seem unlikely, but you never know. It takes all sorts. You said he was appealing in an unconventional, semi-academic way. He might have met someone at a film club."

"That's possible. Now that's a line of enquiry I might follow up. When I get back from Turin."

"If you get back from Turin."

"Oh come on, Sue. Turin's just business. I can look after that without trouble."

She smiled and took my arm. "As a matter of fact, I believe you. Business is a vicarage tea party compared with the Art Fund. I shall start worrying when you come back and take off after Henry once again."

"Good girl. Come on, Let's head south and find somewhere really lavish for dinner. Somewhere of which Brillat-Savarin would have approved."

"Shouldn't we call on the aunt at Whitby on the way south?"

"Oh, I don't think I can face that today. Whitby's well over to the east of the motorway. Besides, Henry definitely said the painting was up in Newcastle, by which I'm sure he meant here, not Whitby. I'll sort out her print, the Florence Engelbach and all the other things she's due when I go through Henry's things properly. After I get back."

She smiled at my prevarication in understanding, then her face clouded as she looked out over the lapping shingle, with its seagulls keening above.

"When you go through Henry's things" she said, musingly. "Like someone else maybe did. And maybe listened to his answering machine. With your message on it. Before he or she wiped it off?"

Chapter 17

The Egyptian Museum in Turin, near the Piazza San Carlo, has its entrance on the Via Accademia delle Science and is within easy walking distance of the Porta Nova Train station. I, however, had driven down the broad Corso Vittorio Emmanuele II from the Po river bridge, turned off at the Via Lagrange, and parked my rental car in a side street nearby. My call to Emilio Bonnetti, using the details Sir Richard had given me in Bobbio, had not met with any live response. I told his answering machine that I would be at the museum by six o'clock, it staying open until seven. It seemed to me that if Sir Richard White had intended to use the museum as a rendez-vous, I could do the same with impunity, not being inclined to sit in my car nearby and await destruction.

Bonnetti hadn't called me back but I was in Turin anyway, so it was no pain to visit a little culture.

The ground floor of the celebrated museum is noted for its statues: Theban, like Amenhotep II as an offerer; Karnakian in the form of the lion-headed goddess Sakmet in diorite; and Nubian, not to mention the odd limestone head from Giza. It is perhaps the first floor, with its hall devoted to Religious and Funerary Traditions, which causes the mind to reflect, som-brely, on the Transitory Nature of Life. One does not have to stroll through such a cavernous diversity of macabre equip-ment, monuments and methods of corpse preservation to bring thoughts of the brevity of existence to circle disturbingly in the sub-conscious, but they certainly emphasise it. Uneasiness was seeping into every pore.

A memorial service to Sir Richard was being organised for a date following the release of his remains from their next examination and I would certainly be attending that when I got back to London. In the meantime, it was sobering to pon-der upon whether he had trodden these same halls, after buying his entrance ticket, in the same way I was doing. All those slabs enclosing kings and their consorts, the many painted limestone steles of homage to the gods - so many gods - canopic vases with heads of humans, baboons, jackals and beaked predators; had Richard paced along their serried ranks? Had he admired, as I was now doing, the painted caskets with their white backgrounds and domed lids, elaborated with brown, yellow and beige figures and hieroglyphs without knowing that, within a brief space, he would be able to do so no longer? The more I looked at swathed mummies on painted and stuccoed sarcophagi, and preserved corpses of the Protodynastic period, or fragments of cloth painted with depictions of hippopotamus hunts, the less stimulated I was culturally and the more tense in anticipation of what Bonnetti might have in store.

Would he arrive, all flustered and apologetic, with disarming excuses and protestations of never having met Sir Richard? Would he be cool, suave, immaculately tailored like so many Torinese, calmly professional and objective, blankly and blandly enquiring the purpose of my visit as he forced a necessary smile? Would he wait, accompanied by suitably muscular retainers, until I emerged at closing time, forced out into the street and vulnerable? Whose side was he on? Had someone perhaps got to him, if they had got to Sir Richard, and immobilised him as well?

At half past six there began to be signs of closure. The last visitors started to drift downstairs. An attendant near me walked over to the windows and began to fiddle with catches that might close blinds or something similar. An air of anticipated desertion stilled the noises of footsteps and shuffling in the halls. I went back down to the entrance area and its stone stairway leading to the street, in case Bonnetti was waiting there, the logical meeting place. I was conspicuous, English, looking about hopefully. I had no doubt that any Italian expecting me would assume my identity to be that of the man he was seeking.

There was no one there. The last visitors ambled past me. The ticket office was shut. A woman attendant looked at me disapprovingly. I took the hint and went outside into the September evening, to stand on the pavement by the entrance.

It was warm and slightly misty. Traffic motored past sporadically. Not far away, if I looked up, and craned suitably, I would be able to see the famous Mole Antonelliana's dome and pointed spike dominating the skyline, like the Eiffel Tower does Paris. Here, I was a dwarfed pedestrian standing uncertainly poised, waiting for what?

I looked at my watch. It was quarter to seven. At seven I would be certain to be ejected, a point in time any assailant could depend upon. Bonnetti wasn't coming. If he was, he was bloody late. I got out my mobile and tried his number. The answering machine responded again.

I turned away from the entrance and walked steadily back to the Piazza San Carlo to find my car. The kerbs were lined with vehicles testifying to the parking problem in all European cities. I'd found a place for my small Fiat down a side street close by, catching, a bit of luck, a space as a car left. At the corner before it, I paused to stoop and tighten a shoelace. I'd put on my heavy brogues with a good leather welt and plenty of solid heel to them.

Down the line of cars, a shadowy figure flitted between fenders into a doorway. On the back of my neck, tiny hairs crawled at a step somewhere behind, a warning of a following presence. There were probably two people, then. Perhaps more. Straightening up, I walked briskly the remaining twenty metres to my car, got out the key, walked round the back of the vehicle into the road, inserted the key, then jumped quickly to one side.

The figure you make as you open the car door and stoop to enter is one of the most vulnerable you'll ever present. You are half-bent and off balance, rear and side available for crippling blows to the kidneys, liver, back of the neck, whatever your attacker favours. By whipping round, leaving the door shut, I came almost face to face with the man who'd stepped forward, arm raised, to deliver a downward chop at a key organ with something held in his hand. The downward chop dissipated itself, checking to avoid hitting the car door instead of my neck or spine. Surprise made him blunder into me. He was chunky but short; I brought my knee up sharply into his groin, achieving a satisfactory grunt of pain. Then I stepped clear and hit him, hard, in the face. He staggered back about a pace but stayed upright, arms half-raised in defence. He was holding a short, thick rod of some kind.

Round the other side of the car, on the pavement, another man, also strongly built, had grabbed the passenger side door handle in anticipation of pulling it open. I guessed, the fleeting split second I saw him, that they had been going to bundle me into the front of the car then carry out their purpose from each side, out of sight, whatever their purpose was. I had a moment or two to spare before the second man could get round the car to join the partner in front of me; stepping forward, I trod hard on his foot with my right one and hooked him under the chin.

The great thing about this old booth fighter's manoeuvre is that the victim can't ride with the punch. His foot is pinned to the ground and he takes the full force of the blow. With any luck the impact, shoving him backwards, damages the foot tendons as well. There was a snap of teeth slamming together as my fist slammed under his jaw and a thump as he dropped the rod and bounced off the car onto the road. Otherwise he didn't make much noise except for a sort of gasp as he hit the ground. Well, he wasn't able to, I suppose; a good hook is one of the most effective blows in the whole pugilistic repertoire.

I turned, ready for number two.

He paused to steady himself as he came round the end of the car, then brought his right arm forward with a slivered glint to it. A knife; I might have expected a knife. Shots would attract attention. An apparent mugging job, my wallet removed, maybe my watch, for verisimilitude. Could happen anywhere, any city. Gone wrong because the victim resisted and was killed. The blade was more professional than a chance mugger's, though; longer, broader, shinier. He shoved it forward and stepped towards me to close, quickly, for the kill.

I used to be known, in my rugger days, for a really high punt kick, an up-and-under, that gave time for the whole scrimmage to get below it, elbowing and gouging each other, by the time it came down. You have to be quick and accurate with it, otherwise it doesn't work. I used it now, lashing out with a right foot clad in hard leather to get him on the kneecap; no good trying higher up, where it would hurt most, because the knife would be at that level and, in any case, he might grab my leg. There was solid contact; good cartilage-bashing contact. He let out a cry of pain but choked it off quickly as he still moved to close in, hampered by a bad leg. The knife swept in a savage arc at my stomach.

He wasn't fast enough; the leg slowed him up. I was able to jump backwards, almost treading on his partner, to avoid the sweep of the blade. Ducking, I got in a straight left to the jaw, in and out quickly, that slowed him a bit more as it jerked his head back. He didn't move further but called out, softly, at a pitch that carried, to a point behind me.

For a moment, I thought it was a bluff intended to make me turn instinctively and give him an edge, but from somewhere behind I heard a car door open. Number three, doubtless the getaway driver, was being called in for reinforcement.

There was no time to lose.

He was drawing his right arm back for another stab at me but I hopped back over the recumbent form of number one, out of range, whirled round and sprinted ten metres down the street to where a man was stepping out of a medium-sized Alfa onto the road. His feet were actually on the ground but he wasn't quite out yet. A look of real terror came over his face as, turning inside the door, he realised I was going to catch him the way they'd intended for me.

By then it was too late.

I slammed the door into him, banging his head between frame and roof before jamming it tight. Holding the door hard against him, I stamped right-footed on his ankles in a classic trample, first one, then the other, getting screams of pain. Then I opened the door and, grabbing his arm with my left, did him real damage with my right. He couldn't get away; I hit him so hard, three quick times, that blood spurted from each place on his face as I hit it. Gagging, he slumped back over the front seat. I then quickly whirled round, clear of the car, and got back my balance, ready to deal with the knife wielder.

He'd followed me down the road, pretty gamely considering he'd had a good left to the jaw, his knee must have been agony and he couldn't move too fast. As he stabbed out at me, rather stiffly, I grabbed his arm and clamped it with both of mine, in the classic arm-breaker's lock. He gave a premonitory cry of pain and tried to hit me with his left.

I was battle crazy by now. Mad, furious, out of control. I'd had too long to think about Sir Richard and what he'd meant to me before this happened. I didn't believe in any heart attack. I'd had too little time since putting my key in the car door to think about anything but murder and ferocious survival. I believed they were going to kill me. The Waldensians had nothing on me; I broke the bastard's arm without compunction. Ignoring his high-pitched scream as the knife clattered to the ground, I let go and went for him, left, right, left, another right. The thumps made him hiccup before he slumped down onto the tarmac. I kicked him to make sure he wouldn't get up again.

Up the street the first man I'd hit started to get to his feet. I ran over and kicked him too, back off them again, so that he ended in a sitting position. Then I leant over and bashed him as hard as I could on the side of the head. He keeled over, into a silent bundle.

Then sanity returned. I paused to get my breath back, my systems buzzing.

All of the action could not have taken more than a minute but suddenly there were shouts, cries, flashing lights. Not one, but two police cars screeched into the street. I leant up against my hire car, heaving for oxygen, and closed my eyes. The knuckles on my right hand were skinned and starting to sting. When I opened my eyes again, I saw that uniformed men were jumping out of black and white coachwork under whirling blue bulbs, calling out things like "*Alto!*" and "*Atenzione!*" and other warnings I only half-understood. They had guns, and one of them, running towards me, even brandished one.

"I suppose" I said wearily to him, as he arrived to stand, half-crouched aggressively in front of me, mouthing unintelligibles "that you wish me to accompany you to the police station? In order to make a statement."

His torrent stopped. He blinked, then said something else I only half-understood.

"I'm afraid my Italian's a bit scanty." I said.

He peered at me incredulously. "*Inglese?*" he queried.

"Yes." I nodded.

"Please" he said, in his best Italian-English tourist-comprehension school accent "to come with us. To the police station. Immediately."

Chapter 18

The Italian equivalent of the duty sergeant at the police station was scrupulously correct. He said something sharp to the rozzer hanging about beside me, took in my appearance and asked to see my documents, which included both passport and driving licence. He told the armed rozzer to push off and then, through an English-speaking uniformed man, asked me to describe the events in the street.

Which, up to a point, I did.

At this juncture I had decided to treat the whole thing as a mugging attempt. My attitude was one of bemused bewilderment. To add any deeper, further information, such as my calls to Bonnetti, and then inevitably the story of Sir Richard, would lead to enormous complications, complications which would undoubtedly drag in Bertrasconi, not to mention maybe Shauna Spring and the story of Belley. I dearly wanted to avoid all that. The bank's business is the Bank's business and whilst I could trust dear old Nobby to hold his horses in respect of information passed, the sergeant's desk at a public police station in central Turin was quite another matter. I wanted this to be over simply and quickly.

The sergeant listened to it all, said something like *felicitazione* to me and I was asked to sit down, in a corridor along with various miscreants and complainers. Time passed. Phones rang. An ambulance had collected, or rather scraped up, my assailants and taken them somewhere under guard, so there was no sight of them.

After about an hour, the translator asked me to return to the sergeant's desk. The sergeant had a large form in front of him. He asked me to fill it in, in English, and I obediently took it to a small hard wooden table to oblige. I kept it pretty succinct. I stated that I had lost nothing and was not injured. Then I carried it back. The translator wrote, in pencil, over my writing, in Italian. The sergeant raised his eyebrows, read it through, nodded faintly, spun the form round and asked me to sign it. I obliged.

"The sergeant asks me say" the uniformed translator had a slight tinge of Soho accent, as though he'd learnt his English in a Dean Street trattoria, "that he regrets this assault upon you during your stay in Turin. It has been confirmed, by questioning the three attackers, that they were simply muggers. They will be severely dealt with. We have the name of the hotel where you are staying. You are free to go."

"Thank you."

"We thank you for your patience. These occurrences are, regrettably, a feature from time to time, of city life."

"Indeed, unfortunately, that is the case."

"You are sure you have lost nothing?"

"Sure."

"You are not injured?"

"No."

"Your hand appears to be bleeding slightly."

"Just a graze. My handkerchief, as you see, is hardly stained."

"We can arrange for a hospital to - "

"No, no. No need, thanks."

A door behind the sergeant opened and a man dressed in a grey herringbone tweed jacket, blue shirt with patterned tie, and dark trousers came out. He glanced at me, glanced at the translator, looked at the sergeant and beckoned to look at my form. The sergeant handed it over, answering a question with the suffix *inspetore*, or what sounded like *inspetore*, anyway, then a couple more queries.

The grey-jacketed man looked up from the form and spoke in English. "Mr Simpson?"

"Yes."

"I am Inspector Renzetti."

"Inspector."

"It seems that you have had an unfortunate experience."

"'Fraid so."

"But, on the other hand, you have been able to resist, yes, I think resist is the word, your attackers."

"Er, yes."

"Resist, in fact, to the extent of putting them all in hospital."

"So it seems."

His eyes ran over my face, taking in, rather obviously, my broken nose. "You have, perhaps, some professional training in this kind of resistance? Or pugilism?"

"No, none, really."

"Did you expect to be attacked?"

"No, not at all. I was simply visiting the famous Egyptian Museum."

He gestured, almost apologetically. "Forgive me for perhaps a personal observation, but your nose - "

"Rugby."

He smiled for the first time. "Ah! The famous rugby! You know we in Italy, we beat the champions, Scotland, last season?"

"You did indeed. It was a remarkable match. Your first big success."

"So. And England won the series but also lost to Scotland, at the end."

"We don't like to mention that."

He grinned. "One day, perhaps soon, we will beat you, too."

"Why not? I can't imagine why a nation so good at the lesser game shouldn't triumph at the bigger one."

His face clouded in mock disapproval. "The lesser game? Football - soccer - is not a lesser game! But what is the famous saying? Rugby is a game for hooligans played by gentlemen, and soccer is a game for gentlemen played by hooligans?"

It was my turn to grin. "Dead right. And watched by hooligans, too."

He smiled knowingly back, then dropped his eyes to my

form. A moment or two passed. He tapped the form and looked up.

"It is unusual, Mr Simpson, for a tourist visitor to do such damage to not one, but three muggers, in the way you have."

"I was lucky. And very angry."

"You played rugby for England?"

"No, no. Just for my university."

"Which was?"

"Cambridge."

"Ah. Very distinguished." His brown eyes held mine for just a moment longer than was comfortable. "You are here as a tourist or on business?"

"I am here on business."

"What business?"

"I work for a merchant bank in London. What is called an investment bank elsewhere. I am visiting our Turin representatives. A matter of possible electronics investment by certain European companies. Nothing to do with mummies or sarcophaguses. That was just tourism."

"I see." He made a note on a scrap of paper. "Your attackers are unknown to us. They say they are from Milan. They say they just made an opportunistic assault. A foreigner, well dressed and off guard, possibly an *Inglese* or a *Tedesco*, who would have some cash with him. You think it was the same?"

"What else could it be?"

"You can think of no other reason?"

"I'm at a loss. What reason other than immediate monetary gain could there be?"

Those three were clearly not going to reveal the name of any employer. They'd be in hot enough water for their failure without implicating their boss or bosses as well. Sticking to the story of a simple mugging was their best bet. And mine.

Renzetti was looking pensive. "I do not wish to embarrass you, Mr Simpson, but if I were a mugger, I would not choose you as my opportunistic target. You are not of the build, appearance or of the age with which most muggers would feel confident."

"There were three of them. And I suppose they hoped to surprise me."

"But they didn't." His eyes held mine again. "They didn't surprise you at all. And they are very badly mauled. Very badly. I am not sure that the game of rugby qualifies its players for such expertise." A pause followed, while he seemed pensive again. Then: "How long will you be in Turin?"

"Just a day or two."

"And we have the details of your hotel - let me see, yes - but not the name of your company? Your bank?"

I got out my wallet, took out a card, and handed it to him. He looked at it and nodded faintly. Then he got out his own card and handed it to me.

"If anything occurs to you, Mr Simpson, anything that might indicate why this attack should have taken place, I ask you to give me a call, yes? It is possible that something may occur to you, subsequently, some explanation of this event. You will call me?"

"Yes. Of course."

He held out his hand. "Thank you. We have no reason to detain you any further. Our apologies for this unpleasant episode. I hope your stay in Turin, from now, will be successful. My colleagues will see you back to your car."

I shook the hand carefully, keeping my skinned knuckles clear. "Thank you." I smiled at him, turned and left, walking carefully between two uniformed men as I fought the desire to break out into a run.

How long before his computer told him those three were probably contract professionals? How long before his computer connected White's Bank with the Sir Richard White found dead in his Jaguar near the Egyptian Museum only a short time ago? If the database was good, not long. Then he'd be back after me. Wanting a much better version of events.

There was no time to lose.

Chapter 19

Whereas Inspector Renzetti favoured the sports coat, albeit of grey herringbone, and grey trousers most Italian businessmen use for everyday office garb, Giorgio Deserti disdained such informal wear. He was clad in a dark three-piece suit, its waistcoat shaped for only those of slender build, the outfit indeed emphasising his wiry, narrow frame, lending emphasis to the spare, harassed, wrinkled expression creasing his pale face.

"It is very disturbing," he said to me.

I had arrived at his office the moment it opened the following morning. The weather was fine and cool, the city brisk with activity. One of those starts to the day which make you believe you can get on, really accomplish something. Giorgio Deserti's office was in a professional, modernised building, which retained the style of a previous era, giving a feeling of continuity rather than novelty. Its atmosphere was serious. The few staff I had seen moved about quietly or sat at their desks and monitor screens in grave contemplation. There was none of the litter we generate in London, nor were voices raised in laughter or discussion. I hadn't had much to do with the Bank's Italian operations and agents, so Deserti was new to me and I, quite clearly, posed a conundrum for him. He wasn't sure whether I was the bulldog London had sent to bite chunks out of him or whether I constituted reinforcements of some kind. His manner was cautious and guardedly expectant whilst showing me that he was extremely preoccupied.

"I can imagine" I answered, sympathetically or, at least, what I hoped was sympathetically.

We were discussing the corpse of Sir Richard White, still residing in the Turin morgue. As local representative, Deserti had had rather a lot to do with the distressing events after Sir Richard had been found in his car, and the responsibility had clearly given him sleepless nights. There had been official representations, meetings with lawyers, messages and calls from London, queries about the post mortem. He was, literally, the man on the spot, despite the fact that Richard had not advised him of his visit, of his presence in the city. A look of reproach came over Deserti's face as he mentioned this, as though Richard should have kept him informed of this incursion into his territory. For someone senior from White's Bank to steal into Turin and then die in his vehicle, leaving Deserti to clear up the mess was, evidently, an act of prodigious discourtesy.

What was bothering him now, though, was that the authorities were proving dilatory about releasing the body. There was, officially, no reason for them to retain it once the post mortem was completed and the cause of death pronounced to be without suspicion. Yet application for its removal had met with vague bureaucratic obstacles, polite prevarications, mentions of documents not so far completed due to the unfortunate absence of the necessary signatories who were away in Rome, and other uncooperative excuses.

"This is not normal" Deserti said, irritably. "By now all these matters should have been cleared."

"Could there be some other reason?"

He pursed his lips. "I have the impression - it has no basis in fact - that somehow or another, there is a query against the analysis produced for the Coroner. I can not say why I have this impression, it is just a suspicion you understand, from the way in which my questions have been answered. No one has said anything, no one at all, but it is the way, the implication, inferences of the answers, which just set off this idea in my mind."

"They couldn't have heard, perhaps, that Freddie Harbledown has ordered a second opinion once the body's back in England?"

His dark eyebrows rose and fell as his eyes flashed significantly. "I certainly have not mentioned it. This is a very confidential, internal Bank and family matter, of course. Very, very confidential. My lips are absolutely sealed. Yet yours is a very good question. Although our lawyers are under the same vow of professional secrecy, I have a very vague suspicion that somehow, I really do not know how, maybe the authorities have heard of Lord Harbledown's intentions. If so, they will certainly delay."

"Why?"

He pulled his mouth down at the corners in a grimace at the innocence of my question. "They would not contemplate the chance that they might have missed something, would they? Allow some minor evidence overlooked to enable London to make them look unprofessional? Quite unacceptable. It is likely they will ask another expert, another medical professor, to make a thorough re-examination. If what I suspect is true." He spread out his hands. "After all, Sir Richard is not just any old fellow found dead in his car, is he? He is an aristocrat, a man of business importance, even a war hero. Lord Harbledown is of the same family and could make a lot of trouble via his connections in high society. Not only in England; Lord Harbledown is quite well known in Tuscany, where he owns a vineyard."

"So he does. Bottles his own chianti, like Osbert Sitwell."

"There you are. This puts me in an invidious position. From London I receive increasingly impatient messages. Here, I receive dilatory answers. I am the unfortunate shuttlecock - shuttlecock, yes? - in the middle. Maybe Lord Harbledown has already mentioned his intentions to one of his Italian friends. At such levels, news can travel very quickly." He shook his head regretfully. "I was an admirer of Sir Richard and his death is a sad blow to me. Did you know him well?"

"Quite well, yes. We collaborated on several projects. I too am an admirer of his."

Deserti perked up approvingly. "You were working with him recently?"

"Not on this electronics project. We had an, er, another potential project."

"In Italy?"

"Internationally, I think one should say. To do with tourism. Across several countries."

"Ah. You met him recently, then?"

"Quite recently, yes."

"I have wondered, ever since this distressing event occurred, why he was here."

"Didn't the electronics project, in which I am now involved, have a major element in Italy?"

"Yes, of course. But he did not advise me, as I have said, of his last visit here. And why, I wonder, do you think he was in the region of the Egyptian Museum? In his car?"

"Ah. Well." I gave my skinned knuckles a quick glance. "I was coming to that. As a matter of fact - "

Too late. A phone on Deserti's desk interrupted me. He gave me a glance of apology and picked it up. There was a rapid interchange in Italian. Since I speak Argentine Spanish and French French, I can understand a lot of Italian, but I don't like to let on. The exchange wasn't good news. Deserti's eyes widened and rested on me. His brow furrowed. Another rapid interchange. His face set. He stared at me again, putting his hand over the receiver.

"There is" he said disbelievingly "here in our foyer, a policeman. Two policemen, in fact. One is an inspector. His name is Renzetti. He says he insists on seeing you. He has a sergeant with him."

My heart had already sunk. "Oh dear. If he insists, then I'd better see him, hadn't I?"

"Indeed." He spoke rapidly back into the receiver, then put it down. His stare had become intense.

"If you wish," he said, "I can call our lawyers - "

I held up a hand. "Wait."

The office door opened. Renzetti came in, still wearing the same herringbone jacket. The man with him was bigger, younger; he eyed me expectantly. Renzetti nodded at Deserti and they exchanged a few words. Then he held out his hand and I stood up to shake it.

"Mr Simpson" he said, quite genially. "Our rugby-playing English tourist, yes? So interested in Egyptology, yes?"

"Ah. Well. I was going to explain - "

He let go of my hand. "Who works for White's Bank. The same Bank as Sir Richard White, whose body is in our morgue. Who was found near the Egyptian Museum, yes?"

"Ah. Yes. But, you see - "

"Who was, presumably, like you, also a tourist. And keen Egyptologist? I did note down quite carefully what you said."

"You did."

"And, would you believe it, Mr Simpson, who said he went to the Museum as a tourist and who could not imagine why anyone would attack him except for some casual muggers, even though his distinguished chief was found dead there a few days earlier, something very strange has happened?"

"It has? What?"

"Have you ever heard of a man called Bonnetti?"

"Never met him."

He smiled a wide, false, stage smile. "How punctilious an answer. Not that you have not heard of him. You do not answer that directly. Just that you have not met him. I am pleased to hear it."

"Why?"

The stage smile vanished. "Because his body was found on the outskirts of the city this morning. He had been murdered. Shot. And when we went to his flat to investigate, we listened to his answering machine. Guess whose voice could be heard on it?"

"Oh God. Mine?"

"Good! Good! At last! Some genuine information! And an admission! Yes, Mr Tourist Simpson, yours was the last voice on his machine! The very last! Arranging to meet him at - guess where - I'm sure you know where - the Egyptian Museum!"

"Oh."

"Where, by pure chance, yesterday, you were set upon by three men. Men you said were casual muggers and who you injured severely. But who are, in fact, known to the Milan police for quite different reasons. Do you know what reasons?"

"Look, I realise that this may seem a bit - "

"I must ask you, Mr Simpson, to come with me. Now. To answer some very detailed questions. You have not told me the truth."

"Look, I didn't lie to you, I simply - "

"Now. To the police station. Where my time is better employed."

I nodded resignedly. Deserti put his head in his hands. He didn't say what he was thinking, but I knew it anyway.

It might, now, be weeks before Richard's body got to London.

Chapter 20

"The reason I am buying this breakfast" Nobby Roberts said, as the waitress put down the full works in front of me, "is by way of apology."

I ran my eye over the two fried eggs, the rashers of bacon, the fried bread, the tomatoes, mushrooms and the two sizzling sausages on my plate before raising my eyebrows interrogatively. If I had been in Newcastle, I would have expected black pudding as well, and there are those who say that a proper breakfast is not a proper breakfast without American hash browns or indeed a sea of baked beans. But we are not all as active as we used to be and I did not want to seem excessive. When Nobby indicated that breakfast was to be on him, I ordered plentifully but not with greed; curiosity had the better of my appetite and a wrangle over content might have delayed things.

"I indicate an apology" he went on "despite the inconvenience of having to answer to the Turin equivalent of CID about your character, integrity and generally inconvenient mode of behaviour."

There is, apparently, deep in the computerised recesses of the Metropolitan Police records, a big yellow and black flash which comes up every time my name is punched into the official memory. This flash is labelled 'Refer to Chief Inspector Roberts for further info' and many is the time poor old Nobby has been quizzed because of it. Not usually from such international spots as Turin, but it can happen - Paris has featured a couple of times. He is wearily tolerant of the enquiries he gets but in return usually extracts Danegeld of a sort from me in the form of breakfasts, lunches and even pints of ale when off duty.

Which made this votive offering all the more curious.

"There is" he said, as his own plateload of steaming

cholesterol was placed proudly in front of him "an established procedure for dealing with vehicles which have been the subject of a serious accident. This procedure is especially strict if the said vehicle has been involved in a fatality."

Suddenly, the hot attractive plateful in front of me faded as a chill struck my spine. Outside, Victoria Street was already bustling with traffic under a September sun and the day was once again mild and ripe. But I started to feel cold. I put down my knife and fork to stare at him.

He actually licked his lips in a sort of flinch at my stare.

"In the case of the death of Henry Weaver" he continued, carefully, "there was no reason to suspect foul play. The deceased was alone in his car and no other vehicle or persons were involved. The deceased had taken alcohol to an amount which would have put him over the limit had a breath test been given. Not excessively so, but in excess nevertheless."

"Nobby - "

He held up a knife to stop me.

"The amount of alcohol may not have impaired his driving ability all that much. I shouldn't, as a police officer, say it, but you and I know damn well, Tim, that despite the effect on the metabolism, a lot of people have one or two over the odds and still get home without veering off into a stout oak tree."

"So - "

"Wait, wait! Let me finish before you get your twopennorth in. The Allegro in which Henry Weaver died was not exactly the stuff of which our assessors - or any insurance assessors - are enamoured. It was old and in seedy condition. Agreed, before the accident it was in sufficiently sound condition to pass an MOT test, just about, but at a pretty minimum level. The examiner who looked at the car after the accident - it was taken to a garage which has an authorised, lockable pound - found nothing to indicate anything suspicious."

"He wouldn't. He wasn't looking for - "

"Hang on! Just be patient! Eat some of your breakfast, it's going cold. I hate to see good hot food congeal."

155

Obediently, I picked up my knife and fork as he continued, talking in part through a mouthful of his own.

"The car was badly damaged by the accident as far as the front end and the roof was concerned. The rest of it was not that much affected but, not surprisingly, the front axle and steering were pretty bent. The examiner wasn't looking for anything dodgy, so it's possible he didn't take too great pains. He dealt with several cars that day. His report is perfectly adequate in the light of the circumstances. The brakes were OK. The tyres were legal. The rust wasn't too structural. The guy was reported to have been over the limit and to have fallen asleep."

"The steering and the seat belt fixings were buggered. Sammy said so."

"Sammy said so, yes, but only to you. After the event. And he's dead."

"So? You can still check his findings, can't you?"

Even as I said it, I knew he couldn't. They couldn't. That was what this breakfast was for.

Nobby wiped his mouth carefully with a napkin. "Foster of Hastings CID responded to my call the day after I spoke to him. I couldn't ask better than that; none of us are sitting around waiting for work, Tim."

"So?"

Nobby shook his head slightly, as though it was necessary to dislodge the words. "When he got to the pound, the Allegro had gone."

"Gone? Gone where?"

"To the wreckers. It seems there was a mistake. There were three or four wrecks in the pound. The others had all been cleared. The wrecker's man showed his papers, the pound man knew that the Allegro had been checked, so he released it. All the wrecks went on the one lorry. Foster drove to the recovery yard to find it was too late. All of them have been hydraulicked. Henry Weaver's Allegro is a bale of scrap metal now."

"What? What about insurance? What about me as executor? Don't I get a look in?"

"Please don't shout! People are staring at us! I think you'll find the insurance was third party, fire and theft. Not comprehensive. No payouts for writing off your own car. They didn't need to inspect and even if they did, our examiner's report would do for them. That car wasn't worth a light."

"Jesus Christ. Bloody hell. I've never heard of anything so lackadaisical. We've no means of knowing whether Sammy was right now, none at all."

"You have my apologies, on behalf of the Force, for the slip in procedure. These things happen, though, Tim, every day. We all make mistakes."

"You can say that again."

He flushed slightly. "I suppose you never passed a wrong investment down at the Bank, did you?"

"Sorry, Nobby." I gave him a contrite look. "Didn't mean to pi-jaw you. It's just that Henry's death bugs me terribly. Things seem fated to obscure what really happened. Did Foster find out anything about Sammy Simes? "

"Nothing significant. To all appearances it looks like an accident."

"It can't be! Sammy may not have been successful but he was a good mechanic. He wouldn't make a mistake like that."

Nobby sighed. "Tim, I used to cover a lot of ground as a uniformed man. Accidents like that happen every day. Ask the Health and Safety Inspectorate. Foster checked with them. No suspicious aspects."

"Was no one seen around at the time?"

"Nope. I know it's screened by trees but there's only one drive into that place."

"You could cut across fields."

"Maybe. Foster hasn't asked around for fear of starting a flap of some sort. Apart from the fact that this isn't an official enquiry and his boss'll cut up if he spends too much time on it."

"Shit!"

"Try to keep calm. Finish your breakfast."

There was a silence while we both ate ruminatively for a while. Nobby ordered more coffee. When it came, he wiped his mouth, drank a draught and looked at me speculatively.

"What?" I demanded.

"Come on. Cough up. The Weaver story is over. You've been attacked now, in Turin, so things are different on the Italian front. These guys murdered Sir Richard White and some geezer called Bonnetti, did they?"

"Is that what Renzetti told you?"

"Never mind what Renzetti told me. He's a good guy, one I've come across before. But it's me you're talking to now. I don't need any edited versions, the Bank's interests safeguarded and all that crap. I vouched for you to Renzetti. I've apologised for the Weaver cock-up and spent time on it. It's come-clean time for Timmy. So let's have it. The real it, that is, not another yarn of some sort."

I sighed. "There is always such a price for your hand-outs, Nobby. Are all policemen the same?"

"Worse. Much worse."

"Actually, I don't think that Renzetti really thought I might be a suspect in the Bonnetti death. Not at all. I rather liked him. I think he thought I was a sort of Bank dick, an amateur sleuth with fisticuffs. All policemen resent men like that on their patches." I shook my head as a mental picture of the sardonic man in a grey herringbone jacket came to me. "In my case, he seemed to act as though I was a mixture of James Bond and Bertie Wooster. It's dreadful how foreigners latch on to these fictional English stereotypes."

His mouth opened for a moment, closed, opened again, then closed. He picked up a cup and drank a draught of coffee.

"The thing is, Nobby, to look at the facts we know. By accident, Richard saw three suspicious collaborators in Belley. Someone then fixed a bug to him. He met me at Torre Pellice, then went to Turin, making an appointment with this Bonnetti, who he said he'd used before. A business investigator who presumably he intended to brief about Bertrasconi's associates before getting him to dig for facts. We don't know if they met. We can assume their meeting was known to the opposition, whoever the opposition may be. Richard is dead. I am certain, now, that he was murdered. I make an appointment with Bonnetti and I, too, am meant to wind up dead. Meantime, Bonnetti is dead. Why? Did he squawk to someone? Was he already in the pay of the opposition? Was he murdered to make sure I couldn't get to him? Did he ever receive my message or did someone have access to his flat and answering machine? Was he killed after the attempt on me went wrong? Renzetti wouldn't tell me the time of death; he wasn't in a mood to humour visiting private eyes. Although people at the Bank knew I was going to Turin, I told no one about intending to meet Bonnetti, so it has to be my phone message that sets up the attack. It was entirely fortuitous that I noted his name and telephone number when Richard showed them to me."

Nobby grunted. "Did this chap Deserti know you were coming to Turin?"

"Of course. I'm now officially a member of the electronics project team with Italy as my co-ordinating brief. I had to go there to see him and get all the necessary documentation. Which I now have."

"And?"

"And it's a big project. A very big project. There are quite a few firms involved. Rationalisation would provide a European challenge to the American, Japanese and other Far East competition. A concept thing which, if not right in practice, could be a disaster. Like the Dome."

"So?"

I scratched my chin. "It lacks the right balance of medical electronics. Guess who's got a good line in those?"

"Bertrasconi?"

159

"Right first time. If this thing bombs, which it could, Bertrasconi would be well placed for a result, Trevor. Very well placed. He'd step in, pick up the shambles for a song and add his medical side to it. Then he'd be in clover."

"What about White's Bank?"

"White's Bank would be up the creek. In need of a white knight, oh, sorry, no pun intended. Maybe it'd get a black knight. Like the Baddy Risk."

He glanced at his watch and signalled for the bill. "It is strongly rumoured that the Baricot wants a substantial London footing. It is also looking at Paris. Funds of a major order are moving in these directions. Where do your Maucourt crowd fit into all this?"

"Theirs is a central role. They've been given a leading position. In a sense, if the project goes ahead, Maucourt will drag White's in with it, willy-nilly. Richard was a very important link in the chain."

"And he was old, part-time, and perhaps very trusting."

"Except that he was interested in gastronomic history. Which included Brillat-Savarin's birthplace in Belley. Odd how a hobby can affect life, isn't it? If it hadn't been for gastronomy, Richard would be alive and we'd be up the creek."

"What are you going to tell Jeremy?"

"I rather fancy Jeremy is going to go off the deep end at me. He may not listen to anything I tell him."

Nobby grinned. "I have bosses like that. When they tear me off a strip, I act all contrite then do what I want to do anyway."

"Thanks. So do I."

He stood up. "I'll leave you to face the music. May I take it that the Henry Weaver affair will not cause any further strain on Inspector Foster? That I can trust you to behave yourself at least in that direction while this Italian business occupies your time?"

I stood up as well. "Thank you very much for the breakfast, Nobby. Doubtless it will be my turn next. But I can assure you that, as far as Henry Weaver and his watercolour are concerned, I shall merely continue to carry out my melancholy duties as his sole executor."

He didn't respond to that. He didn't have to. The look he gave me conveyed his utter conviction that it would be my turn next time.

Chapter 21

People who reported to Mrs.Thatcher during her years in power used to say that there was one mood of hers which, when a subordinate was being treated as a miscreant or for having failed in some way, was far worse to face than that of her anger. It was the 'Nanny is not angry, she is just very, very disappointed' reaction that was the worst to take.

Jeremy took exactly this line. He sat behind his desk, almost a woebegone figure, putting his head in his hands from time to time and speaking slowly, as though to an uncomprehending child who has just burnt a huge hole in the best, beige, fitted, living-room Wilton.

Awful.

"Deserti has been one of our most conscientious managers" he moaned. "A really reliable man. Utterly respectable and well regarded. People like that cannot be valued too highly. His distress was really dreadful to hear. I doubt if he will remain with us despite my assurances. It was an experience completely alien to him. The police. The police, traipsing mob-handed into one of the most respectable offices in Turin, one whose probity and ethics have taken him years to establish, and arresting a senior employee from London for violent behaviour. In front of the entire staff."

"I wasn't arrested."

"Dragging him out to their vehicle - "

"I walked. They were quite amiable. There were no gyves upon my wrists. We are not speaking of Eugene Aram or whatever, though it was a bit misty - Hood, you know - "

"- coming after the suspicious death of a senior director and major member of the family. When complete discretion and the restoration of normality was of prime concern."

"What about the truth?"

"Brawling in the streets with footpads, like a hooligan after an England match -"

"Street, not streets."

"Failing to be absolutely frank and above-board with the authorities -"

"Since when has that been our policy?"

"- drawing attention to - God knows what the banking community in Northern Italy will construe - "

"Merely a minor incident."

"Minor? Minor?" At last, he began to recover some of his spirit. Colour tinged his waxy cheeks. Another little wind-up and he'd be back to normal. "You make clandestine appointments at the most sinister of venues -"

"The Egyptian Museum is excellent, Jeremy, you really should see the sarcophagus of - "

"Don't interrupt! This is no time to be facetious!" His voice took on its usual rich, declamatory tone, like a politician addressing a bunch of sniggering tabloid journalists. "One of the worst aspects of your character is the flippancy with which you treat serious violence! You make, as I say, clandestine appointments at the most sinister of venues, quite deliberately inviting violence instead of pursuing your legitimate business, business which this Bank has entrusted to you in the strictest confidence! The Board are seething! Absolutely seething! Demanding your ejection!"

"Really? How's Shauna Spring taking it?"

That set him back. "She is not here" he muttered sulkily. "She's at some sort of quango conference in Sussex."

"And Freddy Harbledown?"

He blinked. "Freddy is at a dog show in Cleethorpes."

"Cleethorpes? Cleethorpes? Good God. How absolutely appalling. What's a toff like Freddy doing in a seaside dump like that?"

He closed his eyes. "It is apparently, an important show for Old English Sheepdogs. The Yorkshire branch of the Old English Sheepdog Society."

"Good grief. Well the Board'll have to wait for both of those to come back before they can chuck me out, won't they?"

He opened his eyes sharply. "There is no question of the Board chucking you out. I should never allow it. I am merely indicating to you the strength of the uproar with which I have had to deal."

"Oh. I am sorry, Jeremy. Really I am. I never intended to put you through it, you know."

"I'm sure you didn't. But you never seem to realise - "

"And I do think it establishes that Richard's death was suspicious. By the way, it seems that Freddy Harbledown has inadvertently set the cat among the pigeons out in Turin. Further examination is to take place."

"That's what terrifies me. What further horrors are to emerge before the truth is known? Are we all safe?"

"Oh, I don't think any of the protagonists are dangerous except for Bertrasconi. While I'm in England I shall be watchful, but it's unlikely anyone will be targeted here."

"In that case, you must be watchful but I'm glad that you feel safe for the moment. This whole matter must be resolved as soon as possible. Something, clearly, is eluding us. I want a complete analysis of this proposed electronics venture to be done quickly. And put in front of me before anyone else. Is that understood?"

"Yes, Jeremy. The electronics venture is the key to it all, I am sure. So I shall work on it forthwith."

"Thank God for that. Do anything you need to do to get the thing sewn up."

"Right" I said.

"You may have to talk to some of the manufacturers."

"Possibly. Although the research reports are quite comprehensive."

"Nothing like cross-checking, Tim. The research reports may not tell all."

"Right."

"Please try to steer clear of violence."

"Of course."

"Time is of the essence. Maucourt is pressing hard. Inferring that it is we who are dragging our feet. Shauna Spring, too, is making sarcastic remarks about the Board's ability to make speedy decisions. If we're not careful, the whole thing will go through by default. It's amazing how small expenditures like lavatory refurbishment take the Board hours of agonising appraisal whilst huge industrial investments go by on the nod."

"I'm on to it," I said. "Give me a day or two."

"Leave no stone unturned. Spare no horses. I'm nervous about this. Really nervous."

"I have that impression." I said. Which is a French form of locution.

"Good. I'm glad I've made you realise just what this could mean. I was unconvinced at first but this attack in the street changes everything."

"*Plus ça change*" I said, "*plus ça c'est la même chose.*"

My mind, quite clearly, was already wandering in the direction of Paris.

It was Bernard Levin who once wrote that the French could be relied upon to behave badly on any given occasion. One of those jocularly prejudiced remarks to which we islanders are all prone. Like Richard, I am something of a Francophile and much deplore these aspersions on our cross-Channel neighbours. I have played far too many games of rugby over there and made far too many friends to accept these broad disparagements.

On the other hand, you know what they're like.

Chapter 22

The offices of Maucourt Frères, as I have indicated, are in one of those elegant side-streets near the Elysée Palace. They occupy a fine, late-eighteenth-century building with imposing arched double doors to the street, a courtyard where carriages once disgorged their distinguished occupants and long, Directoire-style windows in three-storied tiers. The seasoned floors creak the discreet creaks of old, fine timber. Even the reception desk is a *bureau plat* with ormolu mounts, beside which modern computer and telecommunication equipment is placed.

I, however, was not in the reception area. I was in the grand office of Eugène Maucourt himself, the gelid operational *Président Directeur Général* of the investment bank. His attitude to *Les Anglo-Saxons* has never been warm and he is one of those very formal, upright Gaullists who like to display erudition and intellectual performance of high order whilst discussing matters of mendacious objective. Beside him, the gravid diplomat 'Ice-Cold' Couve De Murville would have seemed like a friendly chatterbox.

Today, however, he displayed a certain pale, autumnal warmth towards me, which was disconcerting. In the past, Eugène Maucourt, the upright, silver-haired, beautifully dressed paragon of diplomatic manners, made it clear that he looked upon me as a relict of Knollys or Dallingridge's rapine marauders from the *Guerre de Cent Ans*, a nasty piratical fixer from across *La Manche* who might be relied upon to do the worst to any chatelaine of a chateau temporarily bereft of its Norman or Burgundian knightly owner and exposed to my licentious grasp. We had, to put it mildly, a distant form of relationship. It was, therefore, a surprise to find that my unexpected, unannounced arrival - itself a rich example of the English lack of understanding how to behave *comme il faut* - had been received without that polite, oblique criticism in which the French specialise. I had been ushered straight into The Presence and my hand shaken with a degree of pressure slightly higher than usual.

"It was" Eugène murmured " a real loss to me when I heard the news about Richard. I was extremely distressed. As I am sure you know, his closest relationship here was with my brother Charles, alongside whom he fought with the Resistance during the war."

I nodded. Charles had been the opposite of his brother. Stocky, powerful, cheerful, always a glint of humour in his predatory eye. Charles and I had got on very well.

"In recent years however," Eugène, I hoped, was not going to go into one of his long, historical *tours d'horizon* in the manner of his hero De Gaulle, but you never knew "Richard and I had drawn much closer. He was a true friend of France despite his particular historical interest. Or indeed perhaps because of it."

Here Eugène gave me a significant look and I smiled faintly back to show that I understood this reference to the distressing curiosity Richard had for the excesses of the Hundred Years War.

"He was an Englishman of the sort we in France have always admired," Eugène said, moving an antique blotter on his desktop a fraction of millimetre to a more satisfactory position. "Courteous, highly intelligent, but above all, practical. A man of sound common sense. His approach was usually much more empirical than we, with our regard and training for theory, would use. More tactical than strategic, one might say. His grasp of the day to day aspects was astounding. It was, thus, an extremely successful relationship with us. The combination worked brilliantly."

"I am sure it did" I responded, tactfully ignoring the inferences tingeing his eulogy. "Richard always spoke of his time here in the highest possible terms. I regarded him as a friend as well as a superior and he confided in me in this particular matter."

Eugène's face did not light up. It never did that. But I detected, moving across its well-bred contours, a slight softening of expression which, I could hardly believe it possible, might be interpreted as evidence of gathering approval of my presence and responses.

He nodded sagely. "His judgement was a great support to us. He had much valuable experience and was able to interpret the nuances of the Anglo-American methods of finance to us with great skill, understanding, as he did, our own methods so intimately. It is a terrible loss. My grandson Christian who, of course, you know well, is away in Russia at the moment but has sent a message indicating his deep distress."

"Ah. I'm sorry I'll miss him." Christian and I had had an adventure together and were friends.

Eugène made a small gesture of sympathy and moved on. "We must await the memorial service in London, when it occurs, for an opportunity for we here in Paris to express our public sorrow. In the meantime, I am glad that you have been appointed to take up the baton dropped by Richard's untimely demise and that we can rely on your usual, assiduous attention to the very important project which preoccupies us all at the moment."

"Thank you." It was indeed a surprise for Eugène to express pleasure at my involvement in anything remotely connected with him. Things had really changed; or were there more pressing reasons for this reception?

"To be absolutely frank with you, Mr.Simpson," he leant forward just a fraction, as though the movement of half an inch towards me brought me into the inner circle of his confidence "this electronics project is one which concerns me greatly."

"It is a very ambitious project, Mr.Maucourt."

"Ah. Well put. Ambitious, yes. And highly important, on a European scale. But, like all ambitious and important projects, it carries commensurate risks. Risks which we, here in Paris, and you, in London, must assess with the finest degree of expertise before any decision is made."

"Absolutely."

"The research is very promising. The mathematical assessments provide most encouraging indications of the probability of success."

"Good."

"When you come to make your analysis I believe that you will find these factors impressive."

"I shall take every due care to give them full consideration."

He nodded approvingly, but with a degree of reserve. "Charville is an excellent fellow, excellent - you know him, of course?"

"Indeed. From the carpet project, you may recall. Mr Malfait's strategy to form a conglomerate."

His expression frosted slightly at the memory. "Ah. Of course. And we were all grateful to you for your intervention. But to the present: Charville, as I say, is an excellent fellow and has performed very well as our Head of Research."

"I am delighted to hear of his advancement."

"If I have any reserve it is that, if anything, his approach is a little too theoretical. You may smile at hearing a Frenchman say such a thing but we in business all know that what looks good on paper may not always proceed in reality with the order and discipline the calculations should indicate."

"Indeed."

"I am therefore glad of your support. Any constructive contribution to what is a critical operation on our part will be received in the most positive spirit."

"How very kind. I shall be glad to assist in any way I can."

"Excellent." He stood up and held out a hand. "Doubtless you and Charville will wish to collaborate on the, er, the technicalities it is so necessary to get right. One must make sure that all the necessary mechanisms are in place."

"Indeed one must." I shook the hand and released it.

"As I say, our leadership in the strategic and theoretical sense is not what concerns me. I am confident of it. However, your tactical, one might say empirical instincts will, I am sure, add useful checks and balances to the assessment."

"They will."

"I leave you to liaise with Charville, therefore," he said, dismissively. "You will see him as soon as you can?"

"You may depend upon it" I answered.

Which, in case you didn't know it, was one of the Duke of Wellington's favourite expressions.

I shot out of Eugène's office, down a passage, round a polished, parqueted bend, and into a reception area. An extremely attractive secretary goggled at me from behind a very expensive modern desk.

I gestured at the nearby pair of reception room doors. "This is Jacques Charville's office, is it?"

"Yes. But he is very busy - "

I wrenched the nearest door open, went through, and closed it firmly. Behind a large desk sat Jacques Charville, still small but fatter than when I'd last seen him. He was holding a large red file. In front of him sat two attractive girls each with horn-rimmed glasses, like researchers or analysts of some kind, both with crossed legs to reveal very shapely knees.

All three of them gaped at me in astonishment.

"Jacques," I said, between my teeth, in English. "I need to speak to you. Now."

"Tim!" His face had gone white. "But I - I - am very - "

I turned to the two ladies. "Excuse us, please. This won't take very long. But it is very confidential. And immediate."

They got up and shot out like rabbits. Charville put down the red file and began to protest as soon as the door shut.

"Tim, this is - you made no appointment - you can't just - "

I leant across the desk and got hold of his tie and jacket front in one fistful before pulling him half upright over his desk. I was still speaking between my teeth.

"Sir Richard White is dead. Murdered. And I'm after his killers. You are in cahoots with them."

"Stop this - let me go - "

"He saw you in Belley with Shauna Spring and Bertrasconi. You followed him so that they could plant bugs on him. You're plotting something big, or at least Bertrasconi is, and you've become his squeaker instead of Maucourt's. You're a traitor. What's the game?"

"Let go of me or I'll ring for the police!"

I let go of his tie and jacket and he slumped back behind the desk. I held up a finger to him.

"I've got all the research reports and the mathematical assessments. I'll go through them like a dose of salts. If you save me the time by coughing up the truth, I might just put a word in for you so you don't get the life term you deserve. Now: what's it to be?"

"You're mad! Violent! You've lost your reason!"

"You deny being in Belley?"

"Of course. I've never been there."

"You never saw Sir Richard's Jaguar in the square by the Cathedral?"

"No!"

"So why is your face as white as a sheet? I'll tell you one reason why: you had to use your mobile phone to call up Bertrasconi's henchmen to fix up the bugs, didn't you? When you were following him from Belley to Aix-les-Bains. And you know something: the police can have satellite tracking information on every mobile phone call made. When and where from to within the square metre. It'll be on the record sheet they get from the mobile phone company. One of modern technology's little inconveniences; we're all so trackable, all the time."

It was a long shot but it hit. He went green.

"That's rubbish!"

"And when you followed him to the Vieux Bedeau Hotel on the Grand Avenue de Lord Revelstoke, you had to call them to tell where he was staying. How will you explain your presence outside his hotel on that day, at that time? Hey? You three couldn't take the risk that he might not have seen you.

You had to check by arranging to stick bugs to him. In his hotel room too, I'll bet."

"You're raving." His voice had gone hoarse.

"Raving mad, yes. I'll get everyone who contributed to Richard's death. Everyone. You may depend upon it."

He stared at me, speechless. Fear was written all over him; he hunched behind the desk like a dog awaiting blows.

"There's another thing, Jacques. Emilio Bonnetti was murdered in Turin. Richard said to me that he was a confidential man used by Maucourt Frères. How did anyone know Richard would contact Bonnetti?" I stabbed a finger at him. "You'd know. When the tracker bugs indicated Richard was headed for Turin, who'd be able to guess that Richard, being no longer too spry himself, would contact Bonnetti? You're head of research here; you're the prime contact with him. The finger points straight at you."

"This is speculation. Madness." He was still terrified. "I had no idea Bonnetti was involved. Or dead."

I shook my head sadly. "How did Bertrasconi get to you, Jacques? Are you stymied for promotion here at Maucourt's? No way past the condescending Eugène and his lofty treatment of technicians? This is the top job you'll get, is it? Not good enough for you, this fine office, a luxurious salary and your pick of ripe research girls and secretaries with brown knees?"

He didn't answer.

"Let me guess: Bertrasconi's promised a big number when his scam goes through. Because scam it will be. He's waiting for a consortium to be set up on the wrong premise, based on research that's faulty, without the right range of products, aimed at markets that'll shrivel. And you'll have made a major contribution. What's it to be? Head of Paris operations? Don't kid yourself; Bertrasconi will drop you like a wet fish once he's got what he wants. He's got some real muscle he'll put into a place like this. Or is it just Head of Research for a bigger, grander organisation? With a bigger car and more short-skirted researchers? Still at the beck and call of anyone who wants a relevant fact? Poor stuff in return for murder and treachery, Jacques; very poor stuff."

He still didn't answer.

"What's the matter? Cat got your tongue?"

At last, it came out, in a dry croak. "You have no proof of any kind."

"No?"

He stared at me from sunken sockets. "What are you going to do? Try to beat it out of me, you violent bastard?"

"Not a chance." I turned and took hold of the door handle. "The next thing you hear will be from the police."

"You see! You have no proof! You haven't even advised Eugène."

I let go of the door handle and walked back to his desk. He flinched and glanced at his telephone.

"You're quite safe, Jacques, so leave the telephone. I wouldn't bother Eugène just now because poor, old-fashioned, obsolete Eugène is one of the old school who believes in loyalty. He'd protect you from me. Take your side. I'll make sure you come to justice quite independently."

"Sir Richard died of a heart attack. You're crazy!"

"You think he died of a heart attack? Bertrasconi is big on medical electronics. He has men who can arrange heart attacks at any time of day. For you, if necessary."

He went a bit whiter then, still with tinges of green, but his mouth stayed shut. I stepped back to the door.

"Think about it. You know where I am if you want me."

He didn't answer. Shock was affecting his blood stream. Whatever role he had been induced to play, it wasn't one important enough for him to be kept continuously informed.

I left. I'd carried out my sortie and, as Wellington said, a good general knows when to retreat.

Chapter 23

"Does Jeremy know" Sue asked, looking out of the study window across to the backs of the houses in Carisbrooke Road, "that, far from pursuing the electronics project requirements he has set you, you have come down to St.Leonards with me to chase after quite a different quarry?"

"No, he doesn't. But I am, in accordance with statutory requirements, pursuing the melancholy duties incumbent upon me as sole executor of Henry Weaver's estate."

"He won't be impressed by that. Not at all. In fact, the said pursuit will, if anything, upset him even more deeply than your neglect of his express instructions."

"Whose side are you on? You jumped at the chance to leave William and come down here with me. I am delighted by your presence. Using our combined resources, we may yet get to the bottom of the Henry Weaver affair. Which to you is far more interesting than any dull old industrial entanglement."

"That's true. But it worries me to think that my husband may be so diverted by the affairs of the Art Fund as to be liable to accusations of dereliction of duty in what is a more important matter."

"Ah. A more important matter, eh?"

"Well, isn't it?"

"Yes, it is. But in view of the events surrounding it, my advice to Jeremy and the Board over this project, if requested, is quite clearly established in my mind."

"And is?"

"To drop it like a hot potato. No good can come of something which, quite clearly, is hedged by criminal intentions."

She frowned. "Jeremy may not have that option."

"True. You are, my sweetheart, as usual, putting your finger on the nub. The events I have set in motion, however, will trigger off reactions which will take a little time to come to fruition. In that time we can comfortably look through Henry's documents yet again and I will also, this very evening, make sure I have digested the documents relating to Jacques Charville's research and calculations in time for reportage to Jeremy tomorrow. If, that is, other matters do not arise in the interim."

"What other matters?"

"To surmise would be mere speculation. Let me just say that my trip to Paris should get things going. Now let us concentrate on the matter in hand."

So far we had disturbed nothing. The flat in Kenilworth Road was exactly as we had left it. Slightly mustier, perhaps. A little unaired, with the same faint traces of aftershave aroma mingling with the onset of damper fragrances.

Sue was anxious to get on and get out as quickly as possible. I was grateful, for all our banter, that she had decided to come with me because, apart from the obvious conjugal reasons, I would be stirred to do what was required as briskly as possible.

"Where would you like me to start?" she demanded.

I handed her the keys to the flat. "I forgot to check the letter box when we arrived. Could you please open it and see if there's anything in it while I go through Henry's desk here?"

She pursed her lips a little at this mundane request but nodded and disappeared. I took a look round the book-lined room, sighed at the dilapidated spines ranged around me, and went back to the papers piled on the surface of the desk. So far, most of them were routine enough; things administrative that needed dealing with. I had appointed an undertaker in the London Road nearby and he was getting on with the arrangements for the cremation. I made a mental note to phone Henry's aunt, Enid May Weaver of Whitby, to ask if she wanted to attend and to suggest who else might want to do so as well. I sat down on one of the two old leather-covered chairs by the large table, got hold of a sheet of paper and began to make notes. So far nothing stimulating had come to light. There were no messages on the telephone answering machine. No reference to his ex-wife had so far come to light, which was odd, unless Henry simply wanted no reminders of a painful past. I had yet to go through all the drawers of the desk completely though; divorce documents might turn up in them.

Sue came in, carrying some post that looked mainly like junk mail, and once again set off the train of thought that had bugged us since our trip up North.

"What do you think, Sue? Did Henry phone me about the Laura Knight painting or was there another? Why the question about whether we only buy British art?"

"You're absolutely sure that's what he asked?"

"Positive. And he was very secretive, as though it he didn't want anyone else to find out about it."

"In that case there must be another painting, a watercolour, somewhere. But where?"

"Not here, or at Cullercoats, for sure."

She smiled. "You're still really miffed about that, aren't you? A good Laura Knight doesn't rate against what I'd sparked off in your mind."

"From the records, a million is quite par for a good Winslow Homer of the Cullercoats period. His Civil War paintings are treasured and so are his tropical and maritime scenes. Is it possible that a Cullercoats watercolour, something from what seems to have been something of a turning point, could still be unaccounted for?"

"I think so, Tim. No one knows how much work he did while he was over here. There are recorded paintings of Flamborough Head and other points on the coast south from Newcastle. Who knows if he didn't call in at Whitby as well? He did a rather Impressionist painting of the Houses of Parliament, a bit like Monet's but maybe influenced by Whistler, who was in London when he visited. He could have stayed anywhere on his way up to or back from Cullercoats - it isn't certain if he went briefly back to the States in the middle of his time here. But it was Cullercoats that seemed to inspire him the most. During his first year he produced some larger watercolours than were those he customarily turned out. They were still only about twenty inches by thirty but he was using techniques for exhibition watercolours that were much more influenced by British artists than American work. Watercolour was much more advanced here, then, than in America. He went on producing work influenced by Cullercoats for two or three years after he'd returned to Maine."

"I wonder if Henry knew anything of this. I never talked art much with him - films and biography were our common subject - but he'd ask after the Fund, usually rather humorously, almost mockingly, from time to time. I had no reason to think of Winslow Homer at all. Still, it's pure speculation. Perhaps he had the wrong idea about the Laura Knight, in some way. He had odd bees in his bonnet from time to time."

"I still think" Sue said, putting the mail down on the table, "that this place could easily have been searched. Quite exhaustively, without too much disturbance to someone who didn't know Henry, but enough to alert anyone familiar with him."

"There does seem to be an odd combination of neatness and disarray."

"There you have it. The neatness is everywhere except in here and the front room, the living room. Where, again, it's not logical. The papers on the table are scattered but the rest isn't."

"That portfolio against the table leg, you mean?"

"Yes. And it's empty. Why prop an empty portfolio up against the table in the front room?"

"Maybe it wasn't empty. The disturbed places are where Henry might have worked, or just read things."

"So someone might have wanted to remove all evidence of what Henry was working on?"

"If he had work. If he wasn't just following some biographical fantasy or another, rather than, say, researching into art.

Henry had yearnings to write biography like his hero, Hesketh Pearson. Maybe he was working on that."

"But who would it be? And how could it affect the water-colour?"

"Your guess is as good as mine." I picked up the envelopes she had taken from Henry's letterbox. There were no more bills. There was a circular for double glazing and a standardised form from a research library saying that the item he had requested would not be available for another ten days since it was out to another borrower. A letter from a market research company stated that the report he had enquired for could be obtained for three hundred and fifty pounds and hopefully enclosed a leaflet. I smiled; some chance of Henry paying that for a research report. A brown envelope, official looking, from Croydon, contained a parking fine notice relating to an offence on the day Henry died.

So he had been to Croydon, as Sammy Simes said.

"What's that?" Sue's voice broke in as I stared at the fine and the name of the road in which he had parked.

I handed it to her. "A parking fine from Croydon. On the day Henry died."

"So he did go there. What for, I wonder? What time did they book him for parking?"

I looked at the document. "Just after five. That's a bit hard; I bet the restrictions ended within the next hour."

She looked pensive.

"He was still parked at Croydon at five o'clock. Yet his accident took place late, after eleven, on the road beyond Whatlington. What was he doing between sometime after five in Croydon and eleven? Even in his old Allegro and in bad traffic it's not more than two hours drive."

"Research, I assume, Sue."

"Tim, most offices close by six at the latest. An outside researcher would be thrown out by then. There's over five hours to account for. Two of them driving, say. What about the rest?"

My mind, for some reason, went into a mental picture of the Royal Oak at Whatlington. A place of high significance to Henry.

What could he have been researching?

I picked up the research report letter and took off the leaflet that was held behind it by a paper clip. The title stared at me unwinkingly.

The Market for Medical Electronic Equipment in Western Europe.

And, at that moment, my mobile phone rang.

Chapter 24

To describe the opening remarks that came through on my mobile phone would be distressing. They were couched in uncomplimentary terms spoken in fury and intemperate haste. There is really no point, I always think, in dwelling upon the unpleasant things in life in detail; one should try to move on to the more positive aspects of human existence.

Jeremy was neither in his 'Nanny is not angry, she is just very, very disappointed' vein nor did he adopt the usual, brayingly insulting mode he uses when uttering criticisms. He was too upset for either of those, upset not only with the events that had occurred but with the repercussions which were still, according to him, thundering down telephone lines into him.

It seems that, shortly after my meeting with him, Jacques Charville left the premises of Maucourt Frères looking white and tense. He had, evidently, at some point gone home to the rather superior fourth floor flat out near Neuilly to which he moved on being appointed Head of Research. Some hours later he had, from the balcony of the luxurious living room with its excellent views over the west of Paris, taken the shortest possible way down to the pavement below.

The impact had made a nasty mess on the pavement and killed him instantly.

After the office had been informed by the police, two lady researchers at Maucourt Frères felt it their duty to advise Eugène Maucourt that I had burst in upon an important meeting they were having with Jacques Charville concerning the electronics project and peremptorily demanded their expulsion. From what they gathered from sounds gleaned through the office door, I had then spent some time being extremely nasty to Jacques. Certainly, they said, when he left the offices shortly afterwards he looked like a man possessed.

Eugène Maucourt's call to Jeremy had given rise to extreme difficulties. It seemed that his warmth, even the autumnal variety, towards me had now evaporated. The Ice Age was back. Eugène wanted explanations and he wanted them fast. Charville had been his, Eugène's personal appointment. There was no excuse to take the confidential remarks he had made to me about Charville's possibly over-theoretical approach to the lengths of abuse and threatening behaviour. The project was now prejudiced by the shocking, self-inflicted death of its principal research manager. If it was aborted in some way he, Eugène, would hold White's Bank responsible and would mulct for damages. Years of friendly collaboration had been destroyed.

"Rubbish" I managed to get in, at this point.

"Rubbish? Rubbish? Do you deny that you threatened Charville in some way?" Jeremy was almost screaming.

"Of course not. You know very well what Richard saw."

"For Christ's sake! You didn't make unsubstantiated allegations to Charville about that, did you? Oh God, what Eugène will do when he finds out! We'll be bankrupted."

"Calm yourself, Jeremy. We'd have been bankrupted if we'd followed Charville's assessments. He was a traitor."

"You accused him of that? You deliberately and premeditatedly went over to Paris to accuse him of that? Oh God! No wonder he was so distressed. And committed suicide."

"Nonsense. Jacques Charville would never have had the guts to commit suicide. Never. He was pushed."

"What?" Jeremy's voice at last sank to a hoarse whisper. "What are you saying?"

"Charville was as guilty as hell. Everything about him shouted it. He may have thought that Richard genuinely died of a heart attack, although that's debatable, but he knew that his involvement with the opposition would lead to his prompt dismissal. That might not have worried him, because he's almost certainly got another job lined up. What was really upsetting was that he knew I'd rubbish his research assessments as evidence of his complicity. I told him his mobile phone would be the giveaway for his following Richard from Belley to Aix-les-Bains. It is an indictable offence to deliberately falsify information on which an employer is going to make decisions. On top of that, I told him that both Richard and Bonnetti, who he arranged to meet at the Egyptian Museum, were murdered. It must have been little Jacques who tipped off Turin about the use of Bonnetti. My knowledge sent him shrieking in fear to those responsible because, at their behest, he certainly followed Richard and knew about the bugs put in the car. Which made him an accessory to industrial espionage and murder."

"But - but - Richard's death has not yet even been - "

"Bonnetti's has. And Richard's will be. I'll bet they don't like panickers in the Bertrasconi camp. They won't like to have had to take extreme measures but so far it's just arguable that these things could be coincidence. Richard old, Charville under stress, my visit tipping him over the edge, et cetera, et cetera. From now on, though, it'll be a bit dodgy if anyone else gets exterminated. Too many coincidences. Which is a comfort to us, eh?"

"For God's sake! Have you any concept of what assumptions you're making? There is practically no evidence to support your case."

"It has all been a bit circumstantial, I agree, but - "

"But! But! But me no buts! Get in here right away! Where are you?"

"I am in St.Leonards, Jeremy."

"*What*?" His voice went back to a shriek. "*St.Leonards*? What in hell are you doing down there?"

"I am pursuing the melancholy duties incumbent upon me as sole executor of Henry Weaver's estate."

"You bastard! You utter bloody bastard! You promised me you'd get on with the electronics project without delay!"

"Don't worry, Jeremy. I promised you, and I will fulfil my promise. I have it in hand and have already taken action on it."

"By going to Paris and duffing up Jacques Charville?" he shouted. "What sort of action is that?"

"The right action. And, if you want a quick and immediate recommendation based on my initial reading of his reports, my advice is not to touch the project with a barge pole."

There was a silence. A pregnant silence. After a while I uttered a cautious "Jeremy?" to see if he was still there.

"It isn't possible" he replied eventually "to take that option, Tim."

"You mean that this is the Last Chance Saloon? That things are so adrift with the Bank's affairs that unless we join in a consortium to finance the major conglomerate the participants propose to form, we are up shit creek without a paddle?"

"To put it in a highly confidential nutshell, yes."

"I wish that you would confide these things in me earlier on, sometimes, Jeremy."

"The Board agreed it was for no one else to know. We did not want to cause alarm and panic. You know how these things can damage a concern."

'So the crux now is to make sure that the assessments and the research establish the correct level of financing, the structure and the share price? And that the venture does not, must not, fail?"

"Precisely."

"Then all is not lost, is it? Yet?"

"I hope to God not."

"Say not the struggle naught availeth, Jeremy. I shall come to see you as soon as I can."

"Sooner, please."

"Done."

The phone went silent. Sue was looking at me with her mouth slightly open.

"Jacques Charville is dead" I said to her. "He sailed off his fourth floor balcony last night. Jacques was a mouse. He wouldn't have had the courage to do that stone cold sober.

And I'll bet he wasn't on any Peruvian marching powders or herbal remedies when he did it."

"Jacques Charville? Wasn't he that little researcher at Maucourt's?"

"Yes, he was."

Sue looked thoughtfully at the mail on the table. "A researcher. Just like Henry Weaver."

I nodded. "Just like Henry, as you say, Sue."

"Don't tell me; you don't like coincidences?"

"I never have, Sue. Although, to my knowledge, Jacques Charville didn't inherit a watercolour."

Chapter 25

"You know how it is with Shauna, Tim. You lean forward to give her a peck on the cheek and the next thing you know, your trousers are round your ankles."

"Eh?"

The speaker, Charlie Macdonald, one of our financial press's most respected reporters, grinned at my discomfiture. Before him, his glass of Burgundy was nearly empty and I hastened to refill it. He gave me a broader grin and cast an appreciative eye at the label on the bottle.

We were sitting in a wine bar off Fleet Street. There are not that many newspapers around Fleet Street these days but Charlie is a superior City reporter full of nostalgia and he likes to meet in that region. Food had been ordered as well as the wine but first things came first; Charlie said he'd had a busy morning. He needed refreshment. Despite a life of disgraceful enquiry, unhealthy business breakfasts and ill-tempered shareholders meetings, Charlie is a tall, thin, good-looking fellow who once played on the wing for Blackheath, for whom he could turn on a timely sprint with the ball when occasion demanded. I've known him a long time, have tackled him on one or two famous past occasions, once when he was in full flight towards the touchline, but he's never borne me any ill will. Nor have I him for a kick in the eye that was borderline for a foul.

"Charlie, what are you telling me?"

His grin stayed in place, like the Cheshire Cat's. "I was, in fact, quoting. The words were those of an acquaintance of mine. One who had to deal with Shauna years ago. Before she moved out of reach of we lesser mortals and was very much within reach for an obliging, virile journalist. One who'd also do her a bit of discreet good in the right financial column."

"Disgraceful."

"Let us be charitable and say that his remark was as much metaphorical as reminiscent, Tim."

"How's that?"

"I think, apart from the obvious we won't dwell on, he meant that in any slight involvement with Shauna, if you showed any indication of willingness to help, she was all over you. She was out to get the most from you. Shauna was ambitious from the word go. Poor old Spring had quite a lot to put up with, I can tell you."

"Spring?"

"Her husband, Tim. Gordon Spring. A well-oiled City man with a number of directorships, particularly in the retail trade. Older than Shauna, of course."

"Of course."

"His attraction to Shauna was a bit obvious. Not that he's not a good-looking, fairly dynamic sort of bloke; he is. In his youth he had quite a reputation. But she was after financial security more than anything. Needed it to take the sort of risks she proceeded to take on her way up. All those well-placed situations and waiting for quangos need patience and investment. And now she's on the board of little old White's Bank."

"She is, indeed."

"And here you are, making enquiries about her."

"Well, you know, just getting myself into the picture."

He chuckled and took another swig at his wine before swilling it round to look at its 'legs' with appreciation. "You pick a good Burgundy for a front row man. How long has it got, Tim?"

"What?"

"White's Bank. Can't be too long, now, can it?"

"I'm not sure what you mean."

"Oh, come on. There's not one of the old merchant bank crowd surviving now. White's is being driven deeper and deeper into a corner. Venture capital and risk money."

"That's always been merchant banking."

"Oh, sure. But with a spread of risk. A bit like publishing, really; you churn out a load of books, most of them steady but uninspiring, some of them real dogs, but every now and then a boomer. Pays for the champagne, don't it? You have to have a good spread and boomers or you're done. But you can't back a winner every time. That's why the old merchant banks have all gone, inside big foreign finance houses with huge funds. There are still some little venture capitalists but White's never thought of themselves that way. The old days have gone, Tim. The rumour is that you'll go too, any day now."

"Rumour?"

"Well why would Shauna Spring, with all her connections despite the odd horrible bomber like Intradeva, go on the Board of White's? Got to be part of some advance move, hasn't it? She's a wooden horse. Waiting for the signal before the warriors are let out to open the gates. You've got some very dissatisfied minority shareholders around, you know?"

"Surely it's just part of a career pattern for her? She's on several quangos still."

"She is. But they're not the sort she prefers. They're stop-gaps. No publicity in them and not much money. Shauna likes the headlines and she needs a lot of money despite what Gordon provides, or maybe because of it. She's not too keen on dependence and its demands. I think she'd like to have her own stash. Nothing personal, Tim, but apart from Jeremy, White's Board is pretty well worked out of the entrepreneurial spirit, ain't it? What's left is dear old Freddy Harbledown and his sheepdogs along with odd conservative cousins and others. Sir Richard's gone, and he was old anyway." He nodded approvingly as I topped up his glass. "What are you planning to do with yourself? There's a few who'd be glad to make you an offer, I'm sure. You've been over in America a bit recently, haven't you? Giving Europe the old heave-ho?"

"I have no plans to move from White's."

"Hey, don't sound so po-faced. This is a friend talking to

you. I'm only telling you the truth, you know. There've been all sorts of rumours about White's being taken over, for years now. It might be the best thing that could happen to you. Lots of the others benefited from those takeovers."

"By Germans, Swiss and Japanese. Who fire them in swathes when things turn down."

"True. City life is much riskier these days. Like journalism."

"I agree. Jeremy and I made a pact years ago that we'd have a bash at shaking up White's and the pact doesn't terminate until the walls fall in. But that's another subject. What else should I know about Shauna? Any steady associations that are relevant?"

"She's a favourite with a few civil servants and politicians. Don't ask me how. The way these City favourites move around and upwards despite their disasters is chronic."

"I know. Piers Hargreaves was a classic example."

He chuckled. "Until you got to him."

"Me? It was his past got to him, not me."

"You're too modest. Are you after Shauna now? Should I start preparing the obituary?"

"Just making a few gentle enquiries, that's all."

"Oh yeah?" He pulled a face. "Like that mate of yours, Nobby Roberts a.k.a Inspector Knacker? A monumental feeler of collars. Used to play on the wing, good he was, before he became a rozzer."

"Nobby's been asking about Shauna too?"

He tapped his nose meaningfully. "My lips are sealed. A journalist's ethics are sacrosanct."

"Dear God."

"Mind you," he eyed me up and down. "Shauna does like a bit of the rough when Gordon's not about."

"Cheeky bugger, you are."

"I mean it. There was one bloke I saw her with a couple of times, a foreign chap. Argentine, really not from her social circle. Goes back to her origins, perhaps."

"Origins? Argentine?"

He frowned. "Jeez, Tim, you really are starting from scratch aren't you? Shauna's maiden name was Hobson but she's related to the Paterson family from Rosario. A niece of some sort. They had a big department store there, like the Hendersons with the Tienda Inglesa in Montevideo. You remember all that fuss about Harrod's, Buenos Aires, years ago? No, it's before our time, the British store abroad, but old jossers used to chat about it when I were a lad. It's what she has in common with old Gordon though: the retail background."

"Good God. I had no idea she was a Paterson."

"Yeah. I think this guy - she actually introduced me, quite brazenly in a night club once, but he only spoke Spanish - was a long-term job. On and off, that is. Enrique, his name was. Shabby, I thought, looked as though he didn't see the light of day much, but then a woman's taste is inexplicable. When lovely lady stoops to folly, and all that. He did have a sort of raffish charm, I suppose. And he was clearly besotted with her, at the time."

"Enrique? Enrique who?"

"Oh God, some Spanish name. Tecky something. Teck, no I can't remember."

Enrique, I was thinking, is the Spanish version of Henry but no, no it can't be; it just can't, life doesn't do that.

But Argentina; both of them?

"You've gone all dark, Tim. Why don't you have another glass yourself? You mustn't worry about White's. You're a marketable commodity, my boy. Business is business. When one door closes, another one opens."

And then he stopped. A radiant beam came over his face.

"What?" I demanded.

"That's it. Door."

"What is?"

"His name. Enrique's. It was Tecky Door. I mean, it sounded like that."

"Oh God. Oh Christ."

"What?"

"You mean it was Tejedor? Enrique Tejedor?"

"That's it. Well done, Tim! Tech-eh-dor. How did you know? Hey, what's up? You've gone as white as a sheet, now."

I hardly heard him. A *tejedor* is a weaver. Enrique Tejedor is straight Spanish translation of Henry Weaver.

Chapter 26

"But" said Sue, sitting, coffee in hand, in the big armchair near the mantelpiece, over which the Medway marine Clarkson Stanfield sailed majestically on forever, "and it is a major but, I still do not see how and why."

"Sammy Simes said there was more to Henry than met the eye. Evidently there was."

"At least we know he really had been married. You found the divorce papers."

This was true. They turned up in the bottom right hand drawer of his old office desk in the flat in Kenilworth Road. All cleared, signed, sealed, granted *nisi* and whatever else you need to extricate yourself from a marriage. On the grounds that he and Sarah Winifred Weaver, née Holdsworth, had been apart for far longer than is necessary for the authorities to grant the said divorce. Well, actually, she went off to Canada with an insurance salesman, according to Henry's accompanying letters, even before he was made redundant. Henry's bibliographical bent proved far too bookish for a girl looking for a bit of excitement and the insurance salesman was making much more money.

Maybe Henry should have married a librarian.

And yet, and yet. Henry had a certain style. Scraps of Spanish phrase, the odd shout of *macanudo!* when excited, an ability to tango; his conversation peppered with literary imagery. There were aspects of Henry that made him different, could lead to attraction. I had a suspicion that Henry should never have left Buenos Aires. Like many Englishmen, he was probably a different character when abroad: easier, less inhibited, much more spontaneous. Something about life in England, the gloomy skies, the sense of everything already being spoken for, repressed his ability to react.

I had contacted the aunt Enid May in Whitby, who said that

she was too old to come to the cremation ceremony but was pleased to hear she'd got the print of Whitby because she'd always admired its broad view of the harbour much more than the pictures she had. She was a bit querulous and see-med slightly upset or flustered, saying that if I brought the print she'd have things ready for me, the place to hang it, and all that. Henry, she said, hadn't visited her for a long time and she relied on the meals on wheels these days. He'd been a kind nephew when he could, especially when you considered that things hadn't gone all that well for him and he had a struggle to keep up. It was sad that he'd started a lonely life so young and she wished he'd found someone else after Sarah left. I agreed tactfully and hung up, thinking about that mee-ting, after the film club, in the Soho wine bar, some eighteen months ago. Had he started his affair with Shauna then? Who had he stayed with after our conversation and his request for my executorship? A friend, he'd said.

"What on earth" Sue was still ruminating "had he got to offer the glamorous Shauna Spring? I mean, how did he even get to know her? She hardly moves in Henry's circles."

"Research. Shauna is often responsible for commissioning research. And far from using the big, reputable companies all the time, there are occasions when you want someone low profile, discreet, inexpensive, unknown. Someone you might pick out of a classified ad or a DTI list, perhaps."

"A failure, you mean?"

"Henry might not have been a success commercially but he could do research. He'd held down a market research job before he got the push. To the accountants who scour our modern organisations Henry might have been just another overhead, someone whose contribution to the immediate bot-tom line was negligible, but he knew his sources and techni-ques. When the profit situation is tough, accountants are only too willing to sacrifice the future for the present. Henry's work was usually to do with the future. So he was expendable."

"That's terrible. It's so short term."

"In the long term, as Maynard Keynes said, we are all dead."

"In Henry's case, not even long term."

"No."

"But Shauna Spring was keen on him. They had an affair. So she would be unlikely to arrange for his demise."

"I suppose not."

"Why the Spanish? Why Enrique Tejedor?"

"It was an illicit affair. A bit of excitement. They found they had Argentina in common. People having affairs sometimes invent another persona for themselves or for their lover."

"Do they?"

"I only speak from hearsay, dear heart, from reading the newspapers. It might have been a bit of fun for Henry to pretend to be an Argentine when they were in public." A thought struck me. "Actually, there might be a practical reason as well. Shauna attracts journalists. A deliberate policy, you might say. An English affair, with a traceable man like Henry Weaver, is not nearly as glamorous as an unknown Argentine called Enrique. Who can disappear conveniently from time to time when not needed. Not back to Buenos Aires, as everyone might think, but to the Hastings hinterland. To unknown St.Leonards, away from prying journalistic eyes."

"So you think Shauna commissioned Henry to do research and then one thing led to another?"

"That's probably it. With Shauna doing all the paying - Henry couldn't afford London night clubs - she had all the control over him she wanted. Could switch him on and off as required. But then Henry came into an inheritance. Not anything great by Shauna's standards, but maybe big enough for Henry."

"Do you think so, Tim? That little house and a Laura Knight? It wouldn't be wealth beyond the dreams of avarice."

"Unless there's another painting."

"Ah, that would be different. That might make Henry

recalcitrant. He might not want to be yet another appendage to her ambitions in life."

"Which I think is what she wants with White's Bank."

Sue put down her coffee, stood up, then came over to sit next to me on the settee. "You're looking so preoccupied, Tim. There's more to it than Henry and this electronics affair, isn't there? Something to do with Jeremy and the Bank?"

"What makes you say that?"

"I'm not stupid, you know. I do read the papers. And although you don't talk much about the Bank these days, I do know that things are not very bright. Do you think it's going to go under?"

"The City seems to be betting on it. And if you extrapolate trends, like any good consultant researcher, you'd expect it."

She took my hand. It's always a bad sign, that. Don't get me wrong; I'm not cynical about Sue's feelings. There are different gestures for different purposes: embraces, an arm hug, a squeeze of the hand, more intimate gestures. Taking the hand without squeezing it is a sign of worry.

"What will you do if White's goes?"

"There'll be time to deal with that when it happens."

"America?"

"I've been offered America before. And turned it down."

"We could still go."

"What about you and the Tate?"

"Me and the Tate? Maybe it would have to become me and an American gallery. I can't expect to stay at the Tate forever, even though it does keep people a long time. There's William to think of."

"I thought you'd got that pretty well organised so far."

"So far, so good. But it's not forever. What I think I'm saying is that I don't want you making the wrong decisions because of me. I know that you and Jeremy are a working item, one that would be difficult to replace, but if White's goes, even if you're offered a job by the takeover people, don't reject other opportunities because of me and the Tate. Right?"

"Right." I leant forward and kissed her. A man with Sue in his life needs to show his appreciation rather often.

Especially if he is going to lunch with Shauna Spring the next day.

Chapter 27

"So" she said, after we'd ordered - no starters, fish for her, fish for me, too - and the white wine was poured out, "so I'm being lunched by Tim Simpson. At last."

We were in a restaurant just off Chancery Lane, a venue I thought a bit appropriate, and she'd arrived just that nicely-judged bit late, so that I was already at the table and she could make an entrance. She was turned out in a smarter suit this time, one that looked pressed rather than crumpled, and the silk blouse under it was pale blue. The people at the restaurant, which I'd used once or twice before, recognised her and were impressed. Their manner towards me perked up considerably. This, I thought, must be what it's like, what so many want to happen: to go to restaurants with recognisable, attractive people and get respect.

"Well" I answered, "it had to happen fairly soon, didn't it, Shauna? I'm glad you could find time at such short notice, in view of your busy commitments."

She smiled attractively. "I always hoped for this, so although I'm very pushed today, I've made time for you. It has been a bit awkward for me to take the initiative, as I'm sure you'll understand, in view of the hierarchical attitude over in Gracechurch Street."

I grinned. "It can take some getting used to."

She took a sip of white wine. "My dear Tim, the place is positively Dickensian. I thought I'd be allocated a high clerk's chair at first, then later perhaps the key to the Directors' loos. Or have to sit at a partners' desk opposite Freddy Harbledown. They seem to think the best way to treat a woman, if they've got one imposed upon them, is like a man. That is the greatest accolade in their book."

"Not Jeremy, surely?"

"Ah. Jeremy is different." She gave me a cautious look from

under lowered lashes. "Jeremy is another subject, perhaps. Gallant, I think, is the word for Jeremy."

I reached across my plate to butter a roll. A break was needed in the progress of the conversation. She appeared not to notice.

"Some of it rubs off, evidently" she said.

"What?"

"The gallantry. I detect a measure of it in you. But whereas in others it is so often a means of avoiding engagement, of compromise, in you it is an accessory to much more masculine qualities."

I smiled. My eye met hers. Hers sparkled back, very briefly. "I'm afraid it takes a few generations to turn out a Jeremy" I said. "In him, gallantry goes deep. In me, as I think you have detected, it is something of a veneer."

"Men who are not dangerous are of no use to women."

"Wow. That's not a quote, is it? That's original, I think."

"Absolutely."

"As befits your reputation."

"Now you're trying flattery. Very pleasant, but not very sincere, Tim. My reputation, if I have one, is not for original or lapidary remarks about the nature of male and female relationships. In public, I'm too sharp-tongued for that. It is, I am sure, the reputation of an ambitious woman who has run a few quite challenging concerns with extreme efficiency and fairly strong control of subordinates. I now sit on two or three official and quite important committees which listen rather carefully to what I have to say."

"And on the Board of White's."

"And on the Board of White's. Of which organisation you are a highly regarded but as yet unexecutive member."

"Unexecutive?"

"You're staff. Assistant to Jeremy. Not a line manager."

"I manage the Art Fund."

The fish arrived, sea bass for her, turbot for me, and she waved a knife dismissively as the waiter put some leaf spinach between us, topped up our glasses, and withdrew.

"The Art Fund" she said, "with all due respect, has earned praise but it is a minor league matter, Tim. I don't have to tell you that. In the machinations of White's Board, such as there are, the Art Fund hardly figures. They like the publicity it gets them from time to time but they look upon that as PR. Not real investment activity."

"I agree."

She put down her knife and fork to look directly at me. "So I wonder what you are waiting for."

I met her gaze full on. "Waiting for?"

"Oh, come on, I'm sure you've had all kinds of offers. You're the right age, intelligent, experienced, sound on finance and you've got style. You are also, when roused, a very dangerous man."

"Now who's resorting to flattery?"

She ignored that. "Yet you stay put, buttling Jeremy. There's no other word for it. Just like a butler."

"You've obviously formed the wrong impression. No one can buttle Jeremy. And I have had a roving commission for too long to do so."

She shrugged. "Put it how you like. Every organisation has its king, its barons and its knights, just like feudal society. You're certainly a knight but you're not a baron." She picked up her knife and fork again. "Do you want to be one?"

"Not if it involves treachery."

The knife wavered above her sea bass. Then it plunged into the soft white flesh. "Treachery is an emotive term, Tim. Don't pretend that the City is a nicely-ordered myth like Malory's King Arthur. In real life, the now highly-regarded Malory was indicted for rape a couple of times. And probably worse. Even Arthur's story is one of infidelity."

"That's why it's called a tragedy."

She brought a forkful of fish to her mouth and put it in. While she chewed she seemed to be thinking. A slight frown had come to her brow.

"I know" I continued while she ate, "that everyone in the

City is out for success. That the old idea of a career in one firm is antediluvian. Opportunity is what it is all about. Was that what you were going to say?"

"More or less. Isn't that the truth?"

"Within limits, yes."

"Ah, limits. The old English idea of limits. Of rules."

"There are rules."

"That's the law. One observes the law. Laws should not be confused with career strategies. With the play of competition. You of all people should know that. You've been extremely borderline in some of your more successful projects and the enemies of the Bank have come to sticky ends. If ever a man thought the means justified the ends, it must be you. So what are your own ends?" She looked at me full face again but differently now, not challenging, softer, promise coming into her expression. "Life isn't for ever. Why do so many people live their lives as though they were immortal? We're not. There are things to do, Tim. Nice things, that need doing while we can. And there are heights to be scaled. I'm not going to sit about waiting for things to come to me. I'm going to get them."

"White's is one of them, is it?"

She smiled. "White's could be one of them." The smile faded and she looked at me seriously. "I see, now, that I need your help to do that, though."

"I'm sorry I've got in the way."

"I'm not. I'm glad. I can see how well a baron's outfit could suit you, when the time comes."

I put down my knife and fork. "So the wooden horse theory is right, is it?"

"Wooden horse?"

"Trojan horse, to be more specific. Currently a City theory. You were elected by minority shareholders who are discontent but, amongst those minority shareholders were people who put you in there as part of a much more long-term plan, one intended to open the gates to outsiders. I wouldn't think that you joined White's just for the amusement."

"I'm glad you understand me. Outsiders sometimes have clearer views than those confined to the building."

"I can accept that the City is a predatory place. There are predatory strategies which are part of the life in this jungle. So your coming onto the Board as part of a takeover strategy isn't something I can object to, morally."

Her expression cleared a bit. The slight frown had disappeared. "I'm glad, too, that you are a realist, Tim. You said just now - it took me back just a little - that you'd object to treachery. Are you an admirer of Talleyrand at all?"

"Very much so. According to Duff Cooper he thought that France should adopt a British style of constitution, like America."

She nodded. "Talleyrand said that treachery is only a matter of timing."

"Ah. Napoleon did call Talleyrand *une merde dans des bas de soie*. Which translates simply and directly into a shit in silk stockings."

She smiled faintly again. "But the point was well made. Timing is everything. And time is becoming critical."

"It must be, for you and Jacques and Bertrasconi to meet up in Belley."

The frown returned. "I'm afraid I don't understand that. I've never been to Belley."

I picked up my knife and fork, casually. "I can understand Bertrasconi. He's something you can deal with, as long as you have a bentwood chair and a twelve-foot stock whip. Or a Webley forty-five. Striped animals are easy to understand. Jacques had no excuse. He was a treacherous little tyke, ready to falsify facts so as to give Bertrasconi an edge when things went wrong. A deliberate act of sabotage on a concern which had nurtured him. As they used to say in the old Westerns Henry was so fond of, he got what was coming to him."

Her face showed no recognition of this mention of Henry, but she made a gesture of dissent. "Jacques Charville committed suicide as a result of pressure of work. And the sudden stress which you put on him."

I paused a fraction to absorb how good her grapevine was, then continued. "If you believe that, you believe that Sir Richard White died of a heart attack."

"Which he did."

"Like hell he did. He and Jacques were murdered."

"That's ridiculous. Fantasy."

"Sir Richard saw you three in Belley and was following the matter up. He was getting close. So was the man Emilio Bonnetti he employed. Three dead, how many more to go? Before you and Bertrasconi achieve your objective?"

She stopped any pretence at dealing with the meal. "I have never heard of this Bonnetti. The other two deaths are perfectly explicable and without suspicion. You are letting your imagination get out of hand. I will admit that I think White's is due for a major and seismic upheaval. I might contribute to that, in the shareholder's interests."

I smiled at this cynicism. "Shareholders have nothing to do with it. Personal interests are what count, aren't they? You just said so."

She waved my remark aside. "Several parties have told me they are interested in acquiring the best bits of White's. I'm talking to them too, not just Bertrasconi."

"But he has the biggest, and most lethal, clout."

Her face creased angrily. "This is getting nowhere. You'd better make up your mind. If you want to be one of the bits retained, rather than chucked into the street, when the time comes, you've got decisions to take." She suddenly looked at her watch. "I have to go to a meeting. It finishes late afternoon. I'm staying up in town tonight. My flat's in the Barbican." She drew a small handbag up from beside the table, rummaged in it, and flung a card at me. "Seven o'clock. If you want to progress, be there at seven for a drink. If not, I'll know where you stand."

She got up, abruptly, and started to leave.

"Hang on. There's something else I - "

"No chance. The Barbican. At seven."

She moved swiftly, decisively, with surprisingly long steps, straight down the aisles between tables, out into the street. Then she was gone.

A waiter rushed up. "Is everything all right, sir?"

"Fine. The lady just had some bad news. You can bring me the bill."

He nodded, face still worried, and moved away. I looked at my watch. Dead on two. Was this a technique of hers? Abrupt withdrawal at critical moments in order to faze the opposition? And the Barbican flat, from which husband Gordon would evidently be absent; from it, would drinks be intended to move to dinner and more?

I got up, paid the bill, and went out onto the pavement.

A dark blue Bentley drew up as I stood there and a uniformed chauffeur got out. He came round the bonnet, opened the nearside back door and saluted me.

"Mr.Simpson?" Although one arm was holding the door open, he was close, almost confining me between the luxurious car and himself.

"What?"

"Signor Bertrasconi would like to speak to you. Now."

Chapter 28

I looked round. No heavy men stood near, no menacing figures, their hands stuck into bulging side pockets. The Chancery Lane pavement was busy, with the usual figures clad in subfusc suits and coats scurrying perhaps from legal office to legal office or property dealer to property dealer. A black taxi dieselled past with a throbbing flourish of engine noise, its driver glancing briefly at the gleaming Bentley stopped on double yellow lines, ignoring, like any superior vehicle containing superior persons, the rules that apply to the crowd. There was no one in a nearby doorway taking a bead on me. I turned my head quickly from side to side, but no one else stood close.

"Signor Bertrasconi" the chauffeur repeated, with perhaps more respect in his voice this time "would be deeply obliged if you would join him for a brief moment."

I stepped forward to stoop and look into the Bentley. On the back seat, drawn against the far side so that there would be space for me to sit next to him on the sumptuous leatherwork, sat a man in a grey twill suit, with slender trousers ending in elegant black leather shoes. He wore spectacles with thin gold rims and had thinning hair brushed back from his forehead. He was of average build, not strong, the skin drawing over his jaw line smoothly to indicate lack of fat, a care of diet and health. He might have been a lawyer or a physician dressed without flamboyance, with cream shirt and patterned silk tie, toned down to meet his own profession. He looked back at me almost impassively.

I got in, sat next to him without speaking and watched the chauffeur close the door. He walked round the front of the car and got in. The engine was still running, just a quiet throb, and we drew away from the pavement. A glass partition slid slowly up from the back of the front seat to close us off from the chauffeur so that, presumably, he could not hear our conversation.

Unless the car was bugged.

Bertrasconi held out his hand. I shook it cautiously. It was thin and dry, brown, but not at all weak.

"Mr.Simpson." The voice was educated, no stage Italian's even if slightly accented, the voice of a man who travelled a lot, used English regularly. "Thank you for giving me your time. I am glad that we can meet at last."

"Good."

"You are not, if you will forgive me, quite as I imagined you. Strong, yes, stocky, but not so very big. Evidently you use intelligence and technique more than brute strength."

"I'm afraid I'm not very good at self-analysis." I looked out at the passing pavements and buildings, the red traffic lights where we were slowing down to stop at the junction of Chancery Lane and Fleet Street. "Where are we going?"

He made deprecating gesture. "If you have no objection, I have told my driver just to cruise while we have a brief discussion. I felt that you might object if I suggested a venue, even on some neutral ground, since it could possibly compromise you. Mobility, I think, solves this problem. There is no particular destination in view. Perhaps the Embankment would provide a pleasant outlook?"

"I see. OK."

"Good."

"What do you want?"

He smiled. His features were firm, the pale skin drawn across the cheekbones under brown eyes, the nose finely-boned but straight, not hawkish. His eyebrows were thick but controlled, clipped presumably, like his smooth dark hair, by an expert barber.

"That is precisely the question I have come to ask you" he answered.

"Me?"

"I am sure you must be aware that mine is an organisation

in expansion. We are aware of objectives we wish to achieve and of the obstacles to them. Sometimes we have to overcome these obstacles. Sometimes it is far better to turn the obstacles into assets, to embrace them into our forces by attraction."

"That sounds like being swallowed up."

A perplexed look came across his features. He took off the thin-rimmed gold spectacles and stroked the points on either side of his nose where they had rested, then put them on again.

"It is" he said "a bit like creating Cromwell's Dyke, isn't it?"

Though it took me by surprise, I tried hard to cover up my feelings. "What? What is?"

"White's Bank. Remember, mine is the Cottian Savings Bank. I am from the Cottian Alps, although I am not a Protestant. I think of Cromwell's Dyke at Bobbio Pellice as the sort of anachronism beloved of the English, although those Waldensians were, I suppose, Italians of a sort. Savoyards of the Protestant religion were only Italians of a sort."

"Italy didn't exist until a relatively short time ago."

"Exactly. And Cromwell's Dyke is not representative even of Piedmonte, let alone of Italy. Called Cromwell's but not, in fact, financed by Cromwell. And as for a dyke, it is on a slope and, though it is a flood barrier, it will not hold water. The analogy of what White's Bank has become is too powerful to miss. It will not be financed by Whites - it hardly is now - and it is not really a bank. It is an investment house, a capital venture house, whose competitors are so many, and who offer so many options to the investor and entrepreneur, that its existence as a bank is a technicality."

"You're jumping the gun a bit, aren't you?"

His face registered approval. "I like racing analogies. But this is not a race which comes conveniently under starter's orders. There is no starter. The other participants will not line up obligingly in a frame, under a wire, to await their signal, the gun, from some referee. They are already off and running.

There has already been a huge race, almost a battle, for supremacy. God, it is said, is on the side of the big battalions. I do not have to name the big battalions for you."

"So, in order to become a big battalion, you can justify murder and subversion and criminal fraud?"

"I do not acknowledge that any such things have taken place. What I do acknowledge is that if one is to survive at all it is better to survive a struggle in one piece, whole. Not limp around on a big wooden leg like poor Colonel-General Beckwith, consoling himself and his pain with grinding evangelical activities amongst the disadvantaged. Living life in a small theatre of operation, with tiny triumphs of insignificant scale. Even most of his enemies, losers who survived Waterloo, did better than that."

"I wouldn't bet on it. But I'm beginning to lose track of the metaphors here. You think that we will be remembered with gratitude and affection? Or that White's is lame? Or are you threatening me?"

He shook his head. "I would not dream of insulting you with silly threats. Like you, I am a man of action. I want to know what it is you want. It is quite within my capabilities to provide what most people in business want. In your case, position and a very generous remuneration would be quite easy. You are very acceptable to those I have earmarked for power. Power would also come to you."

For some reason, at that moment, the idea came to me that he and Shauna had been operating some kind of listening system during lunch. Other than a fixed time, had she worked to end the lunch on receipt of a signal of some sort? One based on his listening-in to our conversation?

My silence prompted Bertrasconi to continue. "I have, as you know, very strong interests in electronics, quite apart from my financial activities. The proposed conglomerate to which that geriatric waxwork, Eugène Maucourt, has so committed himself and, with him, his bank and White's, will fail utterly unless it acts ruthlessly to some of the participants.

They will be reluctant to accept the terms. There is, also, the question of the level at which it is financed and the range of its products. Unless it can induce the right producers of medical electronics to come under its wing, it is lost. Yet the momentum to proceed is irresistible." He paused for a moment to smile wryly. "It is like an aeroplane at the moment the pilot calls 'rotate'. It must now take off because to abort would be to crash. Yet it must be certain that the power is there and the speed sufficient. It is the most perilous moment of the flight."

"They haven't called 'rotate' yet."

"They are rushing up to the moment. The momentum is irresistible. If they call off the flight, the City will lose what little confidence exists. Every operation will be discounted and ruin will follow."

"And that will suit you. Either way, you aim to pick up the pieces, cheap."

"I will have good positions to fill, generous offers to make. Shauna is very taken with you." His thin gold rims gleamed significantly as he lowered his voice to speak softly. "Working with her would, surely, prove a very rewarding experience. I think she has made that clear."

"Not really. That will, I imagine, only be made clear if I accept her invitation for this evening."

"Ah. I did not know of it. And will you accept? Have you decided?"

"Oh, I shall be there. But as to the rewards and the experience, I am not a beginner."

His expression relaxed. "Excellent. Then the right terms can be finalised." He took off his glasses again, massaged the side of his nose, put them on again and looked at me, sharply. "What further questions do you have for me?"

"Right now, no more. Can your driver drop me at Blackfriars Bridge?"

"Of course. I shall be glad, now that you have made your decision, to arrange it." He pressed a button and the sliding division went down for him to give instructions. We turned and headed back along the Embankment.

"You know why I've chosen Blackfriars Bridge?"

"Perhaps. You are attracted by symbols from the past, I think, like Cromwell's Dyke. I am much the same."

"It's where they found the body of Roberto Calvi, the Banco Ambrosiano man, hanging from scaffolding with stones in his pockets. He was a major fraudster, into hundreds of millions, and events caught up on him. They say that it was the P2 freemason's lodge in Rome, who he'd betrayed to the police, who got him."

"I know. I also know the real truth, but I can not tell it to you."

"The story I liked most about Calvi was the one about his ruse when he was a young cavalry officer, fighting the Germans. His men had lost all their horses and were starving. Calvi persuaded a farmer to sell his horses to him against a promissory note, giving the impression that he'd continue the fight. The farmer agreed. Once they'd ridden out of sight, Calvi and his men butchered the horses, ate them, and made their way home. The promissory note was, of course, worthless."

"I'm not sure, now, if I follow the analogy you are making."

"Think about it."

The Bentley came to stop on the throughway by Blackfriars Bridge, ignoring the no-stopping signs. I leant forward and opened the nearside door.

"I'm not sure, either, why Shauna ended our lunch so abruptly. I think you had something to do with it." I moved into the open space ready to alight onto the pavement. "She still says she thinks that Sir Richard White and Jacques Charville died without suspicious circumstances. Well, that's as maybe. But I want to talk to her about someone else who's dead. A man called Henry Weaver. She left before I could get the subject out in the open." I got out of the car. "That's one of the reasons why I'll be at the Barbican at seven o'clock tonight."

Bertrasconi sat on his luxurious leatherwork and frowned from behind his thin gold rims. "Who was Henry Weaver? What is he to you?"

"I am his sole executor" I answered.

Then I closed the door.

Chapter 29

Jeremy White sat at his grand desk with an expression looking more like an enigma within a mystery contained by a conundrum than anything else. When I had finished, he put his head in his hands without making a sound.

"Cheer up Jeremy. If hopes were dupes, fears may be liars."

Tea in Jeremy's office is one of the last gestures he makes to past glories. The cups and service are best bone china. The tea is not Earl Grey or Chinese - 'none of that foreign, perfumed muck' - but best Indian or Sri Lankan. The biscuits - I had just consumed a crisp chocolate-covered wafer - come from Fortnum and Mason's most superior sources. It is a lingering, nostalgic ceremony carried out in stark contrast to the plastic cups, crumbly digestives and shouted oaths of the dealing rooms in less exalted parts of the building.

In another chair, Geoffrey Price held his cup and saucer gingerly in one hand whilst looking at me with a sort of wondering expression, one that combined astonishment with gravid, professional concern.

Jeremy took his head out of his hands. "That woman" he snarled "makes Lucrecia Borgia look like Florence Nightingale."

"She will argue that change is needed and that she is merely an agent of change."

"A completely treacherous one. She joined our Board with all the responsibilities and expectation of ethical behaviour that that implies."

"Agreed. And she will say that she did that in all good faith. That the approaches made to her came after she joined and that she has dealt with them discreetly in order to further the Bank's best interests but, more particularly, the interests of the shareholders she represents."

Jeremy was not in the slightest mollified. "Bertrasconi is a predator. He owes us no allegiance. But Shauna Spring should have declared her negotiations. Should have been open with us."

"She never has in the past" Geoffrey intervened. "Her record is one of clandestine behaviour at every turn. It comes with quango ambitions, I always think."

Jeremy stared at him with a look that said he couldn't give a bugger what Geoffrey always thought, especially about quasi-autonomous non-governmental organisations, on which Jeremy usually expresses himself in terms that can not be repeated on a respectable page. "How the hell we were so negligent as to allow a set of minority shareholders impose her on us, I'll never understand."

"It was a rigged meeting." Geoffrey was impervious to Jeremy's stare and hardly allowed any emotion to disturb his tones. "There were few attendees and someone organised a block vote. As I said before, the Baricot style is ruthless."

"And we are the target." Jeremy was turning rueful.

"Amongst others."

"I wish to God we'd never started into this electronics caper. It seems to have crept in like osmosis. Eugène Maucourt has a lot to answer for. Even Richard isn't free from criticism. I know, I know" he saw me opening my mouth "we can't just sit about ignoring opportunities and the world is watching to see how we perform, but this was a very ambitious undertaking right from the start."

"And as such was bound to attract a predatory element." Geoffrey was still quietly unemotional.

"Agreed, Geoffrey, but while one is ready to cope with predatory elements, one does not usually have to deal, at the same time, with rank treachery from within. We are faced, now, with the possibility of utter disaster."

I shook my head. "Or triumph, Jeremy. We are not entirely alone in this. It may be, in yon smoke concealed, our friends chase even now the fliers, and but for us, have gained the field."

"Dear Heaven! I wish to God you'd stop continually

misquoting that awful Arthur Hugh Clough 'Say not the struggle' stuff."

"Misquoting? What do you mean, misquoting?"

"It's comrades, not friends. And it's possess, not have gained. Your scansion is right off the rails."

"Oh. You obviously know it well. I've always thought of friends being alliterative with fliers and - "

"Stop it! I can't stand that appalling Victorian optimistic-sentimental stuff, never could. It was drummed into us at Eton along with, even worse, Sir Henry Newbolt's *Vitai Lampadi* all about playing the game. Cut it out."

"Right."

"We have really serious things to deal with and you sound off like a flippant parrot squawking stale nostrums."

"Wow. You really are getting going. May I point out that, were it not for me, and of course your uncle Richard, you would right now be steaming full speed straight up shit creek without a paddle?"

"You may. I will allow you that."

Geoffrey Price coughed politely. "The objective now, if I may summarise what we have been discussing, is to ensure that the conglomerate of electronic producers formed by this project is put together at the right cost, with the right, stream-lined producers, and that it includes a strong element of med-ical electronics. Is that correct?"

"In a nutshell. Not difficult, once you've got your objectives clear. It needs hard work, a rapid circulation of the interested parties, new negotiations and a guillotine to come down at a certain date. Beyond which anyone still prevaricating gets excluded. We can set about that instanter."

"For God's sake, Tim! We've been trying to bring that sort of result about for months. Stop making it sound so easy."

"You didn't get the right people onto it."

He hit the top of his desk with an open-handed smack that made the cups rattle. "Christ! You are an arrogant bastard! None of the medical electronics people we approached would come to the party. Not in the way that's necessary. Do you think we wouldn't have - "

Geoffrey's polite cough interrupted him. He turned a savage glare at our financial wizard.

"What?" he demanded.

"It so happens, Jeremy, that I was at the Institute yesterday and - "

"Institute?"

"Of Chartered Accountants."

Jeremy half-closed his eyes. "So?"

"I arranged to meet Harry Deveson. Good chap really, used to open for his Oxford college and then after he came back from Tasmania he played rather well for the Sussex Drifters touring side on Sundays. He and I once put on a century partnership for - "

"Oh God, help me! What are you trying to say? For land's sake cut to the chase, will you?"

"Harry is now financial director of a family outfit, Deveson Diagnostics. His younger brother is the whiz behind it technically. There've been rumours about them going public. You may have read about it in the FT."

Jeremy didn't respond. His mouth had opened slightly.

"Well, yesterday Harry was rather keen on our European conglomerate idea as an alternative because it might provide the broader basis they need to continue their expansion. He's one of these pan-European freaks, keeps banging on about scale and development from within and synergy and all that - and so on. I have to say he's a sound chap financially and his figures always add up. So he's quite willing to bring the medical side to the table; his brother's keen to swallow up a couple of small Dutch companies and he says they're about to sign a deal in Germany."

Jeremy closed his mouth. He swallowed before speaking. "Why the hell haven't you mentioned this before?"

Geoffrey looked hurt. "I have been working on this project since its inception and, like everyone else, have been much exercised by the problem of the medical side. It's a question of timing. They weren't interested before but rapid expansion changes everything. I could only get to see Harry again yesterday. He's not just sitting around waiting for someone to buy him a beer, you know. He's a very busy man."

"Your friends chase even now the fliers, " I murmured.

"Comrades!" Jeremy snapped. "And the smoke certainly has been concealing them."

"The Board shouldn't be so damned xenophobic. All that they achieve is a concern awash with rumour and inaction. You did your best to keep me away from this business."

"God, I can hear you saying, just like Sir George Sitwell: 'So unwise of them not to have consulted me.'"

I grinned. I've always had a soft spot for Sir George Sitwell, who dominates one of the most remarkable, possibly the most remarkable, autobiography of the twentieth century: his son Osbert Sitwell's five-volume work. Henry Weaver was keen on it too, buying the reprint editions for a few pence in one of his customary old bookshops down in Hastings.

Which recollection brought on a wave of sadness and anger, wiping out the grin.

At that moment the phone rang. Jeremy grimaced at the interruption but guessed that Claire wouldn't have put the call through if it were not important. He picked up the receiver.

"Yes, put him on. Hullo, Giorgio. Yes, thank you, and you? Good."

He then listened carefully to what Giorgio Deserti had to say, making encouraging noises until one of alarm and shock followed. Eventually, after saying his thanks, he put the phone down.

"Giorgio Deserti, from Turin. He has been informed, officially, that the circumstances of Richard's death are classified as suspicious. The second examination found a pinprick under the right armpit which corresponds with an injection. The bruises on the wrists are consistent with his being held while an injection was administered. It was almost certainly of a lethal substance - I can't repeat the chemical name - which brought about heart seizure."

"Christ" said Geoffrey.

There was silence for a moment. I thought of that kind, sharp face, breaking out into a smile beside the rough stone flood barrier of Cromwell's Dyke, then his reproach, later, when I suggested that this was too dangerous a business for a man of his age to follow up. If only he had listened - but no, that was not his style, and he was bored. Maybe it would be true to say, of him, that he would have preferred death in action to a long senility.

"There can be no doubt?" I asked.

Jeremy shook his head. "None. We will receive a copy of the official report in due course. I don't suppose Freddy will want to insist on any further examinations here, now."

"So he was murdered. Like Jacques Charville and Henry Weaver and Sammy Simes and Emilio Bonnetti."

Jeremy frowned. "What have Henry Weaver and Sammy Simes got to do with this?"

"Everything. I just need to work out exactly how."

"Tim, I do beseech you not to expose yourself to any unnecessary risks. Leave Newcastle watercolours out of your activities. I really do need you to help us with this wretched electronics project. Without Charville, there is a large hole which needs filling."

"In that case, I hope you can sweet-talk Eugène Maucourt into welcoming me back into the Paris fold. At some point I shall need to delve into little Jacques's raw data as well as dash about here."

"Oh, I rather think Eugène will see things in a different light now that the official news about Richard has come through from Turin. A very different light. He'll still have a very possessive attitude to the project, of course, but there's no change there."

"Right." I stood up. "There's no time to lose, then. I must get on."

215

"Hang on, hang on." Geoffrey was looking at me with real concern. "You're not really going to go to this meeting with Shauna Spring at her Barbican flat now, are you?"

"I certainly am."

"Heavens, Tim, why?"

"I shall be carrying out my role as sole executor of Henry Weaver. Amongst other things."

"This is not a good idea. It is clearly dangerous."

"Don't worry, Geoffrey. I have a friend who'll help me. But I need to phone Sue and tell her I may be late tonight. Office work, you know."

Chapter 30

"Beer? Gin? Whisky? Wine?"

"Whisky, thanks."

"Scotch? Irish? Bourbon? Canadian?"

"Scotch, thanks."

"Ice? Water? Soda? Ginger ale?"

"Soda, for me."

She walked across to the sideboard, where bottles were standing in a decorative polychromatic huddle, paused in front of them, lifted a bottle of Bell's, turned and said:

"No. Why don't you come and help yourself while I get some ice? Then you can mix it the way you like."

"Fine." I moved away from the sofa and easy chairs, where I had been standing in a momentarily awkward pose following my entrance, and went to the sideboard as she disappeared through a side door. I took hold of the bottle of Bell's, which was about three quarters full, thought for a moment, saw an unopened bottle of Black Bush, and opened that. I'm very fond of Irish whisky in the right circumstances and the right circumstances, now, were to ensure an unopened bottle. I uncapped a small bottle of soda and did my pouring and mixing. Shauna Spring came back from a small kitchen, off, and handed me a pail of ice cubes with a smile.

I put three cubes in my drink. "Thanks."

"Come and sit down."

The flat was on the fourth floor, overlooking that big Barbican space with water in it. Away somewhere to the left was the Centre, with halls and art gallery and other auditoria. Here inside the flat the décor was modern, very light, with bits of chrome to give an Art Deco feel. I had a suspicion that an abstract-pattern rug on the light beige fitted carpet was a modernist thing by someone quite important like Marion

Dorn, or maybe her husband, McKnight-Kauffer. A plywood and fabric chaise longue - for one person only - was recognisably by Marcel Breuer for Isokon. Shauna evidently knew what to collect from the twenties and thirties.

She saw me looking, and her smile broadened as she took a sip from a glass of white wine. "Yes, I can see you know what you're looking at."

"I've always wanted one of those chairs moulded from one sheet of plywood. Gerald Summers, wasn't it?"

"Yes. I've got one. In the bedroom. It's surprisingly comfortable to sit on."

There was a slight pause while I took that, and its implications, in. The last time a Gerald Summers chair came up at auction it went for fourteen thousand pounds. Quite a chair to put your clothes on. Bedroom activity-implications, however, needed putting to one side. I hadn't been invited to view the chair. Yet.

"I've met Signor Bertrasconi at last," I said.

"Yes. He phoned to tell me. I'm really glad that you decided to come this evening."

"Then he must also have told you that I still had a bit of conversation to finish off."

Her expression went watchful. The smile didn't fade entirely but the set of her countenance implied the ability to get really difficult, verbally savage, should the talk take a wrong turn. She had discarded the business costume, the suit and blouse stage-managed, efficient appearance, for a much more relaxed, low-cut dress which revealed good shoulders and smooth unmarked arms. It was an appearance which could go either way, it seemed to me, seductive or smart depending on events and approaches.

"You didn't react when I mentioned Henry at lunch" I continued.

"No. I thought it was tactless of you" she answered, her voice low. "I didn't bring up your wife."

"She isn't dead. Henry is. He was murdered."

"That's ridiculous. He was killed in a car accident. It was tragic but it had nothing to do with me."

"But you were - friendly - with Henry?"

She shrugged. "Come on, Tim, what's past is past. All over. Remember what I said about people living their lives as though they are immortal? Henry was like that. He couldn't get off his backside and stop it all slipping away. Oh, he was entertaining in his odd, bookish, romantic fashion. He had all those scandalous stories culled from biographies, from books. Life, to him, was about something that happened way back. But he could sing, too, you know that? Quite well."

"When he'd had a drink or two. I remember his version of *Adios Muchachos compañeros de mi vida* but not much else. That's a rather heartrending song. Perhaps *Adios Enrique* will be a good memorial to him at the cremation."

She shivered slightly. "It's a strong bond, isn't it? Youth in Argentina in common? Like you and me, for instance."

"Mine was a long time ago, and brief. The bond I prefer to remember was the one I had with Henry. Which was so important to him that it killed him. It's a terrible responsibility to bear. I'm ashamed to say that I never realised how important I was to Henry until he was dead. I didn't take him too seriously at all, but he did me. That's why he made me his executor."

She took a deeper drink from her glass of white wine and frowned. "Can't we talk about the future rather than dead Henry? Life goes on, you know. I'd rather talk about what we can do with White's Bank?"

"This is about White's Bank."

The frown deepened. "I don't see how."

"I wondered what Henry was doing when he was killed. Someone, who had a key, carefully took all the evidence of his last research papers from his flat. Someone who didn't want anyone enquiring to know what he was working on. Whoever it was heard my voice on his answering machine, saying that I couldn't get up to Newcastle to meet him. But the post doesn't stop when we die. It goes on, junk mail and the rest. From it, I learnt that Henry was doing research on electronics, including medical electronics. For you."

"No he wasn't. Not at all."

"He was paid in cash. His bank account was in the red and there were very few deposits into it. There were very few movements either; it was nearly static. But somehow he was afloat. If you're working for some money-laundering outfit like the Banco Cottiano, they have stacks of cash to shell out. You were using Henry as a researcher, that's how you met him, and he was paid in cash. You took on a desperate outsider like him for good reasons: you didn't want White's to know you were doing stuff on the side and you needed a check on Jacques Charville. Where you're coming from, no one trusts anyone."

"You're guessing. Without any evidence. Are you interested in making progress in life instead of buttling for Jeremy or have you just come here to speculate and insult?"

"Oh, Shauna, I think we should have our cards on the table before we commit ourselves as a pair, don't you? It's best that we're quite clear about each other. Don't get me wrong; there is every logic in your doing your own research on the side and if you happened to fancy the researcher well, we're all adults aren't we? As you say, that's all part of the past, now. But Henry was serious; he fell for you as only a very lonely man can. He must have been flattered and delighted by your antics in London."

"Does that really interest you? Getting a bit prurient, aren't you?"

"It was fine until Henry realised what you were really doing. He didn't tell me about your affair because he was, I assume, sworn to secrecy by you or whoever you had him nominally working for, or both. Presumably Bracket Electronics in Croydon, who are in the street where he parked that fatal day, were nominally his clients. They're part of Bertrasconi's empire. But the penny had dropped before then, hadn't it? He realised that the research was part of bigger machinations, things that were definitely predatory."

"You think so? You think Henry was as sharp as that?"

"Henry wasn't successful but he wasn't stupid. He certainly taxed you with it. And let me guess: you said so what, Henry? If you want to go on drawing nice chunks of cash and if, even more important, you want to go on having nice chunks of me, you'll have to swallow it. Beggars from bedsits in St.Leonard's can't be choosers. Pick your side, Henry; what has White's Bank ever done for you? And is it me, or your old friend Tim, that's keeping you warm on occasion?"

"Fiction" she snapped. But she didn't move.

"The trouble was, right at that moment, Henry received an unexpected inheritance. Did he tell you about it?"

She didn't answer. She was strangely subdued considering her reputation, which made me believe that I was deliberately being allowed to set out my knowledge.

"Henry thought it was big enough to make him independent. And if he was independent, the cash payments were irrelevant. He might have decided, then, that you were going on to greater things and he wouldn't be part of them when this business was over. You weren't going to divorce your husband so Henry would always be your bit on the side. Well, probably not always; far from it. Time was limited. Either way, he told you. He told you he'd been in contact with me over a painting he'd inherited together with a house and he'd be meeting me in Newcastle with a view to getting the Art Fund to buy it. It was in Cullercoats, to be precise. He'd tell me everything then. Have you got the painting, by the way? It's a watercolour, isn't it?"

"I haven't the faintest idea what you're talking about."

"No? I can't imagine that Henry didn't mention it. Maybe you didn't believe him at first?"

"This is complete fantasy."

"Really? Oh well, let's leave it for the moment. You needed to keep a hold of him until things were set as far as the electronics project was concerned. You knew he was going to Croydon that day. You said you must meet him to talk things over. And guess where you met?"

"We didn't meet."

"Oh yes, you did. You were attending a quango meeting in Sussex. I checked with the Bank after I heard you'd been in Sussex for another meeting afterwards. It was at a country hotel at Battle, on the main line to Hastings. You quango folk like to do yourselves well; the country hotel meeting to ensure concentration, like a management course, and all that stuff. Henry must have been pleased. He told you to meet him at the Royal Oak. All you have to do, he said, is take the road from Battle High Street to Whatlington. It comes out on the A21 right by the Royal Oak. No distance at all for you, only two or three miles, but discreet."

"This is drivel."

"It was very important to Henry. Emotionally it was so significant that he couldn't resist it. That road goes down a deep dip just before it gets to the pub. There's a house called Mill House there, opposite a lane that leads up to Wood Place. The Muggeridges lived in Mill House. Every Tuesday evening, sixty-odd years ago, Henry's hero Hesketh Pearson used to walk Kitty Muggeridge up from Mill House to the Royal Oak for a drink. They were having an affair. The idea, for Henry, of you coming along that same lane to meet him, in similar circumstances, was irresistible. He told you to meet him there that evening on his return from Bracket Electronics in Croydon."

"I was at the hotel all the time."

"No you weren't. The bar staff at the Royal Oak can confirm, from photographs, that you and Henry were in there for at least two hours. You ate ribeye steaks and seemed to be talking, even arguing, passionately. After all, he was going to tell me everything, wasn't he?"

"You're bluffing."

"Oh no, I'm not. They're very sure. One of them recognised

you from the telly and Henry was an old regular they knew well. He drank a bit that night, they say, and they were a bit concerned about him driving. What they don't know is that, while you kept him talking, the man you'd arranged to look at his car in Croydon was outside, in the car park, unshipping his steering and seat belt fixing. There was a choice: if Henry came round to your view, it would be into your car and hey-ho to his flat in Hastings. If not, the doctored Allegro estate for him and back to Battle for you. Which is what happened."

"That's not true!" Her voice pitched up high. "It was an accident! I was shocked and devastated when I heard about it next day!"

"So you admit you were there? At the Royal Oak?"

"You've had confirmation, haven't you? You don't need me to admit it."

"You were the last person to see Henry alive."

"That doesn't mean I arranged to kill him."

I looked at my Black Bush reflectively. "It's ironic, Shauna. Really ironic. He finally got a mistress to come up the side road from Battle to meet him at the Royal Oak for a discreet, evening tête-a-tête. He finally almost levelled with his hero Hesketh Pearson just the once. And she killed him just after his moment of triumph. Just like spiders, it was."

She flushed deeply. "I think you'd better go."

I took a swig of my whisky and nodded. "I will go. In a moment. It's a shame that you had to arrange to kill Sammy Simes as well. I take responsibility for that. But he would have blown the whole story, wouldn't he? Once the police had reason for suspicions, they'd have uncovered all this much quicker than I have."

"Simes would never have died if you weren't a blundering, interfering busybody. Like that old Nosey Parker, Sir Richard White."

I nodded, but something inside me went cold. There'd been a signal somehow. She'd played a very cool hand up to now, admitted nothing concrete, kept her replies noncommittal.

The listening device I had in my side pocket would have provided no proper evidence for prosecution so far. Yet suddenly she was coming out with it. Was it that remark 'I think you'd better go' that was the trigger? What decision did it herald? That I was not going to be obliging, that there was no purchase of me to be made?

Just a little more time would tell.

"Richard wasn't a Nosey Parker. He was indulging in history. With Richard, you had to find your way through a thicket of Crecy, Agincourt and, latterly, Cromwell and the Waldensians. But it was his love of gastronomy which, ironically, took him to Belley. If he hadn't wanted to visit the birthplace of Brillat-Savarin, he'd never have suspected. He wasn't following you, but the past caused the present to be illuminated in a way he could never have foreseen. Even then, if you'd provided a half-credible explanation, he'd have given you the benefit of the doubt. Unlike you, he didn't think that ends justify means."

She was still flushed.

"The ends? You think I need to justify all this? White's is finished. The big boys hold the future. I'm not going to be sidelined, even if you are."

I shook my head sadly.

"That Intradeva fiasco really did knock you off your pedestal, didn't it? The City marked your card after that. A couple of quangos to keep you occupied but no real position came your way. That's when Bertrasconi got to you. You realised that to scramble back to where you wanted to be, desperate measures were necessary. And by God, desperate they've been."

There was, then, the sound of a key in the flat's front door lock. I turned in time to see three men come in. They were of medium build, unremarkable, but fit looking, and they didn't speak as they closed the door and came across to where we were sitting. They stood quite still, without speaking, like three suited executives respectfully joining a business meeting to which they had yet to be asked to sit down.

"This won't work" I said, turning back to look Shauna Spring dead in the eye. "Not at all. Up to now, most of the deaths could just be accidental."

She stood up. "I've tried with you, and failed. You have to go. Yours will be accidental, too. One more accident is quite possible, given your habit of interference in so many things."

"Except that it has now been established that Sir Richard White was murdered by injection."

She didn't answer but her face paled. I wondered how much she had left to Bertrasconi, not wanting to hear the detail, apart from Henry Weaver's meticulous, premeditated arrangements between Croydon and Whatlington. Henry had become a nuisance and now I was a nuisance; evidently, she didn't mind involvement with the disposal of nuisances.

"Stand up" one of the three men said to me. He was dark-haired and, from the way the other two stood slightly behind him, seemed to be the one in control.

I remained seated. Shauna Spring moved away from my chair, backing towards the sideboard. The man took a small automatic out of his pocket and pointed it at my head. "I said, stand up" he repeated.

"You can't pull the trigger. Let me guess; you're going to arrange an accident. Something to do with cars. It won't be any good if your hit-and run victim has a bullet hole in him, will it?"

He smiled a rather one-sided smile. "I think that you have totally misunderstood the situation," he said. "Signor Bertrasconi thinks you should make a decision in his favour." He nodded at the other two, who walked across the living room, over the abstract-pattern rug, to the French windows.

"Open them" he ordered.

Shauna Spring backed against the sideboard, going even paler.

The two men opened the long glass doors, revealing a narrow balcony outside. Cool air blew damply into the warm room.

"Four floors" the dark-haired man said. "Seems to be more than enough."

He nodded again to the two men. They walked back across the carpet and rug towards Shauna Spring, who frowned in a perplexed way. Then her face changed, twisting into a horror mask, mouth yawning wide soundlessly as realisation struck her and the two men grabbed her, one clamping a hand over her mouth. Bottles rattled on the sideboard for a moment as the three figures grappled. Then there was quiet, except for mewling noises from behind a big hand as Shauna was held tight.

"Signor Bertrasconi" the dark man said evenly "feels that this woman Mrs Spring will be a lot of trouble. She is far too ambitious and her way of life is not discreet. Two people will, also, conflict with each other eventually. He needs only one executive to do what he wants. You will be far more effective." He smiled his lop-sided smile at me. "It seems that you have impressed Signor Bertrasconi. I too, find your investigative logic remarkable. Logic, and a practical assessment of human nature, is a combination which commands respect. Mrs. Spring is far too egotistical."

Shauna began to try to struggle, twisting, with arms pinned, still upright between the two men. From her clamped mouth now came terrible muffled sounds coupled with hissing sweeps of air through flared nostrils as she fought for breath. Her eyes, wide open, bulged white as she stared at me or swivelled their pupils to look at the dark-haired man.

"You have a choice" he continued, watching me "when she has gone. You can join Signor Bertrasconi, who will be waiting for you with a very good offer, or we will have to deal with you, too. Despite what you said just now, I am prepared to shoot you. We can dispose of you so that you will never be found and she, there, will not be able to answer questions."

"Another suicide?" my voice was strained and hoarse. "You really think another suicide - ?"

"Of course. Her disloyalty to White's is about to be

revealed by you. The evidence is the same as for Charville. Remorse, or fear of public disgrace, is enough for most people. Enough to convince most enquirers. We will leave immediately she has departed."

He nodded to the two men. They lifted Shauna Spring off her feet and moved briskly across the carpet, carrying her a few inches above the ground. Her eyes, still bulging, swivelled round in one last, desperate stare. I leapt to my feet with a shout.

"Don't try!" The dark-haired man brought the gun up towards my head again as I came upright. "Don't think of it!"

Then, at last, the front door burst open. The dark-haired man turned towards it with an exclamation. I leapt to grab Shauna Spring as the two men holding her went through the French windows onto the balcony. There was a shot from behind me and I flinched, but the reaction was purely spasmodic; the four of us, grappling, had milled onto the balcony. The hand clamping Shauna's mouth came off as I trod on a foot and clouted its owner on the side of the head. Her keening scream pierced the night air high outside the building, almost drowning the shouts from behind us.

"Police! Police! Armed police! Freeze! Freeze!"

As the two men let go. Shauna Spring collapsed onto the cold balcony floor. The flat seemed to fill rapidly with uniformed men in flak kit, most of them pointing guns at us. On the carpet, over the expensive abstract rug, the dark-haired man lay still, bleeding from a chest wound.

"I'm glad you got him, Nobby" I said, to the plain-clothes ginger figure who limped up to the settee. "He'll be the one who did for Richard. And probably arranged for Henry, too."

He smiled faintly back as he gave orders to men who called him 'guv' and handcuffed the two standing men.

My friend, to misquote Arthur Hugh Clough slightly, possessed the field.

Chapter 31

We took William with us this time, installed and strapped into a security child's chair on the back seat of the car. He likes car journeys, staring out at the passing scene from his elevated position, although there is a soporific effect and he soon dozes off. Which Sue says is a nuisance because it disturbs his sleep pattern, but I say you can't have everything; it's nice to take him with us and there's always a price to pay.

The framed and glazed print of Whitby just fitted into the boot of the car, on top of our suitcase and William's extensive impedimenta. The Florence Engelbach was next to William on the back seat. I wasn't playing hookey from the Bank, because it was Saturday. Sue and I had decided to set out very early and take the weekend off with a night at a swish Scarborough hotel where they have special facilities for toddlers and crawlers and even static infants, like people to look after them while you have dinner.

Jeremy might have thought that I should go charging off to Paris or Turin on the Sunday so as to be on tap first thing Monday morning but, after everything that had happened, I wasn't in favour of the idea.

"I still" I said to him "have a duty or two to perform as sole executor of the late Henry Weaver's estate."

"Oh God! You are becoming so tedious as to defy description. Are we never, ever, going to hear the end of that?" He made a cufflink-flash as he pushed back his blond locks. "At least there was no trouble when you took the day off for his funeral, although I kept my fingers crossed. With you, even the dead are dangerous. I was relieved to think that everything was all over. Will you ever concentrate on the project in hand?"

"I am concentrating. Ask Geoffrey. We've spent hours on it."

The funeral at the crematorium on Hastings Ridge had not been a cheerful affair. It was a cold, blowy day and few people had turned up as we said *Adios Muchacho* to Henry. Aunt Enid May repeated that it was too far for her, at her age, to attend. She still maintained she'd have everything ready for me when I came to deliver her picture and went off into another ramble about the shame of poor Henry's lonely and celibate life. I didn't go on to tell her that towards the end it hadn't been so celibate; that wouldn't have been tactful.

Sir Richard White's memorial service was being arranged for a future date, so that the great and the bad from the City could attend.

"Eugène Maucourt" Jeremy had pressed on, "is anxious to get the project finalised. He is impressed by Geoffrey's pal at Deveson Diagnostics but time is critical."

"Well Eugène Maucourt can go fish, unless he is prepared to offer the unreserved services of those two brown-kneed female researchers. Plus unlimited supplies of best chateau-bottled claret to keep me in good humour whilst I plough through Jacques Charville's travesty of the facts with a large red pencil."

"Really! Brown knees! There is no need to be coarse. All I am saying is that there is an urgency to get on. Even if prospects are much brighter, we must not let the grass grow under our feet."

"Acknowledged. But the need is not as pressing now that Bertrasconi is under arrest for fraudulent financial and criminal activities."

This was true. I had it straight from the horse's mouth when I bought the old ginger stallion a breakfast in Victoria Street.

"I'm not sure" I said, at the time, "if this shouldn't be on you."

"Nonsense" Nobby was tucking into fried egg as he spoke. "I saved your bacon, as promised, even though I was sticking my neck out."

"And I delivered to you the career-enhancing result you were after."

"You did quite well."

"What do you mean 'quite'? Quite? I did well, period."

"Up to a point. The two henchmen who survived have shut up like traps. They know what'll happen to them if they talk. We've had to rely on Shauna Spring's version of events, which Bertrasconi's lawyers will make fortunes in contesting."

"Must have given her quite a turn to realise that she was not as indispensable as she imagined. Bit of a shock, when you think you're a queen bee, to find you can be chucked off a balcony like any old underling."

He paused with fork in mid-passage.

"Shock? Her doctors and lawyers have been pleading emotional trauma all through our questioning. Hasn't half hampered us. Fortunately the severity of the charges laid against her have brought a reluctant acceptance of the need to assist us. Once you've survived a murder attempt of that sort, other threats pale into insignificance."

"She can provide evidence of Bertrasconi's masterminding of all those deaths?"

He sucked his teeth. "Up to a point. I've got him on the money laundering we've been working at for months, although the problem about that is that fraud and monetary cases are so complicated they often end up unresolved. The fraudulent plan to take White's over, and his involvement in Sir Richard's murder, and those of Bonnetti, Charville, Weaver and Simes are going to take a lot of work to make stick as well. Especially since, with your leaping about to save Shauna Spring, you forced the police marksman to shoot the key henchman, who turned back to shoot you. Without him, our case is limited. Bertrasconi will plead that he acted without instruction."

"Oh dear, sorry I moved."

"You should have let them chuck her over," he muttered, moodily.

"Nobby! Really! That is no way for a responsible rozzer to be talking. She is, I grant, a nasty piece of work who assisted in at least two premeditated murders. Although the evidence for the first one may be purely hearsay. Like my verbal evidence only. But I could hardly sit by and watch her being hurled over a fourth floor balcony."

"The trouble with you is one of misguided gallantry. That woman is a monster. I thought you'd do anything to get revenge for Sir Richard. Not to mention Henry Weaver, for whom you have interpreted the term 'sole executor' like something from an Arnold Schwartzenegger film."

I managed a smile at this hyperbole. "I thought I was entirely vengeful, too. But I was wrong. There are, evidently, limits to my wrath and guilt-induced desire for retribution."

He smiled and speared some more breakfast. "I'm glad to hear that you haven't changed. If it is any consolation to you, our legal adviser says that Shauna Spring's confession over the arrangements to kill Henry Weaver will ensure a successful prosecution. Your clever bluff over the bar staff being ready to identify her was partly the reason."

"I'm sure the bar staff would identify her, even though I never had time to check. They'd certainly remember Henry."

He grinned. "The key bar staff member was a temp that evening. She wouldn't be a very reliable witness because she's uncertain about timing. She doesn't think she could identify Shauna without reservation. And no one has come forward to verify that Weaver's Allegro was in the car park that evening, even though they do remember Henry."

"Well there you are. I managed to simulate an ace. I must take up poker again."

"It might suit your chancy, irresponsible, superficial character, yes."

I blew a raspberry at him. "She hasn't admitted anything about a valuable painting though? A watercolour?"

"No, she hasn't. And it is not my job to pursue your mercenary and mendacious purposes, either."

I blew another raspberry at him and we moved on to more erudite matters connected with the start of the rugby season.

Sue, William and I had a smooth trip up to Whitby. The famous harbour and fishing port was draped in a wet mist when we got there. Whitby is a charming, historic place, dedicated to the earnest production and consumption of fried fish and chips. In other resorts, even elegant Tynemouth, the Balti and the Tandoori may have curried themselves deep into the high streets, but in Whitby the battered fish and the deep-fried chip reign supreme. Brillat-Savarin would have had something very cogent to write about. The smell of local cuisine wafted greasily through the car ventilation system as we found our way from the quays out to Enid May Weaver's terraced house. I parked outside and Sue plucked William out of the back seat, grumbling sleepily, while I extracted the framed print from the boot. I'd made a list of the other things to which her legacy from Henry entitled her, but she said, after she'd received it by post, that she'd got enough junk of that sort already, in better condition. I could donate it to charity. She just wanted her picture.

The house was neat and clean, with a small front garden. When the front door opened, a tiny, aproned, grey-haired woman regarded us with a bright smile and asked us in. There was a deal of cooing and chuckling over William, who was still sleepy but not grumpy, being intrigued by the dinky old lady.

She took my hand with enthusiasm after we moved into the front room. "I'm so glad to meet you" she said. "Henry often mentioned you. He said how kind you were."

"Well, I don't know - "

"Oh, yes. He said he often met you and you were always so generous. You were at school together, weren't you?"

"Yes" I answered, avoiding Sue's eye "we were at school together. In Buenos Aires."

"That's right. I often thought he missed South America, you know. But he said it was too late to go back; they didn't have the books he was interested in down there. What am I doing? Sit down, please. I've got some tea ready for you."

We sat down and she fussed in and out with tea. A large tabby cat came in and purred when I stroked it, then went to sit in the window. I put the print of Whitby down against a sideboard, so that it could be seen clearly, and leant the Engelbach nearby. Enid Weaver hadn't seemed very excited by them and now, as she put down a tray on a side table, she looked at them critically.

"That's the harbour all right" she said, cocking her head. "My, but there were a lot more boats then, weren't there?"

"I believe so."

"Henry was always fond of it. He used to come to me, often, when he was younger, for a holiday. I haven't seen much of him, the last few years."

"I see."

"And the flowers are a bit impressionistic for me, but Henry meant well, and they're quite colourful."

"Florence Engelbach was well thought of," said Sue. "She exhibited at the Royal Academy."

"Did she? Well, that's something, I suppose. But I shall be glad to have my picture back."

There was a pause. I hadn't quite taken the meaning of this in.

"I've got the space ready in my bedroom as I told you on the phone," she said. "For it to hang where I can see it, last thing at night and first thing in the morning."

Just like your deceased sister Myrtle, I thought, but said "Really?" and glanced at Sue, who was giving William a drink of milk from a plastic bottle. "Would you like me to take it up for you?"

"That would be kind. But have your tea first. I expect it's quite safe, locked up in your car, isn't it?"

She picked up a brown teapot and began to pour out tea into white china cups. Sue frowned at me over William's gurgling head. Is the old dear doolally, I began to wonder, or is there something missing here?

"Miss Weaver, I - "

"Oh, please do call me Enid. Everybody does."

"Enid, I haven't got another picture in the car. These are the only ones I've got."

She put down the teapot to look at me as though I was a bit doolally myself.

"Oh dear." Signs of distress began to appear on her face. "I thought you were bringing my picture."

"I - I haven't - what sort of picture?"

"My lady and the girl. Sitting at the table, with a cat and a teapot on it. It's a watercolour, you know, although I always think it's as good as any oil. By Laura Knight. She was very good, they say. But I just like the picture. It reminds me of my childhood and how we used to sit like that, sometimes, with mother."

I felt as though I had swallowed some hot tea backwards.

"The - the Laura Knight painting is yours?"

"Oh, yes. I bought it at a jumble sale here, years ago. More years than you can believe. Ten shillings, all I had to spend. I had to scrape for weeks afterwards. I didn't know she was at all known then, of course."

"But - but it was in Myrtle's house."

She nodded briskly. "Oh, I know. She always liked it, so I used to lend it to her. A friend who goes up to Newcastle quite often took it. Myrtle always hung it in the same place so that she could see it morning and evening, too. And it was away from prying eyes of course."

"Of course."

Sue was looking at me, with humour bubbling up in her expression over the still-imbibing William. Serve you right, the expression was saying, you looked a gift horse in the mouth and now it's not even yours.

Enid Weaver handed me a cup of tea. I took it automatically, feeling numb, then rallied myself. "I'm awfully sorry" I said. "I hadn't realised it was yours. It's quite safe. I'll make sure it comes to you right away. I'm really very sorry. I had no idea."

She looked immensely relieved. "That's all right. I suppose you weren't to know, if Henry didn't tell you. I'm glad it's safe and sound. I'll be glad not to have to look at those poor fisher girls, all blown with spray and windy, any more."

"I beg your pardon?"

"You can take it with you now, when you go."

"I'm sorry; take what with me?"

She looked at me patiently, as though dealing with a simpleton. "Myrtle's painting. The one she always exchanged with mine. Poor Myrtle, she got the worst of the bargain; she was trying to keep up with me and bought one I've never really liked. Too cold and windy. So I used to lend her mine in exchange, like a good kind sister. I've packed hers up in brown paper for you to take away."

The numbness seemed to be spreading to all my limbs. I drank a draught of hot sweet tea from a china cup. Sue was staring at me still, with eyes that were getting deeper and deeper into their sockets.

"May I see it?" I asked.

"If you want to unwrap it, I suppose so. But I tied it all up with string. It'll be all right, you know. Henry didn't like it much, either, but when he phoned about Myrtle's death and the things that needed sorting out, I reminded him that I'd want my picture back. He inherited Myrtle's. He was going to call and pick Myrtle's up on his way north to change it for me. Bring back my Laura Knight. But then, he had his accident down in Sussex so he never got here. It's all very, very sad."

"Did Henry know this, this painting you've wrapped up, well?"

"Oh, he only remembered the details vaguely. But he asked me who it was by and, when I looked and told him, he got quite excited."

She paused and picked up the teapot.

"Not that I've ever heard of him" she said. "Someone called Homer, it is. Homer. Odd name, isn't it? Foreign sounding. Greek, originally, I suppose. Would you like some more tea?"

Chapter 32

After we got out of Whitby, going over the skinned, withering moors towards Scarborough, I pulled the car off into a quiet layby and we sat for moment without speaking while William went off into a doze in the back.

"A Winslow Homer" Sue said, eventually, wonderingly. "You own a Winslow Homer watercolour of fishing girls at Cullercoats, Tim."

"Poor old Henry. Christ, it's terrible."

"I know."

I wound down the window and let clear, cold, moorland air blow away the damp vapours of Whitby from the interior. A feeling of relief flooded through me, as though escaping from claustrophobia, although this had only partly been a tale of old seaside resorts, the ends of lives, vital fishing places gone to salty decay and protected destitution. Places that lose their risky industries lose, with them, their existence; as long as the Bank's activities were, like sea fishing, inclined to consume lives or at least careers, we knew that we were still among the animate.

It was an invigorating thought as long as you weren't among the losers. Poor old Henry had, for his last eighteen months, come back from Kenilworth Road despair to something like a spark. To have it snuffed out so near to prosperity was Fate at its most cruel.

I got out, went round to the boot, and got the watercolour out to look at it again. We sat in the front seats with it across our knees. It was a good size: about eighteen inches by twenty eight, framed and under glass, with a creamy mount. The two girls depicted were standing with shawls draped over their heads, beside wooden railings. Behind them, men in sou'westers could dimly be descried against a flurried sea surface. To the left was a corner of the roof of the Watch House of the

Volunteer Life Brigade at Cullercoats, with balustered supports and trellised balcony. The women were poised in tense anxiety and one of the sou'westered men was gesturing out to sea.

"It's very like one of the versions of *Perils of the Sea* " said Sue. "Sometime in 1881. Which is what the signature shows. Just 'Homer, 1881' as you might expect, although he did sign himself Winslow Homer as well. The original of *Perils of the Sea* was bought by Thomas B. Clarke, an early patron. It's in the Sheldon Collection now. There are etchings of another version he reworked later."

I sat, holding a fortune in my hands, wondering. "Enid said Myrtle bought this off a friend's mother in Tynemouth just after the war. Around 1947, she reckons, during that very hard winter, when everyone was hard up. Myrtle was only in her early twenties but she wanted to keep up with Enid because she'd got the Laura Knight, which both of them preferred. And Enid still prefers."

"I know. How on earth did this get into local hands? According to most provenances, all Homer's Cullercoats work seems to have gone back to America with him. Why would one quite important one stay behind? So many of the Cullercoats works have been traced back to his family."

"No one knows how paintings leak out of an artist's studio." I stared at the paper surface under the glass." Look at his contemporary, Whistler, if you think of the later watercolours. Stuff all over the place."

"Homer was hardly an aristocratic dandy, like Whistler, parading his wares in front of everyone. Homer was crotchety, reserved, withdrawn, keeping everything to himself. Much more elemental. But maybe he gave this to someone local in thanks for something. To one of the models, perhaps, or a bereaved family. Losses were dreadful among the fishing community then."

"Possibly. It's very unlikely we'll ever know."

She put a hand on my arm. "You own a Winslow Homer.

Of an important period. Maybe worth a million pounds or more. What are you going to do?"

I grinned. "If I were not a responsible executor, I'd hide it. Although I'd have a lot of explaining to do if and when I came to sell it. It's ours, by the way, not just mine; without you, I wouldn't even have started."

"Thank you, kind sir. But what about the Art Fund? Are you going to sell it to the Art Fund? Or keep it?"

"I don't think I can afford to keep it. There'll be big death duties to pay on something worth a million. The fair thing is to put it up for auction, probably in New York. If the Fund has the money, it can buy it."

"Jeremy would want to buy it privately. He'd still offer a fair price. One that saved the odd thirty percent commission."

"Jeremy hates watercolours."

"Not like this one, he won't. It'd be a tremendous asset to the Fund."

I chuckled. "It'd be something for Jeremy to swallow, having to shell out a million or more to me from the Art Fund after all this trouble. Especially in view of all those warnings to avoid Newcastle and get on with Paris and Turin."

She looked out of the window at the rolling brown bracken, then over to the back seat at William, and shook her head. "I can't take it in properly. You realise that you could have enough, even after paying death duties, to do almost anything you want?"

"There'd be at least seven hundred thousand left over, I suppose."

"There are people who'd retire on that, even at our age."

I affected horror. "Retire? Retire? You can't retire on any sum under a million, Sue. Besides, what would I do? I haven't had nearly enough fun yet. And Jeremy needs me. To help save the Bank."

"Oh Tim, really. You are incorrigible. And very smug." She stopped, thought for a moment, then spoke, her voice changing tone to a higher key. "I've just realised; you intended to get involved in this electronics thing all along, didn't you? It didn't happen by accident, did it?"

"Once Geoffrey told me about it - he was dead worried - we agreed it would be a good idea. Richard's fax came in the nick of time."

"So that's that. Until the next crisis. Do you really want to go on?"

"Oh yes. It'll be even more fun now that I know I'm independent. I can carry on without worrying about failure."

"You've never worried much, anyway."

"Me? Of course I have. A mass of nerves, I am."

"Some chance."

I laughed out loud. Elation was beginning to charge through me like electricity. Now was no time to be making decisions about the future or moping about the past. Now was the time to be drinking champagne.

I put the watercolour carefully back in the boot, packed it tight, and got back in to the car. Sue was still staring owlishly into the distance, like someone who's been up all night. I kissed her carefully and started the engine.

"Come on, Sue. Let's head for the hotel. It's time for gastronomy that'll have old Brillat-Savarin saluting in his grave. After the best champagne that money can buy."

She still stared like someone in shock. "Did you ever think this would happen? Ever? After all the things that have happened? That eventually one of the paintings you've chased after would actually come to you?"

"Of course I did. Never doubted it."

"Rubbish!"

"Absolutely true. I have always said: say not the struggle naught availeth, Sue. Ouch! That's very mean, when I've got both hands on the wheel."

She chuckled and did it again. "I shall do that every time you quote Clough. I can afford to, when I want to. I've got a rich husband, now."